AF576872

Justice, Justice Shall You Pursue

A NOVEL BY

Jules Mermelstein

First in the "Pursuing Justice" series
Dresher, PA
2020

Paperback ISBN: 978-1-7344448-0-3
E-book ISBN: 978-1-7344448-1-0
Library of Congress Control Number:2019920994

DEDICATION

I dedicate this book to my best friend and lover, my wife Ruth. She had the wisdom to agree to marry me while we were still teenagers. And although all around us believed we would fail because we were too young, we grew together and are still growing strong after 45 years.

With Ruth, everything I do is possible. Without her, nothing is possible.

Justice is the means by which established injustices are sanctioned.
Anatole France

Fairness is what justice really is.
Former Justice Potter Stewart

Couldn't help but make me feel ashamed
To live in a land where justice is a game.
Bob Dylan

In its majestic equality, the law forbids rich and poor alike to sleep under bridges, beg in the streets and steal loaves of bread.
Anatole France

Justice, justice shall you pursue.
Deuteronomy 16:20

ACKNOWLEDGEMENTS

A novel may have a single author's name on it but its creation is the work of many. First I would like to thank my beta readers. These include family members; my wife, Ruth, my daughter, Hannah, and my daughter-in-law Cari Armstrong. They include two friends, Stuart Visnov, whose name and company, Echelon Protection and Surveillance, are in the novel itself (and who was gracious enough to write a blurb for the back cover) and Laurie Berman, who has been my friend and psychologist for over 30 years. And last, but certainly not least, they include my senior high school teacher, Adria Mednitsky, who taught me English, Creative Writing, and Current Fiction at Upper Dublin Senior High in the early 1970s.

Those of you who have read the back cover may have noticed the blurb by Dave Keightly. He is an attorney in Montgomery County, and a former prosecutor and district judge. Dave and I have known each other since we were teenagers so I asked him to read the book and let me know what he thought. He did much more, pointing out some technical legal issues that he has dealt with over the years. I made additions and corrections based on his comments and am grateful to him.

Others who helped produce this novel include Alanna Sklover, Amy Spencer, Marcia and Paul Friend, Steve, Candice, Marty and Cheryl Applebaum, Hannah Mermelstein and Gretchen Virkler, Ben Mermelstein and Cari Armstrong, Jess Applebaum and Patrick Foran, and Jacki Hulm.

And, helping me through the process of being a first-time novelist, was my publishing specialist, Darcy Post, of Book Baby. I do not know the name of the professional editor that Book Baby assigned to edit this, but they helped immensely to make my writing clearer and bring it to life.

I also want to thank **you, the reader**. If it were not for you, I would have had no reason to write this. If you would like to see the progress of, and offer suggestions for, future novels in this series, sign up at **https://www.julesmermelstein.com**.

And if you like this book, **please review it** on any book sale site you patronize.

TABLE OF CONTENTS

PROLOGUE

Officer Robert Norman was about to finish his day shift for the Upper Dublin Township Police Department when the call came from 911 dispatch: head to a house on Timber Lane. A victim was nonresponsive and bleeding.

Upper Dublin Township was a sleepy bedroom community in eastern Montgomery County, Pennsylvania. Although it had a business park and was a suburb of Philadelphia, the level of violent crime in the township was far less than that of big cities.

Officer Norman pulled into the driveway of the idyllic-looking suburban home the dispatcher had directed him to; then he looked around the well-kept grounds. It was dusk, but he could still make out the features of the house. The faux Roman columns on the porches. The manicured lawns and symmetrically trimmed shrubs. What he didn't see was anyone on the street, or anyone moving behind the homes. But, of course, he did see neighbors looking out their windows, intrigued by the sight of a police car that had turned onto their street with all its lights on and its sirens blaring. Although he didn't know it yet, Officer Norman was parked in the driveway of one of the township's best-known residents.

He walked to the door and knocked. An ambulance pulled into the driveway behind his car. After not receiving an answer, Officer Norman pounded on the door as the EMTs jumped out of their ambulance and ran toward him. He tried the doorknob and made a mental note that the door was unlocked from the inside. No damage to the door. Was this *not* a break-in?

The door was opened by a man with tears in his eyes and blood on his hands. Silently, the man led Officer Norman into the living room. The victim was lying partly on a small throw rug and partly on the floor, her body surrounded by blood. The man walked over to the body, looked down at the woman, and the tears started flowing from his eyes— was the man the victim's husband? A cellphone sat alone on a coffee table nearby.

Officer Norman did not have long to consider the bloody man's identity. The next moment, the EMTs rushed over to the body and actively began evaluating the victim. As they worked, Officer Norman's attention was drawn to the victim's forehead: a trickle of blood traveled from the center of her forehead and seemed to be a drying creek that had previously flowed into her hairline. Blood had seeped from two similar wounds to the victim's abdomen.

After questioning the man with blood on his hands—he in fact identified himself to Officer Norman as the victim's husband—and learning he owned a handgun, Officer Norman called for backup and walked back out to his car to get his evidence collection kit. Officer Norman asked the man where his gun was. The man led the officer back through the house into a bedroom and pointed to a drawer in the night stand. He took the handgun from the drawer the husband identified, while wearing rubber gloves, and dropped it into an evidence bag. That was when the EMTs informed him the victim was dead. Although Officer Norman knew that the victim's husband was now the prime suspect, there was not enough evidence for an arrest.

Officer Norman returned to the police station, the gun he presumed to be the murder weapon tucked neatly into the evidence bag.

PART ONE

THE CLIENT

CHAPTER 1

I try not to kill people or have people killed. I'm in the business of justice. Laws and rules were set up to protect those with power from those with little or no power, so I don't feel bound to them. Of course, I'm careful. If caught, I would not only be disbarred; I would probably spend the rest of my life in prison.

My name is Joshua Frankel and I'm a lawyer.

That afternoon there was a knock on my door. Susan stuck her head in. "Your two o'clock is here."

Susan is a striking brunette, brilliant emotionally and intellectually—and my executive assistant. That's actually an understatement. Without her, my office would be in chaos, logistically speaking.

"Have they finished the IC form?"

Initial Consultation forms save me time during my first appointment with a prospective client.

"He's working on it."

"Okay, send him in when he's done."

"Will do."

Ten seconds later, another knock. Susan opened the door and said, "Mr. Jones."

"That was quick."

Susan rolled her eyes as she handed me the IC form—which was mostly blank. Following Susan into my office was a tall man. I'm not used to looking up to make eye contact, which meant this man was taller than six feet. Something was familiar about him. I studied his appearance to try to figure out where I remembered him from. He had a full head of black hair, graying around the temples. And he was clean shaven. That certainly distinguished him from me. I have a full beard and a bald head. Both are my choice. After years of complaining that I wouldn't mind being bald, but that I hated my male pattern baldness, it suddenly occurred to me that I could do something about the rapidly diminishing follicles on the crown of my head. Out came my shaver.

But I digress.

The client stuck out his hand.

"Mr. Frankel, I'm pleased to meet you." As we shook hands his dark blue eyes scanned my brown ones for…what? Trust?

"Thank you, Mr. Jones. It's a pleasure to meet you as well." I continued searching my memory for the reason Jones seemed familiar.

We shook hands as Susan left the office, closing the door behind her.

"Call me Peter, please."

"Okay, Peter. Let me glance at your form. Please have a seat."

We both sat. His name, Peter Jones, was the only piece of information on the form. To all other questions he had answered "Personal."

"Peter, you aren't giving me much information to let me know how I can help you."

His eyes examined my office as he said, "I have to be careful."

"I understand that. But if you don't give me more information than your name, I don't see how I can help you. Do you understand attorney-client privilege?"

Now his piercing eyes met mine.

"I do. But tell me your understanding of it."

"Anything you tell me, or anything I discover while representing you, is confidential. If I reveal anything that could be detrimental to you, I could be disbarred. Unless you tell me you are planning to commit a crime in the future, or you commit one against me."

"But you're not my lawyer until I hire you, correct?"

"That is true. But as soon as you come seeking my advice or assistance in a legal capacity, the attorney-client privilege takes effect. Even if you don't end up hiring me."

"What about your staff?"

"Any employee of mine, or any independent contractor I hire, is bound by the same confidentiality."

"And information you discover?"

"Well, if I find out either that you are committing, or you're about to commit, a crime, my duty as an officer of the court requires me to report it. And if I am a victim of anything you do, I am freed from confidentiality. But anything you have already done is between you and me."

Peter was still looking nervous. His eyes darted to various objects in my office—my law diploma, my awards, my undergraduate diploma, my desk—I'm most proud of my Citizen of the Year Award from my township; but Peter hardly glanced at the plaque as his eyes moved to the wood paneling behind it, and then to the window. What was he looking for?

"Please tell me why you are here."

"You're independently wealthy and you only represent people you believe have been wronged or are innocent."

"Okay, that's why *I* am here. Why are *you* here? What happened that led you to want to meet with me?" Prying information from Peter was harder than taking a Tesla from a liberal.

"Do you sweep your office?"

This was getting downright strange. He was the first client I had who had asked me if I sweep my office. Yet I understood he wasn't talking about cleanliness but about a different kind of bug.

"Once a month." I didn't want to completely level with him until I saw where he was going.

"When was the last time?"

"A couple of weeks ago." I lied again.

"Not recent enough."

"Look, I have never had any client information compromised. And I really don't want to share all of my security measures with someone I know nothing about."

"If I hire you, you will be subject to more surveillance than you have ever been in the past."

My curiosity was strong, like my coffee. But I don't like playing games.

"Still, I'm not a mind reader and I don't have ESP. If you want me to help you, you're going to have to let me know why you're here."

Peter got up and started pacing around my office. He paid particular attention to my windows, seeming to examine all possible site lines to the neighboring buildings, not that there were that many. My office was in Fort Washington Office Park. It was convenient to the Pennsylvania Turnpike and the 309 Expressway. It was near the new Upper Dublin Public Library. Office buildings there were limited to four stories, and my building wasn't attached to any other: several parking lots and grassy knolls span the space in between.

"Your windows have rippled glass."

I thought I knew where this was going, based on Peter's concern for security, but I decided to play dumb.

"I like the look."

Peter turned from the window and looked directly into my eyes.

"Did you buy this building after it was already built or did you have it built yourself?"

This question took me by surprise. I do own the building but the true ownership is cloaked behind various corporate structures to keep the other tenants from coming to my office to register complaints, ask for favors, or explain why their rent was going to be late. Peter was the first to have discovered I own it.

"If you know I own the building, I suspect you also know the answer to your question."

Peter's eyes twinkled and he smiled for the first time.

"I did a little research about you before coming here."

"More than a little, I'd say."

Another smile.

"After you bought the building, you did extensive work on your offices before moving your firm in. What kind of work did you have done?"

"Are you an architect designing a building?"

Another smile as he said, "I suspect you had security issues."

"As an attorney, I always do."

"I suspect you may need more security than most attorneys."

Now I *was* getting nervous.

"Look, I don't like playing games or dancing around issues. If you have specific questions about my security that you want to ask before telling me why you're here, ask me."

"Did you line the walls, floors, and ceilings of your offices with metal?"

Again, I was surprised. This level of security knowledge wasn't common. Metal linings, as well as rippled glass windows, can be used to interfere with infrared or microwave eavesdropping technology, not typically used by local law enforcement, but used by federal law enforcement, as well as various intelligence agencies.

I decided to be honest. "I did."

In Peter's eyes I saw something that made me think he was beginning to trust me.

"And you only sweep once per month?" He sounded skeptical.

Again, I decided to level with him. "Actually, once a day."

Peter sat down again, a little more relaxed.

"Who handles security for you?"

"Why? Are you looking for a job?"

No smile. His eyes bore into mine.

"Who handles security for you?"

"Echelon, out of Royersford."

"Excellent choice." For the first time during our conversation, Peter—if that really was his name—seemed completely relaxed.

"So happy you approve. Can we now get to why you are here?"

Okay, getting information from Peter was even harder than taking a Tesla from a liberal. It was more like prying an AR-15 from a conservative.

CHAPTER 2

"My name isn't Peter Jones."

I was shocked. Shocked, I tell you!

I crumbled up the Initial Consultation form and tossed it into the trash.

"How about we start with the truth?" I pulled a legal pad toward me to begin taking notes. I saw "Peter's" eyes watch me with concern. "My notes are also part of attorney-client privilege."

Pause.

"My name is Allen Crosby."

Now I realized why he looked familiar. Crosby's wife had been murdered two days earlier. It was big news in Upper Dublin Township, because homicides are unusual here. His face was on the major media outlets all across the Philadelphia metropolitan area. And he had been a popular well-known figure in the area for some time.

"I'm sorry for your loss, Mr. Crosby. How can I help you?"

"First, you can call me Allen. Second, you can find out who killed my wife and who is trying to frame me for it."

"Okay, Allen. What makes you think someone is trying to frame you for it?"

"Well, for one, I woke up this morning with my hand wrapped around the grip of this."

He reached into his pocket and put a Glock 17 9mm gun on my desk. I stared at it.

"It's not yours?"

"No."

"Exactly how soundly *do* you sleep?"

Allen smiled slightly.

"Usually not very, but last night I went out like a light."

"Did anything different happen last night?"

"I went to the Jarrettown to get a couple drinks to help me calm down before bed. I've been devastated since Deidre's murder Tuesday. As I was getting ready to leave, someone who said he recognized me from the news offered to buy me another drink in consolation. I accepted."

I waited. Silence.

"Did you feel drugged after the drink?"

"Not right away. But after I got home, I felt drunker than I should have and tumbled into my bed to sleep it off, then woke up this morning with this." He nodded at the gun.

"Who was the Good Samaritan who bought you the drink?"

"I don't know. He said his name was Ted."

"What time did you get home?"

"Not late. About eleven."

Damn. If a typical date rape drug was used, it was probably too late to detect now. I told Allen as much.

"The drug is probably out of your system by now; but just in case, I want you to get a complete tox screen. I'm going to call downstairs to Dr. Long on the first floor. His office will give you a blood test prescription. Pick it up now and go straight to Abington Hospital to get the blood drawn. I don't want to get the rest of the story from you now, because every minute you wait is too long. After you do that, come back here and we'll continue."

Allen agreed. He left my office as I picked up the phone to call Dr. Long. Then I buzzed Abby, a researcher in my firm.

"Get me everything that's out there on the Crosby murder. And find out if the Jarrettown Hotel has any surveillance tapes."

CHAPTER 3

I stared at the Glock on my desk. The weapon raised ethical questions and, potentially, more than a few dilemmas. So far there was no evidence that the gun had been used in any crime, other than Allen's inference that it wasn't voluntarily placed in his hand, and that it wasn't his. That indicated an unknown intruder had broken into Allen's home. However, if someone was indeed trying to frame him, or if Allen was lying, chances were that gun was the murder weapon. As an officer of the court, I had a duty to turn the gun in if it was used in a crime. I could keep it to test it...which might result in fingerprints being found on the grip or the trigger or the clip—anywhere, really; but I doubted whether testing would reveal anyone's fingerprints, other than Allen's that is. If someone was trying to frame Allen, they would have wiped the gun clean before putting it in his hand, and so I was willing to bet only Allen's fingerprints would be on it. If this were an elaborate setup, would the killer not have gotten Allen's fingerprints on the gun before the murder? Why would they wait until days after the killing? Was the murder unplanned and *then* the murderer chose to frame Allen? And if Allen was lying, his fingerprints would also be on it. *And* I couldn't test it to see whether it was the murder weapon because I had no ballistics to compare it to. True, I could test the gun to see if it had been fired recently; but even if the result came back positive, it wouldn't have been specific enough to determine whether the gun was the weapon that had been used to kill Deidre Allen.

On the other hand, if Allen hired me, if he got arrested, and I appeared on his behalf, the police would figure out where I got the weapon. And that would violate my duty of confidentiality to my client.

I could hire the president of the Montgomery County Bar Association to represent me and turn the gun over to her. She could then turn it over to the police, honestly saying that she did not know whether or not it was used in a crime but that it was given to her by a client. That would fulfill all of my ethical responsibilities.

But even before I took that step—what tests did I want to run on it?

I called Abby again.

"Put on a pair of rubber gloves, bring a plastic bag, and come into my office."

"Yes, sir."

Abby came in a few minutes later with eyebrows raised and curiosity written all over her face. She's a Latina, shorter than Susan, and a first-generation American. Her parents spoke Spanish at home—one of the benefits Abby brings my firm. Another is the police officer training she received while serving in the Marines. She knows how to defend herself and is a top-notch investigator. All of that, and she's only in her thirties.

"Put the gun in the bag and send it to the lab," I instructed Abby. "Have them get any evidence they can from the gun, specifically fingerprints, their fast touch DNA analysis, and when it was last fired. Ttell them to conduct any other tests they can think of to determine if it was used to shoot someone. Unfortunately, we can't do a ballistics test because we have nothing to compare the results to. Check the serial number to see if it's registered."

Abby carefully placed the gun in the bag; then she closed the bag, writing the date, time, and place where she obtained the gun on the outside of the bag.

"What have you discovered about the Crosby murder so far?"

"Not much more than the media is reporting." She smiled apologetically. "They say her husband was out for an errand and came back and discovered her shot. He called 911 right away. When EMTs arrived, she was dead.

I checked with someone in the Upper Dublin Police Department; but he would only say that the police don't have any suspects yet and are checking all leads, including the husband's alibi. Is the gun related to the murder?"

"Possibly." Now it was my turn to smile apologetically. "Keep researching the murder and the Crosbys. Thanks."

Abby left, and I made a mental note that the alibi hadn't yet been verified.

Susan knocked. She entered the office and said, "Mr. Frankel, Mr. *Jones* is back." Her emphasis on "Jones" made it obvious she did not believe that was his name.

Allen walked in looking a little less nervous than he had earlier. "That was easy," he said. Susan closed the door while maintaining questioning eye contact with me.

"Yes." I nodded. "Usually the lab is not as busy midafternoon as it is first thing in the morning."

He smiled enigmatically at me. "You haven't asked me for any money yet."

"I have not agreed to represent you yet. First, let me get some more information." I pulled my legal pad closer to me then continued to take notes from where I left off.

"Tell me what happened."

Allen sat down. "Do you have any specific questions?"

"I'm sure I will after you tell me what happened."

"Okay. It was Tuesday, early evening. We were planning to drive to visit our daughter, her partner, and our granddaughter on Wednesday, and we realized we hadn't gotten any cash for the trip. I love to walk, and it was still light out, so I went to the ATM. When I got back..." Allen's voice began to quiver. He stopped speaking, composed himself, and continued: "When I got back, Deidre was on the living room floor with blood all over the place."

He paused again. I remained silent, and once again he continued.

"I called 911. They sent police and an ambulance. They said she was dead...but I already knew that."

I remained silent to see if he would add anything. He didn't.

"How did you know she was dead?"

"I couldn't find a pulse, and the blood wasn't flowing any more. She had blood all over her midsection and on her head. After I called 9-1-1 I kept trying to find a heartbeat but couldn't. I tried mouth-to-mouth but she never started breathing on her own."

"Okay." Everything made sense so far. But there were still a lot of questions. "Why did you need cash? I assume you have a credit card, and obviously a debit card if you went to an ATM."

"If we stop at a road stop, and even when we take the girls out in Brooklyn, it's often faster and easier to use cash than a card."

"That's true." I paused. "Tuesday evening was nice out. How come Deidre didn't walk with you to the ATM?"

"Well, she doesn't like to walk as much as I do. She gets…got fatigued easily, due to a chronic condition. I also like the woods and went through the park to the ATM."

"You live on Timber Lane, right?"

"That's right."

"So this would be Sandy Run Park you walked through?"

"Right again."

"And the ATM was at KeyBank at Twining and Limekiln?"

"Correct."

I shifted in my chair. "What time did you leave for the walk and what time did you get back?"

"I'm not sure. A little after five o'clock. It didn't take very long. I called 911 seconds after coming back. I'm sure they have the time recorded somewhere."

"How long would you estimate the walk took?"

"I don't know. Maybe twenty minutes."

"Round trip?"

"Yeah."

"Did you use your landline or your cell to call 911?"

"We don't have a landline. I used my cell. Which I left on the coffee table in the living room, so it was close by when I needed to call 911."

"You didn't take it with you on the walk?"

"No, why?"

"Possibly GPS tracking could verify what you are saying."

"You don't believe me?"

I stared at Allen. "Okay, we need to get something straight here. I haven't yet formed a conclusion about you. But if this goes to court, then what I think won't matter. The evidence will. So GPS tracking to verify the alibi would come in handy." With that I returned to the task at hand. "Did you happen to see anyone on your walk?"

"I don't remember seeing anyone."

I nodded. "Okay. Hopefully the ATM camera at the bank will have an accurate time stamp. Can you think of a reason someone would want to kill Deidre?"

Pause.

He shouldn't have needed to pause. He must have already considered this repeatedly and have already come to a conclusion.

"I don't think anyone would. Everyone liked her. She was a great friend, neighbor. Our kids say that they have never met anyone as nice as she is."

"Did either of you have an intimate friendship with anyone else?"

"We have close friends, but if you mean a physically intimate relationship, then no."

"How do you know she didn't?"

Allen looked offended.

"Besides trusting my best friend, Deidre wouldn't have time. We tried to spend as much time as possible with each other. When we socialize with others, it's as a couple."

I paused, thinking.

"When I asked you why someone might want to kill Deidre, you paused before assuring me that nobody would have a motive to do so. Why did you need to pause if you were so sure? Surely you've been thinking about this since Tuesday."

Allen seemed taken aback. He did not meet my eyes as he said, "You're right. I've been thinking about it. I reviewed my thoughts before answering your question."

I decided to let that go for now. He wasn't yet comfortable enough with me to answer truthfully. I would get it out of him before agreeing to take his case, I thought.

Again I returned to the task at hand.

"Tell me if I've got any of this wrong. A married couple who are very much in love with no outside romantic interests are planning to visit kids and grandkid. Husband leaves for twenty minutes to get cash for the trip, and during that time someone breaks in and kills his wife, who is the nicest person in the world, with no enemies. Said killer or killers then leave before husband returns. Correct?"

Allen frowned. "Except for one thing."

"What's that?"

"Police commented that they saw no evidence that anyone had broken in."

"Did you leave the door unlocked when you left?"

"No. I locked the patio doors when I left and unlocked them when I returned. Police asked me the same thing."

"You went out and came in through the patio doors?"

"Yes."

"What about the front door?"

"It was locked. Had to unlock it for the police and EMTs."

"How about when you left?"

"I didn't check it but we always left all doors locked."

"So whoever did this would have to be either someone Deidre would let in, or someone who had a key. Who had keys besides yourself and Deidre?"

"Just our kids. Oh, and our next-door neighbor in case there is an emergency."

"Any gripe you or Deidre have with your neighbors recently?"

"No, they're great people."

"We both know you're into security. What kind did you have at home?"

"We had an alarm we set when we went to bed. We also have a safe room. And I have a gun."

I tried not to flinch. "What kind of gun?"

"Glock 17."

Same model he found in bed with him.

I paused a moment, thinking.

"Okay. Let's move to the attempt to frame you. Before last night, did you ever see the person who bought you the drink at Jarrettown?"

Allen shook his head. "Not that I remember."

"And you never saw the gun that you brought me before you woke up with it this morning?"

A pregnant pause.

"I can't be sure of that."

"What? When did you see it before?"

"I don't know if I did. I've seen guns like it. Mine is that model. When I woke up with the gun in my hand, I checked and mine was still where I keep it."

"We'll get back to that. Do you have any idea who might be trying to frame you or why?"

Pause.

"Yes."

"Okay, let's not play Twenty Questions. Who and why?"

"What do you know about me—besides my wife's death, I mean?"

I sighed impatiently. "You're rich. You travel the world making smart investments in good companies—and you get richer."

Allen smiled.

"I am comfortable. Many of my travels around the world are done at the behest of the government."

"Our government?"

"Yes," he replied, with a chuckle.

"Exactly what part of our government?"

"Well, it's often referred to as 'No Such Agency.' "

I let out a low whistle. "The NSA? Are you shittin' me?"

"Absolutely true. Rich people traveling are a good cover for spies."

I thought about the stories I had heard of Frank Sinatra, Greta Garbo, Josephine Baker, Harry Houdini…all doing various classified work while traveling. Cary Grant not only spied for the British, he would have been perfect casting to play a spy in the movies.

"I've heard stories. So what did you do for them?"

"I could tell you but then I'd have to kill you."

I blanched. "What?"

"Just a joke," he said with a smile.

"Very funny," I said without one.

"Basically my job was to see if certain businesses were involved in helping terrorists, or building weapons they were not supposed to be building under the terms of the treaties we'd worked out with them. I did that while appearing to do my due diligence before investing in them."

"And these business owners are the people you think might be trying to frame you?"

"No. They don't know I was looking them over for the government."

"Then who? NSA agents?"

"Some of them."

"Why?"

"It's a pretty long story…"

"Hold on for a sec." I buzzed the intercom. "Susan, do I have any appointments coming up?"

Susan checked. "You have appointments with two prospective clients this afternoon. No court appearances."

"Move the two prospectives to associates."

"Got it." The curiosity in her voice could be heard even in those two words.

I looked up at Allen. "I've got time."

Allen seemed to relax. He crossed his arms behind his head and settled back in his chair. "As I've said, on some of my trips I would investigate particular companies for potential investments as a guise to discover as many secrets about the company as possible. I then come back and report what I saw or was told by the executives. If I discover something those executives are not supposed to be doing, like selling arms to the wrong parties, researching biological weapons, or developing nuclear weapons to sell to the highest bidder, my superiors are very interested. Shortly after that, I typically hear that something 'happened' to those companies."

"What kind of things 'happen'?"

"Sometimes a lab explodes. Sometimes their own government shuts them down. Sometimes a computer virus destroys whatever project they're working on."

"Didn't the business owners ever suspect you?

"My cover seemed to work. Especially since, if I found something unauthorized was going on, I acted impressed and invested a substantial amount in the company. The US government reimbursed me for any losses."

"So, since you are an investor in the company, you aren't suspected of having anything to do with the unfortunate incidents that followed?"

"Correct."

I nodded. "Okay, so far I'm with you. This doesn't yet explain why NSA agents would want to frame you for Deidre's murder."

"On one of my nongovernmental sponsored investment trips, I came across a company that demonstrated how they kept their overhead so low."

"How?"

"Slave children working in their factories. And some of the company's income came from renting the children out at night to those who wanted to use or abuse them. And if a child started becoming too rebellious, they were sold outright."

I stopped taking notes. "Did you report this company to your superiors?"

"Yes, even though the government did not send me on this trip, I did. And to continue keeping myself protected, I invested in it."

"What happened?"

"I made lots of money from them."

"Nothing bad 'happened' to them, like the other companies?"

Allen shook his head. "No. When I questioned my controller, he said not to worry about it, they were handling it. For a while, I accepted that. Then one time I was in the area where this company is located, and I decided to check on them again, ostensibly as one of their investors. Whenever I'm on these trips, I hire a driver and a limo that has tinted glass so nobody outside can see who I am. As I rode up to the executive offices, who should come out the door but my controller and another man! I stayed in the limo until they left; then I entered the building. As a large investor, I was greeted like royalty. They assured me they were continuing to grow, and they asked whether I saw the men leaving just as I arrived. They told me they had just arranged to buy another shipment of children from them."

"My God." Allen's story seemed incredible; nevertheless, I was transfixed.

"My thoughts exactly. I asked the exec where these men get the children. He shrugged as he told me he thinks they are probably purchased from parents who don't want them, or they are kidnapped off the streets. He assured me they weren't expensive. He also assured me, when I asked, that there was no chance of them getting caught, because the chief investor—the buyer of the children—was a close friend of the president and other influential people."

I let out a low whistle. What Allen was telling me was horrible.

"But since your controller and his colleague didn't see you," I resumed, "I still don't see why they would want to discredit you by framing you."

"When I got back, I struggled over what to do. I didn't know if the influential investor and purchaser actually existed, or if he had been made up to assure nervous investors. I didn't know how high up this scheme went, so I couldn't just report it up the ladder. Then I figured that no matter who or how many other people were involved, the one thing they wouldn't be able to stand is public scrutiny. So I told my story to an *Inquirer* reporter who had interviewed me a few times. He told me he would gather evidence and then publish it. He thought it was a Pulitzer-worthy story and asked me not to let anyone else know. I agreed."

"Which reporter?" I figured we might need him as a witness.

"Paul Roberts."

I gasped.

Paul Roberts, an upcoming reporter in his thirties, had died while working in his loft the week before. According to the *Inquirer*, the coroner concluded Roberts's death was caused by carbon monoxide poisoning from a portable heater he had in the loft.

"Exactly," Allen said in response to my reaction. "I was trying to find out what really happened to him when Deidre was murdered."

"But why would they frame you for her murder instead of killing you?"

"I don't know."

"They would have had to time it exactly, knowing you were going out, and how long you'd be gone...."

I paused, thinking.

"Is there anything else at all you can think of that you haven't told me yet?"

Another pause while Allen thought.

"Roberts had told me he thought the investor the execs mentioned was not only an associate of our present president, but also of a prior one. He had been arrested by the feds but then got a sweetheart deal with no prison time."

"Seems like a confirmation of what you were told."

"True."

"Anything else."

Allen shook his head. "I don't think so."

"Don't wait for me to ask a specific question again," I said, scolding him lightly. "As I said, we aren't playing Twenty Questions. No other thoughts you had, no matter how crazy they might seem?"

"No."

"Okay. Keep your theory to yourself for now. . . . In fact, don't talk to anyone about this without me being present. Do you have any idea how the police investigation is going?"

Again he shook his head. "No."

"Okay, if they want to question you, tell them you have an attorney, give them one of my cards, and read them the back of it."

I handed Allen one of my business cards. He read the back out loud while squinting at a paragraph of business card sized type.

> *"My lawyer has instructed me not to talk to anyone about my case or anything else, and not to answer questions or reply to accusations. On advice of counsel I shall talk to no one in the absence of counsel.* ***I shall not give any consents or make any waivers of my legal rights under the 4th, 5th, and 6th Amendments of the US Constitution or under Article I Sections 8 and 9 of the PA Constitution.*** *Any requests for information or for consent to conduct searches, seizures, or investigations affecting my person, papers, property, or effects should be addressed to my lawyer. I request that my lawyer be notified and allowed to be present if any identification confrontations, tests, examinations, or investigations of any sort are conducted in my case, and I will not consent to any of the above."*

Allen laughed. "I guess that makes it pretty clear."

"It also has a great effect on a judge during a hearing to suppress evidence. Usually an officer reads their Miranda card to illustrate that he gave the defendant their rights before questioning them. If the defendant then reads this card to the judge as his answer to the officer before being questioned, the judge often has second thoughts about automatically believing the officer."

Allen nodded. "I still haven't hired you officially, have I?"

"No." I opened the top drawer to my desk then handed him my standard criminal retainer agreement.

He nodded to the form. "Anything I should be wary of in this?"

I smiled. "Not really. It lets me out if you stop paying me or if I find out you lied to me about anything we talk about."

Allen glanced at my rather large hourly rate and the requirement that he reimburse me for out-of-pocket costs.

As I figured, he didn't question the rate.

"There's a blank for the amount of the retainer."

"Oh, slide it back to me."

I wrote my retainer then handed the agreement back to him.

"One dollar? Really?"

"I trust you aren't going to cheat me, and I know you have the resources to pay. As of now, I have no idea if you'll be charged, or exactly what services I will be doing on your behalf. I'm confident we'll settle up. I have to charge something to make this a binding agreement. And, again, if I find you lied to me I *will* stop representing you."

Allen reached for his wallet. He slipped out the dollar then signed the agreement. I called Susan in to make copies. She glanced at the client name and nodded. Then she noticed the retainer amount and glared disapprovingly as she left to make copies.

As I said, she was more than my executive assistant. She handled the finances of the firm as well, for one thing.

"I'll contact both the Upper Dublin police and the Montgomery County DA to let them know I represent you and that they should contact me with anything concerning the investigation into Deidre's murder. I'll let you know if I learn anything. You need to contact me if you think of something you forgot to tell me, if anyone is too nosy about you, if you see people following you—or if the police contact you, of course."

He nodded, confirming my instructions. "I feel like I'm in good hands, Mr. Frankel."

"Oh, and call me Josh."

I stood from my chair and led him to the door.

CHAPTER 4

Bradley Sims was sitting in my office. He was a handsome, clean-cut man and actually could be cast as a prosecutor in a movie. He was white, but tan. Dark hair and eyes. When he came in, I noticed he was a little shorter than I was. I was reading his IC form.

"You're charged with burglary. Tell me what happened."

"Well, when I was taking stuff out of the townhouse a neighbor saw me and called the police."

"Why were you taking 'stuff' out of the townhouse?"

"It's my career." At least he was honest. "I steal things for a living."

"Mr. Sims, are you aware that I only represent innocent people?"

"I know that's your reputation. That's why I wanted to hire you—so people will think I'm innocent."

I smiled curtly. "I'm sorry. I cannot represent you."

"I can pay you double your normal fee. And my friends and I can give you lots of work."

"Thanks, but I don't need extra work. And, without knowing my fee, how is it that you think you can pay twice as much?"

"I'm very successful in my career. Rarely caught. When caught, rarely convicted."

I sighed. "Again, I'm sorry but I cannot help you. I must compliment you on your honesty with me though. Most clients who try to hire me even though they are guilty lie to me, and I need to find that out through research."

Bradley Sims shrugged. "I knew you would uncover the truth eventually, so I decided to be upfront with you."

"Again, thank you for that. But I cannot help you."

We shook hands, and Mr. Sims left my office. He was quite unusual. Most prospective clients tell me they are innocent or try to justify what they have done to try to make me think they were the victim. Usually it takes time and financial resources to uncover their lies. That was why my standard retainer agreement included a provision stating that the client agreed my firm can withdraw from representation if we discovered the client lied to me or any of my employees. It also stated that the client waived attorney-client privilege if we needed to prove to a court that the client lied. If we were too far into the case, we needed the court's permission to withdraw. Although I would not represent someone who lied to me, I might represent someone who was guilty of what they were charged with if it appeared they were actually the victim, or that justice would be better served if they were found not guilty. Many criminal laws are there to protect those who have power from those who do not.

Anatole France, the famous French writer once wrote: "In its majestic equality, the law forbids rich and poor alike to sleep under bridges, beg in the streets and steal loaves of bread." That sarcasm pretty much summed up my feelings about the law. Even though I was rich and a lawyer.

PART TWO

THE PREPARATION

CHAPTER 5

I called some of my staff into the conference room to fill them in on what I knew of the Crosby case and to assign duties to them. I also warned them about the NSA's interest in the case. I told Susan to call Echelon and ask them to increase our sweeps to twice a day, assign more security to the office, and protect each of us while we were traveling to and from the office.

Susan said, disapprovingly, "All of that for a one dollar retainer?"

"One dollar retainer, our hourly rate, plus reimbursement of our out-of-pocket costs. He is also very concerned about security and won't mind paying extra for it. And if Echelon says they can't do it immediately, ask to talk directly to Stu Visnov. He'll get it done."

I turned to Abby.

"Get all the info on Paul Roberts's death. And keep tabs on the progress of this investigation."

"Yes, sir."

Abby didn't seem her usual upbeat self.

"Something wrong, Abby?"

Abby scoffed mildly. "Do we believe him?"

"Well, you're my researcher. Have you found any reason to not believe him?"

"It's just all…I don't know…so fantastical."

"What is?"

"The whole thing. That the NSA would use him as a spy. Aren't they supposed to go about their business unnoticed? Not attracting attention. And that someone in the NSA, actually at least two in the NSA, along with a friend of the president, are involved somehow in child trafficking? And that these two, or others at their command, go to Mr. Crosby's house, wait until he leaves on a short errand, kill his wife in a locked house leaving no evidence of a break-in, then drug him at a bar, sneak into his house in the middle of the night, and put a gun in his hand to frame him?"

I'm honest with all of my staff; I had to admit Allen Crosby's case wasn't typical. "It isn't the usual set of facts. And I have been fooled by clients before." I gestured appreciatively to Abby. "Let's hear an alternative theory. If we conclude he's guilty or he lied to us, we'll stop representing him."

Abby said, "How about the obvious—that he got angry at his wife and killed her and wants to blame it on a conspiracy theory by the NSA?"

I nodded, considering her words. "Possibly. Let me ask you this. Have you begun researching Mr. Crosby?"

"Of course."

"What have you found out about him?"

"So far, mostly just background information."

"Such as?"

"Graduated first in his class from Wharton. Made a killing in real estate investing in Philadelphia. Used those profits to invest in businesses he thought were undervalued. He was right most of the time and made money hand over fist."

"Given that background, do you think Allen is more on the intelligent side or on the stupid side?"

"First from Wharton, studying and being right about undervalued businesses, I'd say he's pretty intelligent."

"Me too." I considered my next words carefully. "Tell me, what do you know about Abscam?"

"I remember something in school about an FBI sting to uncover corruption in Philadelphia."

"Good summary."

"But the NSA involved in child trafficking is different."

"I'm not comparing the two. Let's stick to Abscam for now. Do you remember what the FBI did to uncover corruption?"

"I seem to remember the 'Ab' part of the name came from the fact that the agents pretended to be Arab sheiks?"

"Right. But how would that uncover corruption?"

"Didn't they try to do some deals with city officials?"

Abby wasn't such a slouch. I knew there was a reason I liked her. "Yes. They met with various city officials and state officials based in Philadelphia and discussed investments they wanted to make in the city. But, although they tried to convince them it was win-win, they also sweetened the deal by offering them bribes if they would push the projects they had in mind. Some of the officials they met with they didn't have to convince to take bribes. In fact one state rep, Ozzie Myers, was recorded telling them that 'money talks and bullshit walks.' "

Everyone around the conference table chuckled.

I continued: "The FBI also tried to find businessmen who would bribe public officials on their behalf. They looked for those who had been successful dealing with members of the City Council and other elected officials. One of those they approached was an up-and-coming real estate developer named Allen Crosby."

I had everyone's attention now. "Does anyone here know what happened when the fake sheiks offered their bribery plan to Allen?"

Silence, attentive silence, filled the room. "He reported it to the FBI."

I let that sink in.

"What does that tell you?"

Jerry Lee, one of my senior associates, ventured: "That he has integrity?"

Like Abby, Jerry was also a first-generation American. His parents migrated from China and gave him the decidedly American name of Jerry.

"Exactly. So here we have someone who has built his life and his fortune using his intelligence and his integrity. Do any of you think someone like that would come up with the story he told us if it were not true?"

Silence, thoughtful silence, this time.

Abby again, ever the suspicious type: "Well, we know he either had integrity decades ago or he smelled something suspicious and chose to cover his tracks. We know he's smart…so maybe he figured out the scam. Also, when you think you're always the smartest person in the room, you might be arrogant enough to come up with this outrageous story."

"Good," I agreed. "Keep thinking and researching. If anyone finds anything that can back up Abby's theory, or if you come up with one of your own, let me know. As you know, I firmly believe in the saying that if two people agree on everything, one of them isn't necessary. And I'm sure none of you wants to be unnecessary. Right now, I tend to believe Allen, but I could be wrong." I paused. "Does anybody have any other theories they would like to discuss now?"

After thirty seconds without anyone volunteering an answer, I said, "Okay, you all have your orders. And protection from Echelon will help you do your jobs unmolested. Be careful out there." I paused. Nobody moved. "What are you waiting for?"

CHAPTER 6

That night, as I slid down my long-time lover's striking body, licking my way to her satisfaction, I couldn't help thinking about Allen and Deidre Crosby. My mind is usually on other, more appropriate thoughts during these activities, but as hard as I tried to keep my mind on the matters at hand—or rather, at mouth, if you will—it kept drifting to Allen and Deidre.

Here was a happily married intelligent, wealthy couple with a couple of kids and I didn't know how many grandkids. He volunteered some of his time for his country's needs. I knew that he was a big philanthropist, trying to make the world a better place for those who were not as fortunate as him, intellectually or financially. He never griped about his taxes, in fact publicly advocating for more taxes on the wealthy.

With a twenty-minute walk, their lives change. She was dead, he was missing his best friend, and he was probably the leading suspect in her death. Although, as far as I know, the prosecution had enough facts to prove opportunity but not motive. Proving motive wasn't required; but as a practical matter, it was needed to convict someone like Allen. They definitely needed more than just opportunity. Was that why the Glock had been planted in his hands? But if the NSA wanted to kill Allen, why did they come by when he wasn't home? Surely they had enough resources to know who was home and who was not. Why did they kill Deidre? Did she know something Allen didn't know? Did she also work for the NSA? I made a mental note to ask Allen about that.

Or was Abby right? Was this a scam being run by a very smart Allen Crosby? He knew people would think he was too smart to commit this crime when he appeared to be the only person with opportunity. Was that part of his plan? To use his intelligence to actually bolster his unlikely tale?

My thoughts were interrupted as my lover started getting excited. It seems my motion was filed and was being actively considered. So actively that her butt raised from the bed. When that happened, I noticed two eyes over the edge of the mattress; I had to keep from laughing. It seems there was at least one observer in the court this evening. I decided I would talk to her about that later.

With one loud shout, she granted my motion and gradually came back to earth.

"You have to do something about the dog while we are otherwise engaged."

Her dog was adorable, half chihuahua and half miniature dachshund. She says he's a *chiweenie*. Anyway, he's the one who was watching us. Owing to his split heritage, she named him Taco Hund.

Susan laughed.

Did I mention that she was more than my executive assistant?

CHAPTER 7

Abby observed that the Crosby home had that happy, lived-in look rather than the museum quality that seems to pervade homes of some other wealthy people. She noticed many photographs of an apparently happy family. There were many candids, in addition to the few posed studio pictures, which looked less authentic.

"I like your home."

Abby also noticed that Allen seemed to be avoiding the living room, which she remembered was the scene of the crime.

"Thank you," Allen replied.

After getting Allen to repeat his story about the evening of the murder, and hearing that it did not differ in any material matter from what Josh had told them in the conference room, she said, "Show me."

"Excuse me?"

"Act out that night, beginning when you left for your walk to the bank."

Allen led her out the patio doors and turned to lock them—but only after the four security men from Echelon exited with them. A good sign that that, in fact, was Allen's habit. Or was he just remembering his story and acting it out? He led her on the pathway toward the parking lot of KeyBank and a generic office building. Along the way, Abby took notes. Security followed at a discrete distance.

"What are you writing?"

"I'm looking at the site lines from your path and making notes as to which neighbors might have glanced out their windows and saw you walking that evening."

"I'm not a stranger to this park," Allen replied. "I'd be surprised if they would remember which day they saw me."

Abby registered that Allen's reasoning might be a defense in case nobody stepped forward to confirm his alibi.

"It's been my experience that on the day of a traumatic event, if a neighbor or a passerby sees something that somehow relates to what happened, many people actually remember which day it happened. Certainly hearing that a neighbor has been murdered and seeing her husband walking in the woods at approximately the same time as the murder could stimulate an association."

"I see." Allen did not seem nervous about that reasoning.

They reached the parking lot, where Allen led Abby along the asphalt lot to the ATM.

"Was there much traffic that evening?"

Allen gestured to the street. "Well, this is the corner of Limekiln and Twining, and it was rush hour, so..."

"I mean in the parking lot. Were people leaving the office building? Were there many cars at the bank's drive-through window? Anyone else walking through the parking lot? Any other movement you can think of?"

Abby studied Allen's face as he considered her questions. Was he trying to remember the circumstances...or trying to decide what would make his story more believable?

"I really didn't notice. Or, I should say, I don't remember. I'm sure I was careful walking through the parking lot so I didn't get hit by a car. Probably there was some traffic, given the time. Also people traveling home from work sometimes stop to use the drive-through window."

Abby looked around the ATM in all directions, making a mental note to come back at about the same time, and on the same day of the week, as Allen's walk the night of the murder.

"Okay, let's head back the way you did that evening."

"I always go back the same way as I came," Allen said, making no movement to start.

"Okay then," Abby smiled. "Let's go back, I left my car at your house."

Allen smiled. The two of them, followed by the security men, headed back.

"Did you hear anything unusual either on your way to the ATM or back?"

"No, nothing out of the ordinary. Rush hour traffic, a little honking. Inside the park I'm sure I heard some birds; but if it were something out of the ordinary I would remember."

They continued walking. Abby heard the sounds of children playing in the woods. "Were there any kids in the woods during your walk that evening?"

Allen thought for a moment. "Honestly, I don't remember. My guess is there were not, since they're usually home by rush hour."

Abby noted that his answer again negated the possibility that anyone had witnessed his walking through the woods.

As they reached the house Abby said, "Okay, now try to reenact what you did that night."

Allen stepped up on the patio, reached for his keys, and unlocked the doors. Again Abby thought, *This is a good sign. He didn't try the doors first, which means he's used to unlocking them after his walk.* But again she wondered whether he was simply remembering the story he had told Josh? He slid the door open and turned back to Abby.

"I probably called out to Deidre that I was back."

"Don't narrate it," Abby told him, "pretend it is that night and do it."

"Honey, I'm back!" Allen paused. "Deidre?"

Another pause as he walked through the kitchen toward the bedroom areas in the large rancher. Abby noticed that Allen could either turn right—as he did now—or left, into the living room, after he entered through the large patio doors. Why did he head to the bedroom instead of the living area to look for Deidre when it was so early in the evening?

"Deidre, are you packing?"

Well, that explained why he headed to the bedroom first. He glanced in the master bedroom then headed back the other way. This time he glanced in the den and continued calling his wife's name: "Deidre? Deidre?" When he got to the living room, he stopped for a second and stared at a location on the floor. Abby could still smell the disinfectant used by the crew that had cleaned up the crime scene. Allen turned to Abby, and Abby saw the tears in his eyes. Were they real or crocodile?

"There was a throw rug Diedre was on. They took the old one during the cleanup." A tear escaped his eye.

Abby nodded. "Keep acting like it's that evening."

"I'm not sure I can."

More tears started rolling down Allen's cheeks, and he took a tissue from the coffee table and wiped his face. Either he was an excellent actor, or he was telling Abby the truth.

After Allen had composed himself, Abby said, "Try to keep going. What did you do when you came in and saw Deidre?"

Allen nodded then knelt on the side of the coffee table across from the sofa.

"Deidre!...Can you hear me?"

Allen reached for the cellphone on the coffee table. Abby noted that he had left his phone on this walk exactly where he had said he left it that night. Substantiation…or acting out the story? He turned and looked at Abby.

"You don't want me to actually call 9-1-1, do you?"

"No, but say what you said to them as best you remember."

Allen held the phone to his ear. "My wife's on the floor bleeding and she's not answering me. Send help please! She looks like she's been shot!"

"Did they ask for your address?"

"Yes, but I'm not sure why since they're supposed to be able to tell on these new cell phones."

"To verify the information. Okay, what next?"

"The operator told me not to hang up, that help was on the way. She asked if I could tell anything about Deidre's condition. I tried to find a pulse in her neck and couldn't. I told them that. The operator asked if I could tell if she had actually been shot. That's when I noticed she wasn't actually bleeding, she had bled, but the bleeding had stopped and she was lying in a mess of blood. I told her that there was a lot of blood around her chest, but couldn't tell for sure what caused it. But there was a hole in the middle of her forehead that looked like a bullet hole. I don't remember if there was anything else to our conversation. Then there was a pounding at the front door. I also realized I had heard a siren. I opened the front door for the officer just as an ambulance crew came running to the house. The officer told the operator he was on the scene and gave me back my phone. He told me I could hang up, so I tried to thank the operator but she had already hung up."

"What did the officer do?"

"First he asked me if the perpetrator could still be in the house. I told him I didn't know. He had me wait out front while he searched the house. Then he had me sit down in the den while the EMTs tried to help Deidre. He asked me exactly what happened and began taking notes."

Abby stared carefully at Allen. "Is there anything you forgot to tell him that you've told Josh or me?"

Allen thought.

"Not that I can think of."

"Is there anything you told him that you forgot to tell Josh or me?"

"Again, not that I can think of. The officer's questions were thorough. He asked me if I owned a gun and asked me to lead him to it after I said I did. He put rubber gloves on and put the gun in a plastic bag. He said it had to be tested."

"Did you tell him about the NSA?"

Allen looked over at the security detail nervously—they had remained in the hallway—then went to the front windows and looked out toward the street. Then he turned on the stereo a bit loudly.

"Please don't ask me questions like that outside your firm's secure office."

"Sorry."

Abby thought Allen's paranoia either resulted from his story being true or his putting it on to make it *seem* it was true.

"No, I didn't tell them. It hadn't yet occurred to me as possibly being related. I thought it had been a robbery gone wrong."

"When did you change your mind?"

"Later that evening."

"What made you change your mind?"

"While the officers were here they had me search the house to see if anything had been taken. I couldn't find anything missing. They said maybe the burglars had thought nobody was home, Deidre surprised them, they shot her, and then they fled in panic before taking anything. I thought that was possible. Then I remembered the child trafficking issue. And then I thought of Paul's sudden death."

"Paul Roberts, the reporter?"

"Yes. And none of the windows or doors were unlocked or broken. I put two and two together."

"Sounds like you came up with four, but let's hope for all of us the real answer is five."

"Yeah."

"Anything else you want to add before I go?"

"That's the same thing the officer asked. I'll tell you the same thing: not that I can think of."

Well, Abby thought, *that still leaves the possibility that he could add new details to his story later.*

CHAPTER 8

Abby left Allen's house. She had noticed that the park Allen walked through went behind most of the houses on the street. She walked over to the house next door to Allen's, the one closer to the bank. She rang the bell.

From behind the door a woman's voice inquired, "Who is it?"

"I'm Abby Garcia, investigating the death of Deidre Crosby."

The door opened an inch but the chain was still attached. Abby always chuckled inwardly when people did this. As if someone up to no good couldn't push their way in, breaking the chain's hold on the door.

"Could I see some identification?" the woman asked

"Sure."

Abby showed the woman her ID identifying her as an investigator. It looked genuinely official and always worked to convince potential witnesses that she was who she said she was.

The door opened. Always the investigator, Abby noticed the woman's features. She was in her forties. Height about five foot four. Weight about 150 pounds.

"You can't be too careful in this day and age."

"You're right," Abby agreed, thinking the woman was not being very careful at all.

"I'm Abby Garcia," Abby repeated, extending her hand.

"I'm Marge Tablou," the neighbor said while shaking Abby's hand. "Come in. Such a horrible thing, Deidre's murder! I'm not sure I can help you though. As I told the last officer who was here, I didn't hear or see anything."

That answered Abby's first question, but she decided to verify it.

"You were home at the time, correct?"

"Yes. I am home most of the time."

"I may have a few questions the officer didn't ask. For instance, did you see anyone walking through the park behind your house that evening?"

"I don't think so. I don't remember."

"When you do see people walking as far away as the park, can you identify who they are?"

"If they are someone I know, usually."

"Have you ever seen either or both of the Crosbys walk in that park?"

"Yes. Although usually it's just Allen."

"If you had seen Allen that night, do you think you'd remember?"

"Oh yes! That would have stuck in my mind." Pause. "Such a lovely woman. Who would have wanted to kill her?"

"That's what we're trying to figure out, ma'am." Abby was always sure to talk like a cop and not identify who "we" are unless specifically asked. She didn't want to lie. Nothing could derail a client's defense faster than the client's lawyer appearing to hire investigators who lie. How could the men and women of the jury believe any details about the case the investigator might testify to at trial?

Abby returned to her questioning. "You said you didn't see or hear anything. No sound that might have seemed like the backfire of a truck, too loud for this residential street?"

"I don't remember anything. But sometimes I hear backfires from the parking lot at the end of the park, or the supermarket parking lot across Twining. They have loud trucks that make deliveries."

Abby nodded. "I'm sure." She cleared her throat then continued: "Did you see anything, like a car or a van across the street, or in the Crosby's driveway, that was unusual?"

Marge thought.

"Other than the PECO van that was across the street, I don't think so."

PECO. The Philadelphia Electric Company. Abby was interested in this piece of news.

"Was electricity out in the neighborhood?"

"Not here. I don't know if any of the houses across the street had lost electricity."

"Were there any storms that day?"

"No, it was a beautiful day. Not too hot and not too cold."

"Was an electric wire down across the street?"

"Not that I noticed."

"Okay, Marge. Try to think hard. Did you see any PECO employees working out there? Maybe climbing one of their polls? Maybe walking around inspecting?"

Marge paused, thinking.

"I don't remember. I may have. But I wouldn't have thought anything about it. Do you think the PECO men had anything to do with this?"

"I doubt it. Just trying to locate other possible witnesses."

"Do the police have a suspect yet?"

Abby shook her head. "I don't know."

"Wouldn't they tell you?"

"I'm running an investigation separate from the police."

Marge looked confused.

"Well, thank you for your help today, Marge. Here's my card in case you think of anything else."

"Thank you," Marge said, still unsure.

Abby left before Marge could ask who she was working for. Then she went to several other neighbors' houses. She spent considerable time interviewing the neighbors, but she discovered no new information.

CHAPTER 9

I loved our local Friends Meeting House, where the memorial service was held. It was built in 1814, and looked like it. The original stone walls were still intact, and a horse block five steps high sat outside. Parking was limited, so arrangements had been made with area churches and synagogues to allow parking and busing of congregants and well-wishers from the lots of those houses of worship to the Friends Meeting House. In fact, the meeting house had been there so long that the road it was on was Meeting House Road.

Deidre's memorial service was very moving—and very crowded. An overflow audience had to wait outside to greet Allen. Friends and colleagues unfamiliar with Quaker ways were surprised to find no pulpit in the meeting house, and no leader for the service. Friends, family, and colleagues stood up to speak as the spirit moved them.

All four sets of pews faced the center of the room. And all four sets were packed with men and women wanting to honor Deidre's memory. Although organizers brought in extra folding chairs, many of the attendees were standing, crowded into the aisles. Elected officials from the area were in attendance, in recognition of Allen's position in the community. Nobody had sought out the town's fire marshal to enforce the posted limitation on the number of people allowed in the room.

Speaker after speaker memorialized Deidre as a great friend, a compassionate person, and a loving wife who possessed a great sense of humor.

The speakers gave numerous examples of her spirited wit that made all of us smile, laugh, cry.

A cliché states that murderers like to watch the results of their work—the investigation, the effects on survivors, any memorial service or funeral service held to commemorate the victim's passing. The reason it's a cliché is because it is often true.

My staff was spread throughout the meeting house. Echelon agents were surreptitiously snapping pictures of those attending. Abby remained in the lobby, pretending to be too broken up to enter the sanctuary; actually, she was watching to see if any attendee did not sign the guestbook on their way in.

After everyone else left, my staff and the Echelon agents met briefly to discuss if any of us had seen anything suspicious. We had not. The Echelon agents would print out their pictures later for us to review and stick in our file; but as far as all of our observations were concerned, nobody at the service had stuck out as being a suspect.

Perhaps Allen was correct. Maybe nobody had a reason to kill Deidre.

CHAPTER 10

Jerry Lee was packing up his briefcase after winning an acquittal for a client falsely accused of rape and murder when the chief homicide prosecutor in Montgomery County walked over to talk to him. Tom Fanucci was quite tall, with a head of dark hair and a youthful appearance that belied his years of experience.

"Congratulations, Jerry."

Jerry smiled appreciatively. "I was lucky to find the evidence proving my client was set up by someone else."

Tom shook his head. "Jerry, you make your own luck. It was your hard work that uncovered that."

At his client's trial, Jerry had presented E-ZPass records proving that his client's car was too far from the scene of the crime for him to have had time to commit the crime, contradicting the testimony of the Commonwealth's lone eyewitness. And he had subpoenaed the photographs taken at the E-ZPass booth his client had driven through, clearly showing the defendant at the wheel.

"Well, mine and the rest of the firm's," Jerry allowed.

Tom smiled. "It's about lunchtime. Want to grab a bite to eat?"

Jerry returned his colleague's smile. "How about the Bar Association? My car's parked there. By the way, you don't sound upset that you lost the case."

"Your case convinced me." He extended his hand and slapped Jerry lightly on the shoulder. "I'm never upset when I think justice has been done." He turned to go. "The Bar Association…Give me fifteen minutes, okay?"

When Tom walked into the Burly Dove Bistro, Jerry was already sitting at a table. He waved Tom over.

"Here's a menu."

Despite its name, no fat doves were on the menu.

"I already know what I want."

Tom had eaten at the bistro often enough to not need a menu.

"Ah, an expert. What's good?"

"I like the Colby-Jack grilled cheese with tomato soup."

Jerry glanced at the menu then snapped it shut. "Looks good to me."

After they had ordered, Jerry approached the topic of the Crosby murder carefully.

"Hey, I don't mean to talk business over lunch, but . . ."

"Go ahead," Tom assured him with a smile. "You're among friends."

"Well, I was just wondering . . . that murder near my office?"

"The Crosby killing?"

"Yeah."

"What about it?"

"Any progress?"

Tom shrugged. "Some."

"Do you have a suspect yet? Can we expect an arrest soon?"

"Yes, and I'm not sure how soon. We're still investigating."

"Anything you can share about it? As you might imagine, we aren't used to violent crimes out in Upper Dublin…."

"I know." Tom relaxed back in his chair and stared candidly at Jerry. "We have someone who had the opportunity, but we're having some problems with motive."

"Lots of people on that street must have had the opportunity. Anything pointing to your suspect more than anyone else?"

"Well, they had a relationship. And the suspect in question gave an alibi that is false."

This struck Jerry as strange. He assumed that the time stamp on Allen's withdrawal slip at the ATM would verify Allen's story. As would the camera at the ATM.

"So, why not arrest the suspect for lying to the police during an investigation?"

"Because he'd be out on bail in a matter of hours." With a smile Tom added, "Say, your curiosity isn't related to the fact that your firm notified us you represent the husband of the deceased, is it?"

Jerry smiled. "No comment."

Tom knew that was exactly why Jerry was asking. But he didn't mind sharing the information, since he knew the Frankel firm sought justice. They would "fire" any client who lied to them.

* * *

Jerry dialed Abby as soon as he was in his car.

"Hey, PinYin, how's your day going?"

PinYin was Chinese for Abby and Jerry's pet name for her.

"Pretty good. And yours?"

Abby knew they couldn't use their cells to talk details about their cases, unless they wanted their conversation to be overheard.

"Excellent. I got the Rogers kid off of that rape and murder. It's a shame he had to go through that."

"Yeah, the police always assume it's the romantic relationship."

Jerry could have told her this back at the office. She was wondering why he was calling.

"I had lunch at the Bar Association with Tom, Tom Fanucci."

Ah, here comes the reason, Abby thought.

"Yeah?" she said. "How was lunch?"

"Pretty good. Their Colby-Jack grilled cheese is really good."

"I'll have to try it when I'm up there."

"And you know that murder near our office?"

Here it comes.

"The one on Timber?"

"Yeah, how many murders near our office are there?"

Abby laughed. She had to make this sound like a casual gossip conversation instead of information being passed on a case they were working on. The prosecutors and the police already knew they were representing Allen, but they didn't know whether the NSA, or any other interested party, knew.

"Well it seems they have a suspect but no motive. All they have is that he lied about an alibi."

"Really?"

Abby wondered about the camera and time stamp on the ATM. She presumed the suspect was Allen Crosby. She could understand if the coroner's estimate as to time of death was too wide to narrow it down to the twenty minutes Allen said it took him to make the trip to the ATM, but lied? How could that be? And if he lied about the alibi then what about the rest of his story?

"Yeah. But they won't arrest him for lying in an official investigation because Tom said he'd make bail quickly. I guess they don't want him to guess he's a suspect."

"I guess not." The call from Jerry gave Abby time to start trying to get evidence in favor of, or against, Allen's alibi before the next meeting about the case.

CHAPTER 11

Like many in the legal profession, Tom Fanucci had gone to law school because he wanted to pursue a vocation in which he could pursue justice. The more he learned in law school, however, the more disappointed he became.

He learned the law; but the emphasis in the classroom seemed to be how to use the law on behalf of one's clients, not on behalf of pursuing justice. In his class on criminal law, he had once asked his professor what he should do if a client he did not want to represent came to him.

"Charge them too much money. Maybe they'll go somewhere else."

The class had laughed, but Tom had not been satisfied. "What if they agree to pay it?"

"Hopefully you picked an amount that would make it worth your while."

Again the class had laughed.

Tom had thought about becoming a public defender, and he had even interviewed with several attorneys who held that position; but he decided against it, because public defenders had no choice over the cases they accepted. In addition, the attorneys at his interviews made clear that he needed to question the honesty of any witness against his client, even to go so far as to suggest *the witness* committed the crime, even if Tom had no evidence of that.

He didn't want to open his own office; the logistics of running a business held no interest for him. He was a lawyer, not a businessman. And he knew the financial pressures resulting from the office's overhead costs would compel him to accept cases and clients he would not want to handle.

Tom's revelation finally came during the criminal prosecution clinic he enrolled in during his final year. He learned that prosecutors had the discretion to not prosecute if they thought the evidence of the crime did not merit it. He began to think that was the way to go. He could pursue justice while practicing law after all!

The Montgomery County District Attorney's office hired him immediately after he passed the bar examination.

Real life, of course, does not always match what a student learns in academia....

As Tom's caseload at the DA's office grew, he came to the conclusion that most of the defendants whom he felt were guilty of *some* crime were nonetheless being over-charged by the police and the prosecutors. When he complained of this practice to his superiors, they told him that over-charging defendants was how the defendants became convinced to plead to whatever crime the police thought they were actually guilty of.

"But what if they aren't guilty of anything? Doesn't it unfairly pressure the defendant to plead guilty?"

The only reply Tom ever received—usually with a patronizing smile—was: "They won't plead guilty to something they aren't guilty of."

Tom knew that wasn't true. He had read many stories of innocent people either confessing or pleading guilty to crimes they never committed. Often, the police lied to them, telling them if they confessed, they could go home; or there had been some other trick or lie the police, with the blessings of the courts, had used. The defendants who plead guilty were often those the courts said made too much money to have an attorney appointed to represent them. Yet these defendants really could not afford a full-fledged defense. Certainly not one to defend the charges against them in a jury trial and, if necessary, an appeal. And if they were convicted of the more serious charges, they would face longer sentences than they would have faced if they accepted a plea agreement. They might even be facing mandatory minimums.

Tom protested some of the cases in which he concluded the defendant was likely innocent, and in which he wanted to drop the charges. The police objected. They had "closed" the case and gotten a "bad guy" off the street. His supervisors always sided with the police, partially to keep good relations with the police and partially to keep the office's conviction rate at close to one hundred percent. They reminded Tom that he was the prosecutor, not the judge and jury. If he had evidence that a crime had occurred, he should present it and let the finders of fact make the ultimate decision.

As time went on and Tom's colleagues left the DA's office for more lucrative private practices, Tom moved up the line of seniority. He also became skilled at convicting those defendants he thought were guilty and not exactly doing his best against those he thought might be innocent. Along the way he developed an interesting reputation for a prosecutor. He was known as a prosecutor who was unwilling to plea bargain. He would unilaterally drop the excessive charges and try the defendant based on the evidence he had. He also objected to "open pleas" by defendants who were not represented by a lawyer. He argued that pleas without an agreement stipulating the sentence the prosecution would recommend violated the defendant's Sixth Amendment right to have an attorney represent them.

When questioned by his superiors, Tom argued that his approach resulted in fewer appeals that resulted in an order for a retrial. That saved office resources. There was grumbling among his colleagues, but the statistics on his cases versus cases handled by other attorneys backed him up.

Tom's reputation for hard work preparing cases and doing the right thing led a newly elected district attorney dedicated to criminal justice reform to appoint Tom as chief of homicide. Even though his new position gave him a little more leeway, Tom still did not like the tension he felt between his office and the police whenever he dropped a case—and between himself and defense attorneys, whenever he refused to accept a plea.

He was never upset at losing a trial in which, by the end of the trial, he was not convinced beyond a reasonable doubt of the defendant's guilt. He truly believed the old saw: better for one hundred guilty people to go free than one innocent person to be convicted. He became upset at losing a trial only when he was still convinced of the defendant's guilt. But he usually blamed himself for the jury's verdict and vowed to work harder.

CHAPTER 12

I called for Reese to come into my office. He was tall—a few inches taller than I was—and about three hundred pounds, seemingly all muscle. All muscle *and* brains, that is. His DNA had not chosen between strength and intelligence: it had combined the two to form one person. Reese grew up on the streets of Philadelphia without much parental support. He was self-motivated, driven to succeed. Unlike many of his friends, he studied hard, and he had worked hard at physically demanding jobs to help support his family. He did well, graduating first in his class at Germantown High School, an inner-city school so rough that it was eventually closed by the school district. At Germantown he played offensive tackle on the football team. He received a full football scholarship to Penn State and graduated near the top of his class in criminal justice. He was hired by the Philadelphia Police Department and quickly rose within the department. Unfortunately, some of his colleagues believed that a black police officer who was advancing quickly through the ranks could not be doing so solely based on merit. His colleagues were jealous; to explain why Reese was advancing while they were not, they blamed his promotions on "affirmative action"—or, as they liked to call it, "reverse discrimination."

Reese's colleagues decided to make an example of him, in case any other "uppity" colleagues decided to try to "take advantage of their race." After Reese led a raid on a major Philadelphia drug dealer, an officer on the scene made sure to accurately record the amount of drugs and money that had been seized...and then made sure only about half the drugs and half the money were turned in as evidence. The missing drugs and money were used to frame Reese. He was arrested and suspended with intent to dismiss. He was fired while awaiting trial.

Fortunately for Reese, he came to my office seeking an attorney to defend him. A few weeks later, Abby managed to discover that one of the officers who had framed him was feeling a bit guilty. After some time, but before trial, Abby convinced the officer to agree to wear a wire while speaking with his colleagues. This took time and persistence on Abby's part, because that blue wall of silence was less penetrable than any wall President Trump hoped to erect along the Mexican border. Also, recording someone in conversation without their permission is a third-degree felony in Pennsylvania.

I didn't use the tape at the trial until the cross-examination of the main officer behind the conspiracy to frame Reese. After I led the officer into stating unequivocally that the other officers had not framed Reese, I used the tape to impeach his testimony. I was able to get the tape admitted into evidence over the prosecutor's objections by pointing out to the court that the allegedly illegal evidence was not being used to prosecute the officer whose rights were allegedly violated; it was being used only to impeach that officer's testimony.

The reporters covering the trial reported on the tape. The DA dropped all charges against Reese and successfully prosecuted those involved in the frame-up without needing to use the tape. The list of crimes the police can prove once they actually know the truth and don't have to work to discover it is amazing. Just amazing. And just as I had calculated, the DA did not bring charges against Reese for the recording. That would not have been great PR.

The PD offered Reese his old job back. Although he accepted the back pay, he did not want to return to the department that had not even investigated the possibility he had been framed. He blamed it on institutional racism, despite the naysayers who said institutional racism didn't exist.

Later, when I bumped into him after his acquittal and we went for a cup of coffee, John told me he wanted to find a job that would allow him to genuinely pursue justice. I asked if he wanted to pursue justice even if he had to bend, or even break, a few rules. He thought about it then told me it seemed many of the rules were instituted to ensure that those with money or power would never be brought to justice. So, yes. Since he had just restated my philosophy of life, I hired him on the spot. Although Abby was an excellent investigator and could hold her own in a fair fight, she was only five two and about 120 pounds. Reese had the necessary investigative abilities and had proven several times that he could hold his own in a fight decidedly tilted against him.

* * *

A few moments after I had summoned him, Reese came in and closed the door.

"What can I do for you, boss?"

* * *

Thirty minutes later, I gathered the staff working on the case together in the conference room. Well, most of them.

"Where's Reese?" Abby asked.

"Busy elsewhere."

Abby raised her eyebrows. She knew better than to ask for details when I was intentionally being vague.

"So where are we?" I asked.

Jerry relayed that Tom said Allen lied about the alibi. Then Abby described her day with Allen and his neighbors.

"So none of the neighbors saw Allen walking, or heard—or saw—anything suspicious?"

Abby nodded. "Except for the PECO truck."

I sighed. "Without more to go on, a PECO truck on a street serviced by PECO is not suspicious."

Abby begged to differ. "Nobody saw a PECO employee working on the poles or walking around the street. No neighbor on either side of the street had problems with their electricity."

I decided I would give Abby the benefit of the doubt. "Check with PECO to see if you can find out why they were there. Tell them we represent a client on that street and that nobody reports any problems with their electricity."

"Yes, sir," Abby replied.

"By the way, good job in court, Jerry."

Jerry raised his coffee mug in a gesture of appreciation. "Thanks, boss."

I nodded back to Jerry then resumed our discussion.

"So, with no charges filed yet, does anyone have any ideas how we can get a look at the ATM video or the time stamps?"

Abby spoke up again: "I've gotten Allen to request an account history for the last month, in as detailed a manner as possible."

Thanks to Jerry's heads-up, I knew.

"Good move. Did you tell Allen the police said his alibi was false?"

"No… Is it really an alibi? I mean, how precise could the coroner's time of death be? Isn't it possible that he killed Deidre, then went for his twenty-minute walk?"

I nodded. "Good question. Generally, a coroner's time of death is recorded as a range. Find out what range the coroner estimated the time of death was for Deidre Crosby, and ask them what calculations they used to reach that estimate. I'm suggesting we do that because there are several ways to come up with an estimate, usually relating to body temperature and surrounding ambient temperature. What assumptions were made and what were the calculations? When will we have the bank's report to put a time on Allen's ATM visit?"

"Within a couple of days?"

Abby didn't sound very sure of her answer. She jotted a note to contact the coroner.

"That long?" Jerry piped in.

"Normally you can get an account history online. But if you want a detailed history, down to the time of each transaction, it has to be prepared by the bank, and you have to pick up a hard copy in person," Abby explained.

"Okay." I looked around the conference table. "Who else has progress to report?"

Again, Abby spoke up. "Before you go on to others, I have a question."

"Yes, Abby, what is it?"

"When Allen gave you the gun he said was put in his hand about thirty hours after the murder, did he tell you how he knew that it wasn't his gun?"

"Yeah, he said he checked and his gun was still where he kept it."

"He told *me* that a UD officer bagged his gun for tests when they came to investigate. Did he have more than one gun?"

Silence. All around the room.

I didn't like this. It looked like a lie.

Finally I said, "Okay, let me talk to him about that. Anything else, Abby?"

"No."

"Okay, who else has progress to report?"

After everyone who had something to add had done so, I told them to keep pressing, and then I gave them each a gift.

"Burner phones," I said. "Use them from now on. There's a sticker with your name so you know which phone to take. Susan will give you a list of everybody's new number. Take the batteries out of your smartphones; leave them in a drawer of your desk for the remainder of this case. The NSA can listen in on our smartphones even when we think we've turned them off. When you've used up the time on your burner, let Susan know. She'll give you a new one and update the list of numbers."

After that, we adjourned for another day.

CHAPTER 13

"Allen, give me your cell phone." He was in my office for our scheduled appointment. Allen seemed perplexed. "Why? It gets no reception here anyway."

"I know. Part of our security. We're a dead zone." I slid a burner phone across my desk. "Here's a burner for you to use. I'll keep your cell and its battery in my drawer until the case is over. Then I'll give everything back to you."

He nodded, taking his phone from his pocket and sliding it across the desk. After I removed the battery and had placed the phone and the battery in my drawer, I looked at Allen again. "I have a question. You told me that when you woke on Thursday with the gun in your hand, you checked where you keep your gun and it was still there, right?"

"Yes."

"Abby says that you told her an officer bagged your gun for possible evidence Tuesday evening."

"That's also true." He hadn't hesitated in his answer. "When it occurred to me that the NSA might be involved, I figured I should be armed. So I bought another one."

"When and where?"

"The next day, Wednesday, at Clayton's."

"Over in Horsham?"

"Yeah. It's where I do my target shooting as well."

I pondered the possible confusion of three Glock 17s. "Clayton's gives you paperwork when you buy a gun, correct?"

"Well, they offer the receipt and the background check. But I always tell them to recycle it."

"How did you pay for the gun?"

"They know me there. I run a tab and they bill me at the end of each month."

"Keep it when you get it next." Another thought occurred to me. "If you got the gun to protect you, why didn't you have it on you? I assume you have a license to carry a concealed weapon?"

"I do. Although I don't usually carry it, I have since Deidre's murder. My habit when I go to bed is to put the gun between my mattress and my headboard. I used to keep in in a drawer in my night table but, again, since the murder I've wanted it easily accessible even at night. When I woke up Thursday morning in my clothes, with a gun in my hand, I was worried that I hadn't put my gun away. But it was where it belonged. So this was a different gun."

"Okay. By the way, the tox screen came back clean."

"But alcohol doesn't usually affect me so much."

"Date rape drugs, even the one that might not affect you until 30 minutes or more after you take it, leave your bloodstream quickly. That's why I sent you down to toxicology immediately, in the hopes that some remnants of the drug would still be in your system." I stared at him candidly. "You still could have been drugged, even if the screen was clean."

He frowned but nodded his understanding. "Okay."

"None of the neighbors Abby has been able to contact so far saw you on your walk to the bank. And they didn't hear anything unusual. The only activity that might possibly be suspicious was a PECO truck parked across the street from your house: nobody was working on the electric lines. Some of your neighbors saw the truck, but none of them had any problems with their electricity, at least not the neighbors we've contacted to date."

"So the PECO truck," Allen said, growing excited, "that's them! That's who killed Deidre."

"Let's not jump to conclusions." I stared at Allen deliberately. I wanted to make sure he calmed down a bit. "Maybe it was PECO workers goofing off on a quiet residential street between service calls. We're investigating. Did you notice the truck that day?"

"No."

"Okay. Have you thought of anything else since we last spoke, either something you remembered that you hadn't told me before, or any other theories?

"No."

I had anticipated his answer; so the lack of any new leads didn't' disturb me.

"We've also heard through the grapevine that the DA's office has determined that your walk to the ATM never took place, at least not the way you described it. Your alibi is false."

"What? There should be video and a time-stamp!" He seemed honestly shocked. Or at least a very good actor.

"I know. That's why Abby asked you to request your detailed history from the bank. Your habit of not keeping these receipts may be a problem. We're trying to figure out how to get to see the video before any charges are filed."

"If they think I lied, why haven't they arrested me?"

"Because they have no motive. Although criminal law doesn't require them to prove motive, juries like to understand why someone did what they are accused of. With you being an upstanding member of society and all, and no record of any domestic violence or any reason you would benefit from Deidre's death, the DA's office realizes they have a losing case so far."

"That's good. Because I can't think of any motive I could possibly have."

"Good. If anything comes to mind, even if it wasn't really a motive for you but could be argued as such, let me know."

"Will do. You still believe me, don't you?"

"If I find evidence you are guilty, I'll withdraw from your case. Until that happens, I believe you. I trust we will not need to withdraw."

"I guess I'll have to be satisfied with that."

"I guess you will."

CHAPTER 14

"Gun reports are back, but I don't think you're going to want to hear them." Susan was sitting comfortably in front of my desk. She crossed her legs, her skirt riding up the length of her shin. She knew I didn't mind that—in fact, I rather enjoyed it. The whole time we talked, she stared into my eyes, swinging her leg attractively and dangling her shoe on her toes.

"Tell me."

"The only fingerprints and DNA the lab found were Allen's."

"I figured. That could mean either he's guilty or he's being set up."

"And the gun had been fired 'recently.' "

"Now if they could only tell me when and where—and at whom."

"We also researched the serial number by calling Clayton's."

"And…?"

"It was purchased by Allen at Clayton's on Tuesday morning, the day of the murder."

I put my head in my hands. Another possible lie?

"And Clayton's has no record of Allen purchasing a gun on Wednesday."

I felt like I had set a new speed record and had outrun my lungs. I was waiting for them to catch up to me so I could speak.

"Are you ready for some good news?"

"Absolutely." I looked up hopefully.

"PECO has no record of having a truck on Timber that day."

My lungs must have caught up to me then, because all of a sudden I had a lot to say. "Would they know if their workers were just goofing off between jobs?"

"They have no record of any work in this area of the county at all."

I nodded. "That is promising."

"What now, boss?"

When in the office, Susan called me "boss" like the rest of the employees. I'm sure the others knew we had a special bond, but I'm not sure they knew it was romantic. We didn't really hide it, but we never flaunted it either. They knew how we met, so they might think that our closeness is all due to that.

"Get Allen here as fast as you can."

"Yes, *sir,*" she said with a smile.

* * *

Susan poked her head in my office ten minutes later. "Mr. Crosby's here.

I glanced at my watch. "That was fast."

"That's why I make the big bucks."

Susan moved aside and let Allen enter. I closed another file I was working on and pushed it aside. Susan closed my door as she left.

"Why the sudden call?" Allen asked as he sat down.

"I'm trying to make sense of the information we're getting. When did you last fire your gun?"

"This morning at Clayton's. Why?"

"Not that gun. I mean before Deidre's murder."

"I usually go to Clayton's once or twice a week to shoot."

"When did you last go before the murder?"

Allen thought.

"It would have either been that morning or the day before."

"Did you buy another gun that day?"

"The day of her murder?"

"Yes."

"No, not until the day after her death."

"Okay, here's what we've got. As we suspected, the only fingerprints on the gun you woke up with are yours. The lab discovered it had been fired recently."

"So it may have been the murder weapon."

Interesting that Allen would be so quick to guess that a gun that only had his fingerprints was the murder weapon.

We traced the serial number. Clayton's reports that you purchased that gun the morning of Deidre's murder. And that you didn't buy one the next day."

"That's wrong!" Allen was clearly upset. But upset that they were wrong, or upset that he had been caught in a lie? I watched him carefully.

"Gun records are kept electronically, so it's possible someone, such as the NSA, could have hacked into the system and changed them. And I assume the bill they will send you at the end of the month is based on the same database. Check it when it comes in to see the date it says you bought the gun. It will probably be the date of the murder. I'm not sure we can prove they've been changed. Is there anything you can think of that would help us prove it?"

Allen was standing by now. He turned away angrily and ran his hands through his hair. Then he took a deep breath and seemed to calm himself. When he turned back to me the expression in his eyes seemed a little desperate.

"When I bought the gun Wednesday, Bob, the clerk there, offered me his condolences. I explained that the police had taken my gun, so I needed to purchase another in case the murderer came back. He should remember that conversation."

"Good," I said, taking notes. But I was thinking that Allen was awfully quick with that memory.

"I'll go talk to him."

"No, you stay away," I told him. "Let our firm handle it. We don't want it to look like you tried to get someone to lie for you." And I didn't want him to actually *get* someone to lie for him. With his money, that would be possible—I know because I've done it. And although I'm wealthy, I don't have as much wealth as Allen.

"Okay," he said, "but it's frustrating not being able to help."

"I understand. But by not contacting witnesses and giving the prosecution the ability to say you either coerced or bribed them into lying for you, you *are* helping. By the way," I added, "there is some potential good news."

"What's that?"

After all the bad news I had given Allen, I avoided cracking a joke by defining what "good news" was in answer to his question.

"PECO says they had no crews anywhere in our area on that day."

"Then they did it!"

I had a bad sense of déjà vu. He was as excited as he had been the last time.

"Hold on, we still have no proof they did it, although it is suspicious. Give the jury the choice of believing that some anonymous people in a PECO truck killed Deidre or the husband of the victim and they will pick the husband."

"But it's good enough for reasonable doubt, isn't it?"

"Possibly, when combined with no motive for the killing." I returned to the question I had asked him the other day. "Have you thought of anything the prosecution could use, or twist into, a possible motive?"

"Not yet."

"Neither have we. And neither has the prosecution."

"How do you know the prosecution hasn't?"

"They haven't arrested you yet."

CHAPTER 15

"Boss, I'm back."

"So I see. What did you find out, Reese?"

Reese slid some papers and photographs across my desk. I looked them over and let out a low whistle.

"Great work."

"Thanks."

"We need to substitute your phone for a burner phone."

"Susan already did that when I showed up."

"Good. Now put all this in a report to me and label it, in large letters, 'Attorney Work Product.' "

Unlike evidence turned over to us by someone involved in the case, like the possible murder weapon, which we had not yet turned over, our research does not have to be turned over to the authorities. We simply classify it as "Attorney Work Product." That includes photographs taken by my staff.

"Got it."

I asked Susan to get Allen in to look at what Reese had brought back. But I told her it wasn't an emergency. He could come at his convenience.

* * *

Abby pulled off Easton Road into the parking lot. For this afternoon's research, she wore her lowest cut top, no bra, a miniskirt, and more makeup than usual. She checked her face in the mirror then got out of her car and locked it. She walked into Clayton's swaying her hips as she approached the counter.

"Is Bob here?"

"Not right now, sweetie." The large balding man behind the counter let his eyes linger on Abby's bust. "Is there anything I can help you with?"

Abby seethed at "sweetie." She made sure she didn't show any reaction on her face. "Well, you can tell me when Bob will be here." She smiled seductively. "Sweetie."

"I'm Rich. What do you want with Bob?"

"Oh, you're rich?" Abby was trying to deflect the question. "Maybe you can do something after all. Want to give me about ten grand?"

Rich laughed. "No, sweetie. My name is Rich. Is there a particular gun you're interested in buying?"

"Maybe. But I need to talk to Bob."

"Well, I guess that's my loss then." Rich glanced at his watch. "Bob's due in about thirty minutes."

"I'll be back."

Abby swayed her hips as she left, hoping Rich would make Bob look forward to her return.

* * *

Susan walked in with an IC form and said, "Your eleven o'clock is here. Help this woman."

Susan didn't often tell me to help someone who had come in, certainly not before we'd done any investigation. When she did, she was never wrong.

Susan left the office. A woman with sunglasses and a limp entered. I glanced at the IC form.

"Ms. Glass, pleased to meet you," I said as I held out my hand.

"Please, call me Betsy," she said. She sat down. "Mr. Frankel, I need your help."

"Okay, Betsy. I haven't had a chance to read your info yet. Could you summarize for me why you're here?"

She took off her glasses. I saw a large bruise around her left eye. The white of that eye contained some red streaks that looked more like blood than strained eyes.

"My ex keeps attacking me."

"Have you gotten a restraining order?"

"Yes, but it doesn't stop him. And every time I go to court, he attacks me again."

"You said 'every time.' I assume you've called the police?"

"Yes. But my ex is a police officer himself. They won't arrest him. They just issue a summons for him to show up at a hearing. The judges won't lock him up, because as an officer he would be a target for other prisoners."

"There's protective custody," I suggested.

"The judge says that's the equivalent of solitary confinement. He doesn't think my husband has earned that." Betsy smirked.

My teeth were clenched. My gut hurt…and I understood why Susan wanted me to help Betsy. Even in this day, the law is still woefully inadequate when it comes to protecting women from abusive spouses. Or ex-spouses.

"That's horrible, how the courts are treating you. I am truly sorry. What is it that you think I can do for you?"

Betsy shifted uncomfortably in her chair. "Well, uh…I've heard that you can help clients who have problems getting help from the law."

I was silent for a few beats.

"Who did you hear that from?"

Was Betsy part of a sting operation in an attempt to catch me? I had to be very careful.

"Just rumors. I'm a paralegal for Smith and Robertson. People talk."

" 'People' meaning former clients?"

"Not really. Mostly just lawyers and other paralegals. They privately admire your work but wouldn't dare try it themselves."

I was happy to hear that my former clients weren't talking. At least "not really." The lawyers and paralegals had to have heard about my services from somewhere. I was also pleasantly surprised that privately there was admiration for my extra-legal efforts. And I fully understood why others would not so engage in my "justice above the law" approach.

I glanced at my computer—specifically at the top right corner of the monitor. There was nothing indicating that Betsy was wired or bugged in any way. There's an app for that, provided by Echelon. And I had to be careful if I was going to engage in any extra-legal remedies for Betsy.

Betsy appeared unhappy with my silence. "I asked my boss, Pat Robertson, what I should do after last night. He suggested I come see you."

"Tell me what happened last night."

"Well, after yet another hearing where the judge just slapped Donnie with another fine, he broke into my place and attacked me again. This time, he really banged me up—and he raped me. He kept punching my face and twisting my leg, saying that he was going to make me so ugly and gimpy no man will ever want me."

I watched her quietly. Tears welled up in her eyes.

"Did you call the police?"

Betsy shook her head. "No. He said if I ever call the police on him again, he'll come back and kill me. So I waited until I went to work this morning and asked Pat what to do. That's when he told me to come see you."

I looked down at the IC form to read whatever information she had filled out. She lived in Philadelphia, which had multiple police precincts.

I pushed the form across my desk.

"In the space where the form says to fill in any additional information you might want us to know, write down all contact information you have for Donnie. Is his last name Glass, or did you change your name after your divorce?"

"No, it's Glass."

"Okay, put down everything. His home address, which precinct he works for. If you know his cell number, give me that. If he has a landline and you know the number, give me that. If you know of any close friends give me their names and any information you have on them. If he has any relationships with other women, give me their information as well. If in doubt about giving me the information, give it. If I don't need it, I won't use it. This is confidential information," I assured her, "it won't go past my office. We are all bound by attorney-client confidentiality."

She held my gaze a moment, as though there was something else she wanted to tell me. "The thing is, Mr. Frankel…I know you charge a lot, and I can't afford much."

I took out my standard agreement, made a few scribbles with my pen, initialed my changes, and slid the form across the desk. Betsy picked it up and read it.

"Is this right?" she said. "I only have to pay you a dollar?"

"That's right. Don't worry about expenses or finances. Let me worry about that. I have resources that can handle that. I would have charged you nothing, but to make our agreement legally binding you have to give me something."

Tears welled up in her eyes. "Mr. Frankel…thank you so much!" She opened her purse and took out a handkerchief; then she dabbed away the tears that had fallen on her cheeks.

"No 'thank you' is necessary. I just ask three things. First, you tell nobody that you came to see me, or that I am handling your case. That is, unless, for some reason, the police come to speak with you. Then you read the back of my business card to them and hand my contact information over to them."

I passed two of my cards over to her. She read the back of one of the cards and smiled. As most of my clients do.

"Okay. You said you ask three things. What are the other two?"

"Call me Josh, and give me a dollar."

* * *

After Susan told me that Betsy had finished filling out the information I asked for, I asked Susan to copy both the IC form and my notes then open a file with the form, my notes, and the retainer agreement. Finally, I asked her to put the copies of the form and my notes into an unmarked folder.

"Yes, sir."

I heard the joy in Susan's voice.

I took the unmarked folder and walked to Reese's office. Reese looked up as I entered.

"What can I do for you, boss?"

"We have a potential new client. Find out if her story is true. If so, solve the problem."

I dropped the folder on his desk and walked out. I had confidence that Betsy would not be bothered again.

* * *

About forty-five minutes after she had left Clayton's, Abby walked through the door of the gun shop again, swaying her hips on her way to the counter. A different man was there. She could tell by the man's smile that Rich had forewarned him.

"How can I help you, missy?"

"Missy" rankled more than "sweetie."

"Are you Bob?"

"I sure am, honey. What can I do for you?"

"I'm a friend of Allen Crosby."

"Allen's a good guy."

"He is. And he told me to ask for you. He said that the day after his wife was murdered he came in and bought a gun, and he recommended the same gun for me."

Bob eyed Abby, feasting his narrow gaze on her clean, nimble body. Then he reached into his pocket and pulled out a stick of gum. He unwrapped the gum and popped it into his mouth. "It's horrible what happened to his wife," he said, chewing on the gum.

"It is. I hope they catch whoever did it—and *fast*."

"Well, Allen always buys the same model. A Glock 17. It's a lightweight Glock." He chewed the gum, still staring at Abby's chest. "You might want something even lighter."

Abby let Bob enjoy his gawking. “You remember him buying the Glock 17 the day after his wife’s murder?”

Bob stopped chewing the gum. He crinkled his forehead and looked at her a bit suspiciously. “I do. He told me all about it. It was before I saw it on the news. I was shocked.”

That’s the confirmation Abby hoped she’d get. It confirmed Allen’s story of buying a Glock the day after the murder. Now, about the rest…

“Did he also buy one the day before? The morning before the murder?”

Bob shook his head. “Not to my knowledge. He usually comes in when I’m on duty, but he could have come in when I wasn’t. Why all the questions about when he bought his Glocks?”

Abby flipped out one of her cards.

“Actually, I’m investigating Deidre’s murder for Allen. He wants an investigation done in addition to the police. By the way, has anyone from the police been in to question you?”

Abby’s revelation didn’t seem to faze Bob. He simply shook his head again. “No.”

“Okay, they might. Anyway, you said that he might have bought a gun from someone else in the store. Is there any way you can check that?”

“We do have computer records,” Bob said.

Abby put on her sweetest smile then positioned her chest in its most favorable posture.

“Could you check them, please…?”

A pause.

Bob chewed his gum for a long moment.

“Okay, for *you*.”

He walked over to the computer and spent some time there, looking confused. “This is strange.”

Bob said the words but did not really seem puzzled. Abby thought maybe he was one of those people who don’t register emotions on their face. Or maybe he wasn’t really puzzled.

“What?” she asked.

"The computer says he bought one on the morning of the murder but has no purchase data for the next day."

"Could someone have entered the information wrong?" Abby had been expecting what Bob had just told her; but she hadn't finished the job she came for.

"Don't know. I thought it got the information soon as we rang up the sale."

"Can you do something to correct it, since you know it's wrong?"

"Don't know that either. Never ran into this before. I'll have to check with my boss."

"Okay, you have my card. Call me any time if you have more information, and to let me know if it's been corrected. And also"—a *very* sweet smile this time—"if anyone else talks to you about this."

Bob smiled, still chewing his gum. "I'll be sure to do that, honey."

Abby swayed her way out of the store.

* * *

"Yeah, it's all true. He's a real scumbag and should be behind bars," Reese's raspy-voiced friend in the Philadelphia Police Department told him over lunch. "He's violent against perps too, but only if there's backup there with him. Otherwise, he's a real coward."

"So why haven't the police arrested him?"

"Do I really have to explain the blue wall of silence to *you*?"

"Thanks," Reese said as he finished his lunch. "And by the way, I never asked you this."

"Asked me what?"

CHAPTER 16

Donnie Glass unlocked the door to his apartment and stepped inside. Tired after his shift, he flicked on the hall light as he looked at his mail, which he had picked up from the floor just inside the door. He sorted the mail into junk mail and items he had to pay attention to. The latter consisted only of bills. He tossed the junk into the trash and carried the bills into the living room, flicking on the light. Suddenly a large arm slipped around his neck and his revolver was removed from his holster. The attacker spun Donnie around. He heard the safety flick and the revolver cock. The bills fell out of his hand, scattering across the hardwood floor.

"Hello, Donnie."

"Hel…lo."

"I bet you weren't expecting me."

"Who…who are you?"

"Your worst nightmare."

"If you shoot a police officer, the force will go all out to find you."

"Possibly."

"They will. I can assure you of that. I have lots of friends, we always keep looking for cop killers until we find them."

"Sit down at your desk," Donnie's assailant said.

The large black man held Donnie's revolver to the back of Donnie's head, with a hand on his shoulder to make sure Donnie didn't try any self-defense move as the police officer walked over and sat at a rolltop desk. It had been handed down to him from his grandfather. Donnie considered how he might possibly turn the current situation around...make some move to knock the gun out of the intruder's hand. But he doubted that he could beat the intruder in hand-to-hand combat, and felt the hand on his shoulder, so he decided to wait and see where this was going.

"Open the desk."

Donnie rolled it open.

"Take out a piece of paper."

As Reese expected, Donnie opened the wrong drawer.

"Surprise! No gun there. Now take out a piece of paper and a pen."

"Okay, okay."

"Write an apology to Betsy for all the violence you have done to her. Make sure it sounds sincere and that you are really sorry."

"That bitch lies!" Donnie scoffed. "I've never done anything violent to her."

Donnie felt the gun press between his shoulder blades.

"Okay! I'll write whatever you want. Just tell me exactly what to say."

"I told you what I want you to say. You put it into your own words."

Reese knew for the note to be believed, it had to be in Donnie's words.

Donnie began writing. He figured if this was to be used as evidence against him he could argue the duress of the situation and get it thrown out of court. And if this was all the intruder wanted, he could escape getting killed.

"Now sign it," the large black man told Donnie.

Donnie did so.

CHAPTER 17

Betsy looked through her peephole after hearing a knock on her door. Two uniformed officers were standing outside. She opened the door.

"Betsy Glass?"

"Yes?"

"May we come in?"

"Yes," Betsy said, remembering where she put her pocketbook with Josh Frankel's card.

They walked in.

"I'm Officer Wayne Torres and this is my partner Wade Pierce." Both were tall. Officer Torres had brown skin. His partner was white.

"And?"

"Donnie Glass was your ex-husband?"

Betsy felt her body tense. "Was?"

"We're sorry to have to tell you this, but it looks like he killed himself last night."

Betsy felt her knees start to bend. Officer Torres grabbed her arm and helped her to the sofa in her living room.

"Why?" Betsy asked when the initial shock has passed.

"Here's a note he left, apologizing to you."

Betsy read the note. Donnie had apologized for all the violence he had wreaked on her. He had signed it too. It was his handwriting…but Besty knew: he never would have apologized to her.

She wondered how Josh had gotten him to sign it.

She looked up, speechless.

"We're very sorry," Officer Torres said, misjudging her lock of amazement for one of distress. Betsy's eyes were filling with tears, which Torres took to be tears of sadness.

"Thank you," Betsy said quietly.

"If we can do anything for you," Torres replied, "please let us know."

Suddenly Betsy felt anger. She shook her head with resentment.

"Now you ask?" Her question merely fueled her fury. "What about all the times I called you because he was beating on me? What about when I called each time he attacked me, violating the protection order I had? You wouldn't lock him up because he was one of you! You wouldn't protect me from that monster!"

Now Betsy was crying.

"We're sorry," Officer Torres repeated, sounding genuinely sorry.

Betsy held her hands up dismissively. "Just leave."

Because the two officers believed she was genuinely shocked by Donnie's death, and because they had no evidence to believe Donnie's death wasn't a suicide, they honored her request.

* * *

Josh was ten years old when he figured out that his mother could not be that clumsy. Her clumsiness was a family joke. Only, his mother never laughed about it.

Joanne Frankel often greeted Josh in the morning with bruises on her face, or a slight limp to her gait. Her explanations were always the same: she fell in the bathroom, or she bumped into the furniture the night before, after Josh went to bed. Sometimes her arm was wrapped tightly in a sling. But Josh was an early avid reader of news. He had read about abused spouses. About their excuses for their injuries. It all sounded very familiar.

His father, a very successful businessman, had received awards from a broad array of organizations—most of which he helped raise money for. He was admired throughout the entire community. But he acted differently in private, when he was in his own home, alone with his family. He was very strict, ordering Josh and his mother to clean up the house by the time he got home from work. "Wipe up those coffee stains from the kitchen counter---and, Josh, pick your clothes off the bedroom floor," he'd say. "Or else there'll be hell to pay!"

Josh's hell was spankings, and his father's refusal to take him to a Phillies or Eagles game, or drive him to a friend's house. Until he turned ten, he never thought about what his mom's hell might be. He did notice her scrubbing and trying to get the house spotless as if her life depended on it.

Maybe it did.

* * *

One night Josh went to bed at his usual time but did not go to sleep. He was in the middle of *To Kill a Mockingbird,* so he snuck a flashlight under the covers to keep reading. After a while he heard a disturbance downstairs. He listened closely. The noises grew louder. Josh snuck out of his bedroom and flattened himself against the wall next to the balcony. He heard his mom's voice. It sounded as if she were crying.

"Please, Sammy," she cried. *"Stop…!"*

A loud slam vibrated the wall Josh was leaning against.

"I'll stop when I'm good and ready!"

His dad's words seemed slurred.

His mom's gentle sobs floated up to the balcony. Then there was a short interval of silence. Finally Josh heard what sounded like someone sitting down on the sofa. He peered out over the balcony and saw his father passed out. A moment later he heard the sink running in the kitchen, and then his mother's gentle footsteps in the living room. He rushed into his room and kept his ear to the door. He heard his mother climb the steps and start walking toward his room. He quickly jumped into his bed and turned away from the door. Soon, he heard his door open.

"He loves us," his mother said quietly. "Do you hear me, Josh? He loves us . . .."

The door closed again.

Josh heard his mother's steps going down the hall as he started sobbing into his pillow.

* * *

Abby stuck her head in my door. "Got a minute?"

"Sure," I told her. "What's up?"

"Allen got the report from his bank."

"And?"

"It doesn't show any ATM withdrawal on the date of the murder."

I sighed. We still couldn't request discovery of the recording at the ATM from the DA or subpoena it from the bank because there was no court case…yet.

"Okay," I said, "let's figure out what to do."

"Does Allen have any right to ask to see the recording?"

I frowned. "I haven't researched the law on this, but I doubt it. If any of us watched the tape we'd probably see other people using the ATM, and the bank probably won't let us do that without a court order. Have Jerry research the law on that."

Abby nodded. "Okay."

"Let's work on the assumption Allen has no right to get the recording. What can a customer do if their bank has no record of an ATM transaction but the customer insists he made one?"

"Don't know, boss. That's your field." Abby tossed a smile my way. "Allen's trying to find the receipt he got at the time of the withdrawal."

Pause.

"And it could be that the bank's records are correct," she added.

"What do you mean?"

Although I asked the question, I knew what she was getting at.

"What if he's lying?"

"Would someone so smart make up a lie that could so easily be uncovered?" I didn't want to believe it.

"Maybe combined with a story that the NSA was out to frame him?" Abby raised an eyebrow to emphasize her point. "After all, they have the wherewithal to change computerized records."

"I didn't think you would still be so skeptical after what you heard from the clerk at Clayton's."

"When you believe a client, it's my job to be skeptical. Or have you forgotten that if two people agree on everything, one isn't necessary? I like my job and would like to continue being necessary." She smiled again.

"I'm glad you like your job." I returned her smile but was still thinking about the video recording. "Let's hope the video contradicts the records. I assume the recording would be digital, not on tape?"

Abby smiled. "Yes, Mr. Dinosaur. What's tape?"

"Ha, ha." I was thinking. "And the digital would be kept electronically?"

Abby smiled again. "That's what *digital* means. It's an electronic technology."

I picked up the phone. "Susan, get Keith up here."

Keith Haddad was our IT expert. We got him off a false charge of hacking into his previous employer's computer system to change his pay. He had the skills to do it. And he was the one who benefited from the hack. But when his first paycheck with the new pay rate came out, he took it to his supervisor to complain that it was too much money. His company turned the incident over to the police.

In any crime, the "usual" suspect is the one who has something to gain from the crime. So it was an easy decision for the police to arrest Keith: their theory was simply that he feared getting caught. That's why he reported it. But we were able to show that Keith's assistant at the firm used Keith's computer to hack into the employer's pay system. Apparently *his* motive was getting Keith fired....while he himself would be promoted. Either that, or he didn't like a Muslim being his boss. Horrible person. Not as bad as the people who saw Keith on the street shortly after 9-11 and beat him so bad he now had to use a motorized wheelchair. But horrible, nonetheless. The end result was that we hired a great, honest, highly skilled IT director.

Keith knocked on my door and rolled in.

"What can I do for you, boss?"

I gave a sideways glance at Abby. "It seems I am a dinosaur when it comes to electronics and digital information." Abby smiled.

"I could have told you that," Keith said as he maneuvered his wheelchair in front of my desk. He parked it next to Abby.

"So I've got two smartasses working for me."

"Way more than two," Keith volunteered.

"Okay." I acknowledged Keith's good-natured banter but needed to get down to the matter at hand. "We are working on a case where a client withdrew money from an ATM but his bank history does not record it. How can we see the video of that day's ATM transactions?"

"Subpoena? Discovery? You said you have a case."

"I don't mean a case that is in court yet—and we don't want to trigger it getting to court. But we want to be ready if it does get to court."

"Are we talking legal or extralegal methods?"

"We're having Jerry research any legal solution for the customer to gain access. I don't think he'll be successful, because of privacy issues. Plus, I'm afraid that if we go with anything like a formal request, it might trigger an arrest."

"Okay. Well, I don't have any legal skills. But I do have a *very* particular set of skills."

Keith smiled. He loved quoting from popular culture, especially movies. In this case, I recognized the quote from Liam Neeson.

"Abby will give you the details," I told him. "Use your '*very* particular set of skills' and let Abby know what you are able to do. And don't leave a trail."

* * *

Susan came into my office with a smile on her face. "Did you see the news today?"

"I always read the news."

"It seems that Officer Glass committed suicide last night."

"I saw that. Which reminds me, have Betsy come in."

"Do you know I love you?"

I smiled.

After she left, I went over to Reese's office.

"Nice work," I said, without explanation.

"Thanks, boss."

* * *

Susan opened the door for Betsy.

"Thank you so much, Mr. Frankel."

I gestured to the chair. "Sit down, Betsy. And it's Josh, remember?"

"Okay, Josh," Betsy replied. "Thank you."

"Well, actually, I heard this morning that your ex killed himself."

"Yup."

"So, since your problem appears to be solved, there is nothing for us to do. Here's your one dollar retainer back."

I slid the check across my desk. Betsy looked at it, at first confused. Then she smiled.

"Okay, I get it. Thanks for the check."

"Honestly, it was my pleasure, Betsy. Have a pleasant and safe life."

CHAPTER 18

Abby entered Keith's office. To Abby, it looked more like a command center for a space mission or a drone strike. A bank of computers crowded a table that stood against one wall. Above the computers, attached to the wall, a row of monitors displayed the live video feed from all the entrances to the firm—and to the building. Other "computer stuff," as Abby called it, occupied virtually every corner of the office.

"What did you find?" she asked, getting straight to business.

"I managed to get footage for the time we're interested in. But either the camera malfunctioned or someone deleted it. There's just static, and then black screen."

"Wow." Abby whistled through her teeth. "Is there any way to tell which it was, a malfunction or deletion?"

"Not that I know of. It's just missing."

Abby frowned. "Shit. Someone is doing a great job of framing our client." She found herself believing Allen's theory.

"Is this Allen Crosby?"

Abby nodded "Yeah. He claims he was withdrawing money from the ATM at the time of the murder."

Keith considered for a moment. "How about his bank history?"

"It shows no withdrawal at that time."

Keith smiled. "Well, at least he gets some free money."

Abby was not amused. "And gets framed for his wife's murder."

Keith turned more serious after acknowledging Abby's observation. "How sure are you that he didn't do it?"

"Not positive, but Josh believes him. His story seems to check out… except for when we need evidence that can be accessed electronically."

"The money they have is his, it wasn't hers?"

"Correct. He built it up with his own work and research."

"I guess insurance doesn't matter since he doesn't need the money."

"Our thoughts exactly. His too, by the way. He hadn't taken out a life insurance policy on her."

"What about outside romantic interests for either of them?"

Abby shook her head. "Can't find any evidence of that. Everyone insists their marriage seemed really great."

"So there's really no motive we know about for him to kill her?"

"Right. We think he hasn't been charged because he has no motive and the prosecution hasn't discovered a murder weapon. He had the opportunity. And there doesn't seem to be any motive for anyone else to kill her. So suspicion falls on the spouse."

"How do you know they don't have the murder weapon?"

Abby paused.

"Because we think we have it."

Keith's eyebrows raised up. "Josh is taking a chance not turning it over," He said.

"He knows. He's trying to figure out how best to protect Allen while not getting us into trouble for obstruction of justice."

"He must really believe in Allen."

"It seems Josh thinks Allen and his wife had the same kind of relationship that he and Sheri did…."

* * *

Josh and Sheri had met when both were students in middle school. They dated on and off until their senior year of high school when it finally stuck.

In between dating each other, they were part of the same group of friends. By high school graduation, they were not only lovers, but also best friends.

Josh's father had wanted him to go to an Ivy League school: his grades were good and the money was free-flowing. To spite his father, Josh had applied only to Temple University. He was accepted. Sheri wanted to be a special education teacher, and Temple didn't have a degree program for that course of study. Her parents weren't in the same financial position as Josh's; they limited Sheri's choices to state schools. Sheri chose Penn State and was accepted to the main campus.

Josh and Sheri's parting in the fall was heartbreaking for them and heart-rending for those who knew how close they were. They were miserable when they were apart, and in total joy during the weekends they visited each other. In less than a month, they decided to get married even though they were still teenagers.

One weekend when Sheri was visiting Josh, they sat down with Josh's parents for the first time. Josh was direct, as he did not share small talk when his father was around. "Sheri and I want to get married next summer," he told his parents.

"As of now, I'd have to say no," his father replied.

"I don't remember asking a question," Josh immediately returned.

Josh knew that he and Sheri would legally be considered adults before the following summer. There was nothing Samuel Frankel could do to prevent their marriage.

* * *

The wedding was the most fun Josh had. Ever. He especially liked the introduction at the reception: "For the first time in public, Mr. and Mrs. Joshua Frankel!"

His best friend, the person he respected most, was now his wife.

He knew he would never treat her the way his dad treated his mom.

Although he enjoyed himself at the reception, he nervously monitored his father's drinking throughout the celebration. As he had grown out of childhood, he had gradually begun to understand the connection between his dad's drunkenness and the way he treated his mom. He had urged his mom to leave his father on many occasions. But Joanne Frankel was old school. Marriage was literally "for better or worse, until death do us part." She felt that she deserved the "worse" because of her failure to thoroughly know Sammy before they married. Besides, who would have thought that a Jewish husband would abuse his wife? This was during a time when stereotypes, instead of evidence, led to conclusions like that. Arguably, we are still in that time.

Throughout the reception, his dad's behavior toward his mom seemed okay to Josh. Josh relaxed a bit and enjoyed the celebration. He and Sheri were set to leave for their honeymoon the next day.

In the morning, Josh and Sheri stopped by Josh's parents' house to thank them for the reception and say goodbye before the honeymoon. They had already stopped by Sheri's parents. When Josh's mother opened the door, Josh saw bruises on her face. She was wearing a long-sleeve shirt and long pants even though the heat of August was in full throttle. He told Sheri to talk to his mother while he went to see his dad.

"Don't do anything, Josh," his mom pleaded. "Anyway, he's still sleeping."

Josh went into his parents' bedroom. His dad was snoring away.

Josh emptied a vase of flowers, filled the vase with cold water from the master bathroom, then came back and threw it on his father's face.

"Wha—!" Samuel stammered, started coughing, looked up to see Josh staring down at him. "What the fuck?"

"The next time you lay a hand on my mother, I will kill you."

Josh turned and walked out of the room.

* * *

Josh and Sheri thoroughly enjoyed their honeymoon in the Catskills. They went horseback riding, wined and dined on gourmet food, swam in the pool at the fabulous resort where they were staying, wined and dined on gourmet food, enjoyed the entertainment at the nightly shows, wined and dined on gourmet food….They came back to their community in high spirits, although a bit heavier than when they had left.

The next time the newlyweds visited Josh's parents, Josh again saw fresh bruises on his mother's face. He went into his parents' room, grabbed his father by the lapels of his pajamas, and pulled him out of the room and onto the balcony outside his childhood bedroom.

Watching from below, Josh's mother shouted *"Stop!"* at the same time as Sheri shouted *"What are you doing!"*

Josh threw his father down the steps leading from the balcony; then he ran down the steps. His father was motionless, his head dangling to one side.

Josh checked. His dad wasn't breathing.

"Call 911," he told his mom and Sheri.

The coroner's report stated that Samuel Frankel died due to a broken neck during an accidental fall at home while drunk. The inheritance made Josh and his mom independently wealthy.

Justice had finally been meted out, outside the law.

* * *

Josh and Sheri had a great marriage. Josh's dad had been a model for how *not* to treat women. Josh knew to not follow that model, and he had no desire to do so.

Also, Josh did not drink.

Shortly after their wedding, Sheri started feeling weaker than normal. She became clumsier. She started choking when swallowing liquid. She began a long string of doctor appointments during their sophomore year. Most of the doctors found nothing wrong with her, concluding her symptoms were the result of nerves: she was a sophomore in college and had married quite young.

Josh knew that was wrong. Sheri was very smart, easily earning A's. Their marriage was wonderful. He kept encouraging Sheri to try different doctors. Finally, an experienced general practitioner researched her symptoms. He suggested Sheri be tested for myasthenia gravis. The test came back positive.

After an x-ray of Sheri's chest, a specialist determined that Sheri needed to have her thymus gland removed. The thymus gland is located near the heart. In most children it slowly gets smaller as the child gets older, until it finally disappears during adolescence. In some myasthenics, however, the thymus gland never gets smaller and is thought to cause some of the symptoms of myasthenia gravis. Because the gland is so close to the heart, surgery to remove the thymus is as dangerous as open-heart surgery. And it was considerably more dangerous decades ago, when Sheri underwent surgery, than it is today.

Sheri was admitted to one of the best hospitals in Philadelphia. With their wealth, she and Josh didn't have to worry whether the insurance would cover the procedure. Josh sat at Sheri's bedside and held her hand until it was time for Sheri to be wheeled to the operating room. As they parted they kissed each other gently.

Sheri died during the surgery. Josh was devastated, and he was determined to find out if the doctors had done anything wrong. After obtaining copies of the medical records and interviewing the doctors and nurses in the surgery, Josh learned that there had been a slight leak at the bottom of Sheri's oxygen mask. Oxygen is heavier than air. As the oxygen leaked, it accumulated in Sheri's chest cavity, which the surgeons had cut open to perform the surgery. During the procedures, Sheri's heart stopped; the doctors had used a defibrillator to try to restart her heart. Immediately, her chest cavity ignited, causing a fire that damaged her heart beyond repair.

Josh was shocked: he had never heard of a patient catching fire during surgery. Through his research, he discovered this type of adverse event happened about fifteen times a week, although it rarely resulted in the patient's death. Sheri's surgery had taken place during the summer before what would have been their senior year. Josh temporarily dropped out to sue the hospital and the doctors involved for malpractice.

Two things worked against him. First, the law did not consider negligence to include a surgeon's failure to notice a slight leak in an oxygen mask. Second, Josh could not prove that, had the fire not occurred, the doctors would have successfully started Sheri's heart again. In addition, fire during surgery was not as uncommon as he had first thought. His case went nowhere.

Josh was not persuaded by the arguments in favor of the doctors. He perceived that the rules protected the powerful against the weak. The medical profession was powerful. Patients injured or killed by the medical profession, such as Sheri, were weak. He decided to become a lawyer and make sure he always sought justice, whether through legal or extra-legal remedies.

* * *

Keith came into my office and asked, "Got a minute?"

"Sure," I said. "What's up?"

Keith closed the door then rolled in front of my desk.

"Abby told me about your problems with the case."

I looked at him hopefully. "Are you able to help?"

He shook his head. "The camera apparently was not working during the time he went to the ATM."

"Not working—or erased?"

"Yes, exactly."

"You can't tell which?"

"No, just that it's blank."

"Damn."

Keith stared at me. "I was wondering why it's such a problem if the police don't have a motive or the murder weapon? Abby told me you think someone is trying to frame Allen…and that you think you have the weapon."

"Correct." I saw no reason to hide the fact from my staff.

"Whoever is setting it up is pretty sophisticated. Abby also told me about the manipulation of the gun purchase records."

"Yup."

"Do you know who's doing it?"

I paused.

"We think it might be some agents of the NSA."

Keith let out a low whistle. "Rogue, or at the direction of the government?"

"I hope to God they're rogue. We don't know for sure yet."

Keith thought for a moment.

"Wouldn't NSA agents be ready for the frame before the murder took place? Unless…"

"Go on."

"Unless they thought Crosby was home, and when they found out that he wasn't, changed their plans to frame him."

"I was thinking about that possibility. Allen left his cellphone at home when he left. If they were tracking his phone . . .."

"I see. So you're afraid they're piecing the frame-up together and eventually will manufacture a motive."

"Yup."

"Have you thought about pushing the prosecutor into an indictment?"

"How and why?"

"The 'why' is so the NSA doesn't get a chance to manufacture a motive."

"And the 'how'?"

"How familiar are you with movies of the 1950s? Especially those with Marlene Dietrich and Charles Laughton?"

"Even if I saw the movie you're referring to, my memory of those old movies are not nearly as good as yours. Why?"

"How about more recent movies, such as those with Richard Gere?"

"How about if you get to the point?"

"Since I know you don't necessarily follow the rules in your pursuit of justice, here's my thought…."

Later, as Keith left my office, I began to think about who I knew who needed a new life.

CHAPTER 19

A few days after I gave him the assignment, Jerry came into my office. "I've done the research on the ATM video."

Jerry didn't know we had already gotten a copy of it.

"What'd you find?"

"Well, it seems the bank owns the video. They can turn it over to whoever they want to turn it over to. Generally, if a crime is committed on the video, banks voluntarily turn it over to the police. They can, if they want to, turn it over to a customer. But they are hesitant to do so."

"Because of privacy concerns?"

"No, actually there is no right of privacy when one does something out in the open. There is no reasonable expectation of privacy when approaching a public ATM machine."

"That makes sense. So what's the problem?"

"The bank is more concerned about the viewer seeing something that incites them to commit a harmful act against someone on the video. Then the bank could be sued for causing that to happen."

"Could you give me an example?" I wasn't sure how the scenario Keith was describing could happen.

"Like, if a married woman has a boyfriend and they go to the ATM to get money for a date. The husband suspects the woman of fooling around and requests the video to figure out who she's fooling around with. The husband sees the other man in the video. Then the husband physically attacks the other man."

Okay. That made sense.

"I see," I said. "But in our case all we want is a video of the customer who is requesting the video."

"Right. But since the bank owns it, it is still up to the bank. They would probably provide it, even without a court order, if there were ongoing litigation about it. If there's not, it's anybody's guess."

"Got it. Thanks. On another matter, how's it going with Lynn Warner's matter?"

Lynn Warner was a client who had witnessed a drug-related murder in her neighborhood. The prosecution wanted her to testify. She identified the suspect in a lineup but then feared for her life when she was not-so-subtly threatened by associates of the suspect. She wanted to do the right thing, but only if she were given a new identity and a new life somewhere else. Lynn's parents were dead, she had no siblings and no strong attachments. If this were a federal case, maybe she could go into witness protection. The prosecution was resisting, though, because the Commonwealth's budget for this type of witness protection was virtually nonexistent. And it was a state case in the cash-strapped City of Philadelphia. Jerry had been trying to negotiate a deal with the prosecution. Lynn had told us that without a guarantee of her safety, her memory of what she saw would suffer.

In the back of my mind, I knew that if Jerry couldn't work something out to everyone's satisfaction, I could arrange it. With my contacts and my assets, I could produce a fake identity and buy Lynn a home somewhere, and possibly get her employment. But I'd rather get the state to do the right thing.

"The Commonwealth is being stubborn," Keith told me. "They say they can't afford to give her a new identity and move her halfway across the country. She says she'll 'forget' what she saw. The Commonwealth says they will subpoena her, and if she doesn't confirm that she saw the defendant kill the victim they'll charge her with perjury, for her testimony, and filing a false police report for her initial identification. They will then let the jury sort it out."

"I see." I considered the matter for a moment. "Have Lynn come in to see me. Have Susan set up an appointment with her."

"Should I be there?"

"Jerry, I don't want you to think I'm excluding you. But if you're there during this conversation and the conversation ever comes to light, you could be disbarred and criminally prosecuted. So, no, you shouldn't be at that appointment."

* * *

After leaving Josh's office, Jerry thought for a moment. He felt put out. But he was even more curious. What could Josh want to discuss with Lynn that would be illegal but would have to do with settling her problem? Jerry figured that Josh had the resources to provide Lynn with a new identity, but doing so would hardly get them disbarred or prosecuted. Even if it could have, the prosecution wouldn't do anything about it, because they get their witness.

Jerry guessed he would have to trust Josh on this.

* * *

A few hours later Susan came to my office. "Lynn Warner's here." Susan led Lynn into my office.

I stood as Susan left, closing the door behind her.

"Have a seat, Lynn." I smiled quietly to her. " Thanks for coming in so quickly."

"Mr. Frankel, I have been so worried about this. When Susan told me you wanted to see me, I came in as soon as I could.

I acknowledged her worry. "How are you doing?"

"Mr. Frankel, I'm really getting nervous. The DA says they won't provide protection and are going to subpoena me anyway. If I lie to them, they'll charge me with perjury."

"So I heard. I have a question for you. This is a hypothetical favor to me that could solve your problem *and* a problem for me. That means I'm not actually asking you to do this, but I'm curious what your answer would be if I actually did ask you this. Do you understand?"

Lynn thought, her brow furrowed. Then she smiled with her brow unfurrowed. "So you're saying if you ask this hypothetical and that's all, then if anyone asks me if you asked me to do whatever's in that hypothetical, I can truthfully say 'no'?"

I smiled. I knew she was smart. "You got it."

"Okay, shoot."

"If I asked you to do something for me that wasn't legal, but that would help ensure that justice were done, and if you did this thing, then I would manage to get you a fake identity—a life in another part of the country, a life with a new home—*and* you could testify against the gangster in your present neighborhood, would you do it?"

I eyed Lynn carefully. I could almost see the gears in her brain turning. "I guess it depends on what law you wanted me to break and why. I need a more detailed hypothetical, I guess."

"Okay," I said. "What if I asked you to . . .."

* * *

Lynn testified for the prosecution at a preliminary hearing the following week. As a result of her testimony, the killer agreed to testify against the gangster who ordered him to make the hit, in exchange for the prosecution taking the death penalty off the table. As far as everyone knew, Lynn Warner then disappeared, never returning to her apartment after her testimony. The prosecution feared she had been killed and dumped somewhere. However, because this case was not a high-profile case in Philadelphia—i.e., there was zero news coverage of it—the whole affair was soon forgotten.

The day after the hearing, Jerry came to my office, concerned that he couldn't get in touch with Lynn to check on her. "What happened to Lynn?"

"She's safe," I assured him.

"Where is she?"

"The less you know, the better for both you and her."

"I guess I have no choice but to trust you...."

I could see Jerry was reluctant to remain outside the loop.

"Trust me. At some point you'll figure it out, but because I didn't tell you, and you weren't here during the meeting, you're safer."

Jerry shrugged. "Okay, I guess."

He seemed a little relieved to be assured he would know the answer at some point.

I led him out the door of my office, putting my arm around his shoulder. "And have I ever done anything to disappoint you?"

"You mean other than not sharing information with me?"

I smiled. "Yes, other than that."

"I don't think so."

"Good. I don't intend for that to change."

CHAPTER 20

As Jerry left, Abby arrived. "Boss, I got some bad news."

Abby walked into my office and closed the door behind her.

"Please tell me it's not about the Crosby case."

I had had enough of trying to line up the bad news we kept getting regarding the story Allen had told us.

"I can't do that, because it is."

I gestured for Abby to sit down "Okay, shoot."

"The coroner places the time of death between 4:30 and 5:00 p.m. Allen's call to 911 came at 5:23. He says his walk took no more than twenty minutes. Even with him looking for Deidre when he came back, it means that if he's the killer, the earliest he left for his walk was a couple minutes after five."

"Damn." I had been afraid of this. I had hoped that the estimate would include the time Allen was out, not exclude it. "Although that's really close to what Allen says, the prosecution could use it to say he killed her, then went out for his alibi walk."

"Exactly what I was thinking. And maybe that's what happened."

Given all of the evidence contradicting Allen's story, Abby's skepticism had returned.

I put Abby's doubt regarding our client aside. "How did the coroner determine time of death?"

"Body temperature. It's what they use when a body is found close to the time of the murder inside a building."

"Okay. Get me the science on body temperature and how it was applied here."

Abby stood from her chair. "Will do, boss."

* * *

A few days later, Susan buzzed me on the intercom. "Allen's on the phone. Says he's been arrested." Susan's voice sounded surprised and upset.

I picked up. "Where are you?"

"At the UD Police. Waiting for a county sheriff's van to take me to Norristown."

"I'll be right there. You aren't giving any statements, are you?"

"Nope. I read them the back of your card."

"Good man."

The police station was only three miles from my office, so it took me just five minutes to drive there. I told the police I was Allen's attorney and wanted to see him. They escorted me to his cell.

"Did they tell you anything about the case against you?"

"Only that I'm being arrested for Deidre's murder. I thought they wouldn't make an arrest unless they found a motive or a murder weapon?"

"We'll see what they have."

The Sheriff's Department was ready to transport Allen at the same time the local media arrived. I didn't think this was a coincidence. Camera crews from the Philly television stations were busy setting up in the parking lot. This, unlike Lynn's case, was going to be a hot, media-focused case. A wealthy semi-famous man accused of killing his wife in an idyllic Philly suburb sells newspapers and gets people to watch the news.

After Allen left, I took out my burner and called the DA's office to give them some grief about not calling me and arranging a surrender since they knew I was representing Allen and he was an upstanding member of the community. The assistant I spoke to in the homicide division said they had gone ahead with the arrest because the extent of Allen's assets and investments around the world would have given him the ability to flee the country. I think they arrested Allen instead of arranging his surrender because they wanted a perpwalk for the news. I also told the assistant that neither law enforcement nor the DA's office had my permission to talk to Allen without my being present. I asked if the assistant knew which ADA was going to handle the case. I wasn't surprised when she told me it would be Tom Fanucci, the chief homicide prosecutor. He wasn't available to talk to me at the time, so I left a message for him to call me.

* * *

Back at the office, I set things in motion. We officially requested the video from the bank. My entry-of-appearance form as Allen's attorney was prepared. We started putting finishing touches on our request for discovery.

"Tom Fanucci for you."

Susan's voice.

I picked up. "Hi, Tom."

"I thought you only represented people you thought were innocent?"

"I do think he's innocent. And I thought you'd give me a call and let him come in on his own since I told you I represented him?"

"Given his resources and how much he's traveled all over the planet, we thought this was safer so he wouldn't try to flee."

"Yeah, yeah. I saw the perp walk on TV."

Tom chuckled.

"For future reference," I told Tom, "innocent people don't usually flee."

"What makes you think he's innocent when you haven't even seen our evidence?"

"I know the man. He's not a murderer."

"You'd be surprised what people do when emotions are involved."

"Sounds like you think you have a motive."

"*And* a weapon *and* opportunity."

"Yeah?"

"Yeah."

"He has an alibi."

"First, it's not an alibi. Second, he's lying about that."

"We'll see."

"I guess we will." He paused for a moment, and I thought I heard one of his colleagues talking to him in the background. Then he returned to our conversation. "Listen, we've been accumulating evidence for a while, so there's a lot to copy. I assume we'll be getting a discovery request."

"Being prepared as we speak."

"Okay, it won't be a problem. After that, you may reconsider your representation."

"I doubt it. But we'll see."

* * *

I immediately went to Common Pleas Court for a hearing regarding bail. The prosecution, as was its wont, argued for no bail, since this was a first-degree murder case. Bail was supposed to be at a sufficient amount to make it worth the defendant's while to show up for trial. Although this wasn't a death penalty case because there were no aggravating circumstances under Pennsylvania law, the standard argument was still used: No amount of bail was sufficient to convince someone to show up with the possibility of life in prison with no possibility of parole.

I argued that the prosecution's case was so weak, and the defendant's character so strong, that the chance of conviction was minimal. Part of this argument was to try to tip the prosecution's hand as to the strength of their case. But apparently their desire for "no bail" was not a sufficient incentive for them to reveal the murder weapon or motive. I also argued that the defendant's reputation in the community was so sterling that it was worth more than any bail that could be set, and that Allen was motivated to show up for trial in order to clear his name.

I pointed out Allen's strong ties to the community, his lengthy residence there, and his lack of ever even being arrested before this. In the end, bail was set at five million dollars, and it was conditioned on Allen surrendering "any and all passports." Tom Fanucci did not give up. He argued that with his wealth, Allen could create a false passport (a fact I knew to be true). I pointed out, again, Allen's lack of criminal history and, therefore, his lack of connections to anyone who could produce fake identifications, and his lack of desire to even obtain a fake ID. The decision remained the same—bail was set at five million dollars conditioned on surrendering his passport. I had brought his passport to the argument expecting to have to surrender it. I did, along with posting bail, and Allen was freed.

Back in my office, Allen was full of questions.

"I thought they wouldn't charge me without a motive, or at least without a murder weapon."

"You do know that, as an officer of the court, I am ethically bound to make sure any evidence of a crime I have in my possession is turned over to the authorities. Once we got back the report on the gun placed in your hand, I had no choice."

Allen looked a bit taken aback. "But isn't that attorney-client privilege?"

"No. The fact that you gave the gun to me is, but the gun itself is not."

"Isn't that easy for the DA to figure out? You turn in a murder weapon you happen to have in your possession and then you're representing the person they charge? Won't they figure out where you got it?"

The conversation was approaching a topic I wasn't entirely comfortable discussing. I smiled quietly at Allen to reassure him I was in full command of the situation. "I have to keep you in the dark about certain things. The prosecution and the police have no idea I caused the weapon to come into their possession."

Allen stared at me. "How did you do that?"

"That's what I have to keep you in the dark about. By the end of the trial, I expect you to figure it out, but I will never be able to confirm or deny it to you. For both our sakes."

"Okay...I guess." He didn't seem entirely convinced. "But as you are showing me now, and as I knew from your whispered reputation, you're willing to paint outside the lines to defend a client you know is innocent. Why couldn't you just not turn over the gun?"

"I wanted to trigger the prosecution to take action." Before Allen had a chance to respond I explained my reasoning: "We believe the NSA didn't plan to frame you before they killed Deidre but are doing so now. We believed they, sooner or later, would let the prosecutors know that either you or we had the murder weapon, and we feared they would also manufacture a believable motive. We wanted to beat them to it."

"I don't understand. So you provided motive as well?"

"No comment. Do you trust me?"

"I did." He fell silent for a long moment, then shook his head as though he realized he had no other choice. "I guess I still do."

I nodded. "Good. Then do that. Trust me. I know what I'm doing."

* * *

"The Crosby case takes precedence over everything else you are working on," I said, opening a rare full-staff meeting. "Okay, everyone?" We were crowded into the large conference room one floor below my office. A thick sheet of metal lined the walls, as was the case throughout my entire office space. It's called a Faraday Cage. I was confident nobody was able to listen in on what we were saying.

"I don't care what you are working on," I continued. "If you are asked to do something for the Crosby case, that immediately takes priority. We are dealing with a client I firmly believe is innocent and is being set up by various government forces. Luckily, I think we have the resources to combat that. You are all bright, hard-working people dedicated to pursuing justice, or else you wouldn't be here. Any questions?"

Just quiet nods and stoic faces. Apparently, I had made myself clear.

"Okay. Everyone can go back to work—except Jerry, Abby, Reese, Keith, and Susan."

After the rest of the staff had cleared out, I said, "Jerry, I want you as second chair on this case. You up for that?"

"Absolutely." This was the first high-profile case Jerry would take part in.

"Abby and Reese, anything yet on reporter Roberts's death?"

Reese answered: "We are trying to piece together the death scene to see if any other causes of Roberts's death are possible. That involves researching everything found at the scene, from the garbage in the trash, to his bed, to the keyboard at his computer. Then we have to research whether there are ways to kill based on what we find. If the NSA did it, it's not going to be easy to prove."

"We aren't trying the NSA in Roberts's death," I reminded them. "We don't have to prove anything beyond a reasonable doubt, just raise reasonable doubt about Allen's guilt. To do that, we have to support Allen's story, which sounds like it is right out of a novel."

Abby's turn. "But we have to have enough solid evidence to get past the DA's inevitable objection based on relevance."

"True. I trust you both will come up with that."

Abby persisted. "How did you get the gun to the DA?"

"I expect you will hear about it at trial. If I were to tell you, it would put all of you in danger legally. Let's just say that it produced the effect I wanted."

"You *wanted* Allen charged?" Jerry asked.

"I was afraid that the NSA was slowly building an ironclad frame-up. I needed to push the DA into acting. I figured out a way."

"Does the DA's office have a motive?"

"Let me work on figuring that out—and destroying it." I glanced at Keith. I was happy to see him displaying an excellent poker face. Of course, he didn't really know if I had acted on his suggestion on motive. Just that shortly after our conversation, Allen was charged.

CHAPTER 21

When Josh went back to school after Sheri's death, he was determined to pursue justice. He had seen how difficult it was to use the law to obtain justice in his father's case and in his lawsuit against Sheri's surgeons. He also had a religious mandate from the Torah: "Justice, justice shalt thou pursue." That was a command from God, a command in which the word *justice* was repeated. As he had learned in Sunday School, the Torah did not waste words. If it repeats itself there is always a reason. Whoever wrote the phrase, whether it was God or someone inspired by God's qualities, they emphasized that they meant *justice*. There were other times when *law* was used—and, as in English, *justice* and *law* are two different words in Hebrew. Thus the command was not to pursue law, but to pursue justice. The Torah's command to seek justice spoke to Josh more than any other part of his religion.

Josh considered training to become a law enforcement officer, but there were two problems with that particular course of action. First, he had not pursued a major in criminal justice. Although he had taken the occasional course in the subject, too many requirements remained for him to graduate in one year. And graduate was something he wanted to do. Temple's campus and classes reminded him too much of Sheri.

Second, if he were a law enforcement officer, he thought going around the law in order to obtain justice would be difficult. He had seen the "Dirty Harry" movies and had identified with the frustrations of following the law that often prevented justice from being served. He had also seen the "Death

Wish" movies and identified with vigilante justice but understood how that line of pursuit could get out of hand, and how easily mistakes could be made. He was majoring in political science and understood that the courts had been created to give victims a place to seek justice *instead* of pursuing vigilante justice. But he also understood that the judicial system was losing the respect of ordinary citizens because the courts could not always accomplish their stated goal.

He started admiring his childhood heroes, such as Batman, even more. The turning point was when he read *The Boston Strangler* by Gerold Frank. He saw that F. Lee Bailey had used the law to achieve a just result for an insane defendant. He then read F. Lee Bailey's book, *The Defense Never Rests.* That sealed the deal for him. He took the LSATs and did very well on them. The fall after his college graduation he headed to law school, as did almost all other political science majors.

While in law school, he began to question another part of the past he had accepted simply because his father had told him. His father, and his father's companies, were almost constantly being sued. His father would say that lawsuits were simply a cost of doing business and that every business had frivolous lawsuits filed against it. Josh began researching the lawsuits against his father. They included suits seeking compensation for deaths caused by poorly designed products; his father could have avoided these deaths, but it would have cost him more money than dealing with the suits. They included suits filed by his employees because of the way he treated them. They included suits by the US government because he wasn't following safety or pollution standards. They included suits by contractors because his father hadn't paid them the agreed upon amounts. In each case, his father settled the suits for much less than it would have cost him to do the right thing to begin with. The results of the lawsuits against his father convinced Josh even more that following the law did not always result in justice being served.

Josh's new understanding of his father's business practices made him even more determined to always pursue a just course of action, no matter the cost, and no matter what the law had to say about his methods of achieving justice.

CHAPTER 22

Susan was happy to see Josh arrive at her apartment that night, but not as happy as Taco, Susan's chiweenie. Taco jumped up and down as if his legs were springs until Josh bent down and picked him up. Taco loved to be at eye level with large humans.

"Hey, Taco," Josh said, scruffing the dog's neck. "What's up?"

"He is," Susan said, laughing.

Josh and Taco were staring eye to eye, with Taco's tail moving like an out-of-control metronome.

Josh and Susan kissed, while Taco tried to nose his way between them. They made their way to the kitchen table and Josh sat, returning Taco to the floor.

Susan had made Josh's favorite: bone-in rib eye with garlic mashed potatoes and nothing green. The fact that Josh did not like vegetables was a source of, well…not argument but *discussion* between them.

After dinner, Josh cleaned up. When he finished, Susan placed a note in front of him.

What's with motive?

Josh took the paper and wrote.

You really don't want to know.

After Susan read Josh's response, Josh took the note to her sink, retrieved a book of matches, and burned the note to ashes. He made sure to run the garbage disposer.

Susan trusted Josh completely, she was just curious. If he wouldn't tell her the information she wanted to learn, she knew the knowledge he was keeping to himself was dangerous for him to know—and dangerous for anyone else who knew about it as well. Now she was concerned, but she wouldn't ask about it again. At least not tonight.

Susan took something that looked like a small, hollow red snowman out of the freezer and they headed to the bedroom, with Taco close behind.

"Is Taco going to make me want to laugh during sex again?" Josh asked.

"I think I may have come up with a solution."

Susan tossed the red snowman onto the floor. Taco raced toward it and started licking out the contents.

"What's that?" Josh seemed amused.

"It's called a kong."

"What's inside?"

"Frozen peanut butter."

Josh laughed as Taco diligently worked on the kong.

* * *

After everyone had satisfactorily completed their second feast of the evening, Susan allowed Taco to jump onto the bed. The three of them cuddled together. Soon Josh was breathing regularly with a slight snore. Susan watched him sleeping and thought back to when she first met him.

It was at a Bar Association event about 15 years earlier. She had come with her boyfriend at the time, a corporate lawyer whose name she intentionally did not remember. Josh had come to the event without a date. He seemed drawn to her immediately, hanging around her during cocktail hour while her boyfriend made the rounds schmoozing. It wasn't until later that she found out why he hung around her, constantly asking her questions: she was wearing a long-sleeve blouse during the heat of summer, and the blouse reminded him of his mother.

They sat at the same table. By the time her date sat down, it was obvious he was a bit tipsy. Susan was embarrassed and glanced at Josh. He was staring at her date, hatred dancing in his eyes. His teeth and jaw seemed to be grinding wheat into flour. Susan was surprised at Josh's reaction, not knowing of his upbringing.

Her date became more and more inebriated as the night wore on, making more and more of a fool of himself. Susan excused herself from their table to go to the ladies' room. Her date immediately followed. Josh came into the hall just in time to hear her date say, "You don't leave the table unless *I* say you leave the table."

Susan's date had a tight grip on her arm, twisting it. Susan's face looked fearful, her eyes welling with tears.

"Is there a problem here?" Josh asked.

"No problem," the date insisted. "Susan was just coming back to the table with me."

Susan didn't know where she dragged up the courage, but she said, "I have to go to the bathroom."

Josh said to her date, "Seems that you and I are headed back to the table while the lady uses the facilities."

Susan's date let go of Susan's arm then approached Josh, purposefully intruding into his personal space. "I'm her boyfriend," he observed firmly. "So I get to say where she goes—and when. *You* leave."

Josh met the date's gaze. "What if I don't?" he asked quietly.

"You'll regret it."

Josh smiled. "I don't think so."

The date took a swing at Josh. He was so drunk by this point that a five-year-old boy could have avoided the punch. Josh didn't. He got hit square on his eye. He immediately slammed his knuckles into the date's windpipe. The date fell to the floor, gasping for breath.

Just then two prosecutors who had been sitting at Susan and Josh's table came running into the hall. Apparently they had seen the fight. One of them shouted something to Josh about leaving.

"Why'd you let him hit you?" Susan was astounded.

"Better evidence for self-defense. C'mon, let's get outta here."

Susan immediately followed him out.

She never went back to her boyfriend again. Josh hired her as his executive assistant, and she had never failed to trust him.

CHAPTER 23

Abby and Reese came into my office and closed the door.

"We have copies of the Roberts autopsy and the coroner's notes, as well as the police reports."

"Good, what'd you find?"

Reese spoke first. "The coroner concluded carbon monoxide poisoning, as you know. He based his conclusion on both the presence of an unvented space heater and Roberts's very red cheeks when he was discovered facedown in his loft."

Abby's turn. "We checked his credit card bills, with Keith's help. It seems about six months ago Roberts bought the space heater—but the one he bought was vented."

"Interesting. Is there a vent in his loft?"

"It's covered up. And here's the really interesting part. The first responders noted a vented space heater in the apartment. But the police reports just note a 'space heater,' which the coroner concluded must have been an unvented heater because of the red cheeks. How else could he have died of carbon monoxide poisoning?"

I was beginning to get the picture. "Okay. Did you talk to the officer who submitted the report, or to the first responder?"

"The first responder insists the heater was vented. The officer never had a space heater, was never trained about space heaters, and so did not know the difference. He didn't notice if it was vented or not."

"Did they keep Roberts's property?"

"Landlord got permission to sell his stuff once the coroner concluded the death was accidental. We spoke to the landlord, who said someone came in and offered him a thousand dollars, cash, for everything in there, including the trash. He thought the guy was nuts but gladly sold it. He didn't get the buyer's name or address."

"The trash?" I shook my head incredulously. "Is there anything in the police report that itemized the trash?"

"There were notes with what appeared to be telephone numbers. I wonder if it's Roberts's notes about following up Allen's story?"

Reese added: "Also, there was an apple core."

I raised an eyebrow. "Is that significant?"

"Maybe, maybe not. He could have been poisoned by something in the apple."

"Would his death still have looked like it was due to carbon monoxide?"

"If it was hydrochloric acid….Remember Alan Turing?"

I thought for a moment. The name sounded familiar. "The British scientist who helped the allies win World War Two?"

"That's the one. He was prosecuted after the war because he was a homosexual. He was sentenced to chemical castration."

Reese's words hit home. "Yes, I seem to remember learning about that. He killed himself, didn't he?"

"That's the official story. He died after eating an apple laced with hydrochloric acid. Some say suicide, some say assassination."

"By an intelligence service," Abby added.

"Exactly," Reese agreed.

I nodded, taking in all the new information. "Good, keep researching that possibility—and any others that come to mind. And keep gathering evidence indicating Roberts's death wasn't caused by carbon monoxide poisoning." Abby and Reese started to leave, but I wasn't done yet. "Did you find out any more about how body temperature can be used to determine time of death, and how it was applied to Deidre's death?

Abby spoke up: "So far, it seems the coroner used standard procedure. The body was in a room that was cooler than normal body temperature. Therefore, the body would cool at about 1.5 degrees per hour. The coroner's office took Deidre's temperature on the scene at 6:02, and it was 96.65 degrees. That would put the time of death at 4:44. But coroners like to give ranges, as you know; hence the 4:30 to 5:00 estimate."

"I see. What else can affect body temperature?"

"If the body were outside and subject to daily temperature changes, and if a longer time period had gone by, determining the time of death would be much more difficult; a coroner would evaluate how badly decomposed the body was, what types of insects had penetrated the deceased's skin and orifices...things like that. But even if the body were inside a building, it might be lying in a sunny area, which would naturally warm the body up before it began cooling on its own. And if Deidre was sick—if, say, she had a fever at the time of her death—her body temperature would have started out being higher. But that would mean that she died even earlier rather than later."

I could see Abby had done her homework. I could also see that determining Deidre Allen's time of death was a complicated matter that required more thought about what further information I needed. But I didn't have the time for that right now.

"Alright, thanks," I told Allen and Reese simply. "I'll work on this."

CHAPTER 24

Some attorneys routinely waive their client's preliminary hearing, which is a safety valve for defendants. Essentially the hearing is a mandated court appearance during which the prosecution has to show that based on the evidence they have 1) a crime has probably been committed; and 2) the defendant probably committed the crime. Notice that the burden of proof in this case is "probably," not "beyond a reasonable doubt"—and that any such "proof" is based only on the prosecution's evidence, not the *totality* of the evidence. In other words, the judge does not consider any evidence the defendant presents at the hearing. It is extremely rare that charges are tossed out at a preliminary hearing and, if they are, the Commonwealth has the right to refile them. Some attorneys consider preliminary hearings a waste of time because even if the defendant gets the case tossed out, that would just force the Commonwealth to make a stronger case before they refile the charges. I consider preliminary hearings invaluable. They act as the first step toward discovering the evidence the prosecution has against my client, as well as getting on record witness testimony for possible cross-examination at the upcoming trial. As to the possibility of strengthening the prosecution's case, I never argue for a dismissal at the preliminary hearing unless I am sure that the prosecution cannot strengthen their case. And I can rarely be sure of that.

With Allen's case, I had another factor to consider. This was a high profile case. The media would be all over every court appearance. Should I allow a preliminary hearing in which the prosecution presents their case, the defendant does not present his, and the jury pool is therefore possibly poisoned, tilting their judgement in the direction of guilt?

I opted for the preliminary hearing even after my motion to close the hearing to the press was correctly denied by the judge. If the press coverage of the hearing were to get out of hand the denial of my motion would add to my arguments on appeal in the event the jury voted for a conviction.

Tom presented Officer Norman, the officer who had taken Allen's original statement—and who had taken his gun. He then called the tech who had examined the gun taken at the scene and found that, although the gun was similar to the murder weapon, it had not been fired recently enough for it to have been the murder weapon; nor did the ballistics match. The tech testified that he had recently been given another gun of the same model to test. He matched that gun ballistically to the bullets recovered from Deidre's body and concluded it was the murder weapon. He then testified that the only fingerprints he found on that gun were the defendant's. I asked about DNA and the tech explained that, since the gun was kept in a plastic bag, the moisture degraded the DNA to the point that it was unusable. A murmur rose through the courtroom at the tech's testimony.

During cross-examination, I asked the tech where the other gun had come from. All he knew was that it was sent to him by a police detective in an evidence bag with a request to test it to see if it matched the weapon used in any unsolved gun violence case. It matched the bullets found in Deidre's body.

Tom then called a detective who had requested and received various computer-generated reports related to the murder. Among these was the bank's report indicating that no ATM withdrawals had been made just prior to Deidre's death, and Clayton's report showing that Allen had purchased the murder weapon on the morning of the murder.

Tom made no mention of motive...which I found interesting. I even tried to goad him by objecting to holding Allen for trial on the evidence, which included a gun that had mysteriously showed up in an evidence bag; the prosecution had provided no feasible reason for Allen to have killed Deidre. Tom answered, correctly, that the prosecution was not obligated to prove motive and that anything I wanted to know about the gun that the prosecution also knew, I could learn about during the discovery process. Allen's case was bound over to the Court of Common Pleas for trial.

I deduced from the preliminary hearing that Tom was planning a methodical, prove-the-elements case and was going to withhold from the defense the information regarding where the gun came from—and any motive the DA's office had learned about—for as long as they could.

CHAPTER 25

Janice McGuire and I were classmates in law school. I often felt we were kindred spirits as we both had a burning desire to pursue justice. Her Catholicism and my Judaism motivated us in that respect, at least partially. Although I had personal reasons for wanting to see justice relentlessly pursued, I never did find out if Janice had any reason other than her Jesuit upbringing. Jesuit tradition is as emphatic as Jewish tradition about pursuing justice. Janice considered pursuing justice through her religion. However, Jesuit religious leadership is limited to men, so Janice pursued law in an attempt to find justice.

Janice and I would often be the only students in our classes arguing against what a professor said the law was, because in our eyes, it did not seem just. Other students seemed willing to merely record what the law was without looking at it with a critical eye or passing it through any sort of justice "filter." After all, their goal was to get good grades in the class so they could get a good job after law school. Learning what the professor said the law was, was essential to fulfilling their goals.

One of the classes Janice and I took together during our first year was Civil Procedure taught by a former "Nader Raider." Neither Janice nor I thought we were going to practice civil law, so we paid only a minimal amount of attention to both the professor's lectures and the assigned readings. But by the end of the class, we respected the professor, who seemed dedicated to seeing justice served, so much that we thought maybe we could pursue justice by practicing civil law after all. When the final came, the professor presented various case scenarios and various rules of civil procedure and asked us how they applied to the case at hand. After the final ended I found out that Janice had been as panicked as I was by the questions, because we had paid little attention to the principles dictating how the cases said the rules were to be applied. So we had both answered in similar ways—that the entire court system was established to see that justice was served. In the case presented, justice would be done if the result were *blah, blah, blah.* To make that happen, the rule must be interpreted as *blah, blah, blah.* Therefore, that is how the rule must be interpreted in this case.

There were seventy-five students in our class. Although Janice and I were hoping that we didn't fail the final, it turned out we earned the only A's in our class.

After school, I clerked for a federal judge while Janice went to work for the Justice Department. She liked to joke, "How better to pursue justice than to work for a department named for it?" Periodically, we got together for a drink or a meal to hash out our careers and next steps. Although I eventually went into private practice, Janice stayed with the government, moving up in the department. When a president was elected who wanted career prosecutors running the Justice Department, as opposed to big donors or partisans who happened to be lawyers, Janice was promoted to US Attorney for the Eastern District of Pennsylvania. We continued meeting periodically to discuss our lives. I was pleased to hear that she continued battling for justice rather than just following orders unquestioningly. She was pleased to hear that I finally had a romantic relationship when I told her about Susan.

As the Crosby trial approached, I gingerly approached a few topics with Susan during one of our get-togethers.

"What if I had evidence that certain employees of the federal government were using their position to conduct an illegal business?"

Janice shrugged. "If the evidence was credible, I would pursue it."

"What if the illegal activity included murder and the framing of an innocent person?"

Janice paused. Then she looked at me uncertainly. "Are we talking about the Crosby case?"

"I can neither confirm nor deny whether I am talking about a real case or a hypothetical."

We both smiled. It was a common answer we'd given each other many times over the years.

Again Janice shrugged. "I would vigorously pursue any such credible evidence. You know I would. Can I see the evidence?"

"Well, again, you don't even know if this is a hypothetical question or not. Yet."

"Okay," Janice allowed. "Then why did you ask it?"

"Curious, I guess. I want to hear your thoughts on the subject. That said, let me add another twist to my question. How capable are you of keeping investigations secret?"

"Very capable."

"What if one of the people involved turned out to be a friend of presidents—present and former presidents of the United States—who had already been investigated and was given a sweetheart deal by your department?"

Janice paused. "I would still investigate, keep it secret, and pursue it if the evidence were there."

"Let's assume I had such evidence, and that I gave it to you. You investigate and determine arrests should be made based on the evidence. Would I be able to set a date, before which you would agree to make no move?"

"No." Janice was adamant.

"That's it? Just 'no'?"

"Yes. I can't let anyone, even you, old friend, restrict my actions in pursuing justice."

"Okay." Good answer. "What if I were to tell you to be in a particular courtroom on a particular day to obtain the evidence? Could you be there?"

Janice considered. "Depends on the advance notice and my schedule."

"What if it involved more than one day? Maybe some testimony followed by more physical evidence?"

"Same answer. How much notice am I getting and what is my schedule for those days?"

"You will probably get one or two days' notice."

"Then it all depends on the schedule."

"I could probably estimate it for you earlier than one or two days before."

"That would help."

"Would it help you if I laid out the allegations to you without you having the evidence? Could you conduct a quiet investigation with only people you absolutely trust to gather any evidence you can gather before I actually hand you our evidence?"

"Maybe." She stared at me, shaking her head mildly. "Why the big concern?"

"Because this hypothetical involves members of the intelligence community in addition to the president's friend."

Janice was silent at first. The FBI was part of the Justice Department. CIA, NSA, DIA, and others were not.

"Are we talking about FBI employees in this hypothetical?"

"No."

"Then I believe it would be no problem."

CHAPTER 26

Part of our massive discovery request were questions concerning the Roberts death. I'm sure this raised Tom's curiosity, but it also raised objections, which we argued in court.

"Your Honor, the Roberts death is irrelevant to the Crosby murder." Tom's argument was succinct.

"Counselor, why do you need information about the Roberts death?"

Judge Sophia Warren was a strict judge. But she was also determined to make sure all defendants' rights to a fair trial were upheld. Her concern for defendants' rights had members of the Montgomery Bar refer to her as the "Warren Court," after the Supreme Court of the 1960s, which attempted to ensure that defendants' guarantees in the Bill of Rights were not just meaningless words.

"Your Honor," I began, "my client is facing a possible sentence of life imprisonment without the possibility of parole. Without revealing my client's defense in advance of trial, the records in the possession of the Commonwealth might help prove his innocence. Mr. Roberts is deceased, so no privacy claim can be made."

Judge Warren turned her attention to Tom. "Counselor, why don't you want to provide this information?"

"Your Honor, we are concerned that this is the beginning of a fishing expedition by the defense."

"Has defense counsel been asking for much discovery you consider irrelevant?"

"No, Your Honor, the Roberts death is the only irrelevant information they've asked for."

"Well, since neither you nor I know exactly what defense Mr. Crosby has, we can't really determine that this is irrelevant, can we?"

"But if it is, Mr. Frankel will just use this information to confuse the jury."

"Counselor, as I think you know, I am not in the habit of allowing totally irrelevant information into trial. I will decide on the relevancy issue if Mr. Frankel attempts to introduce anything you object to as irrelevant."

That seemed to satisfy Tom. Or else he knew further objection would not help him. "Yes, Your Honor," he replied.

"The Commonwealth will provide the requested discovery," ruled Judge Warren.

* * *

I was back in the office soon after the hearing. Susan entered, closing the door behind her.

"There's a woman with a hat, sunglasses, and a scarf on in the waiting room. She won't identify herself but says you will want to see her."

I nodded. "Okay, send her in."

Susan cocked her head at me. "What if she's NSA?"

"I doubt they would send someone into the office in broad daylight to kill me."

"Why not? We wouldn't be able to identify her."

I stared at her, considering whether she had a point. She did.

"Okay, ask the Echelon agent stationed in the waiting room to scan her for metal. Is our Echelon agent today male or female?"

"Male."

"Is Abby in the office?"

"Yes."

"Have her pat down this mysterious woman for any possible weapons that might not be metal. Then send her in."

Susan left the office. About fifteen minutes later my door opened. The woman walked in, closed the door, and took off her glasses.

I blinked. "Janice? Why the disguise?"

Janice was visibly nervous. She rubbed her hands absently, and her face was ashen. "After our lunch yesterday, I went back to the office. When I went home, a man was waiting for me there."

"Who was it?"

"He pulled out an NSA identification. Name is Terry Logan. Not sure if it's his real name."

"What did he say?"

"He wanted to know what we talked about."

I was under surveillance. Neither I nor my Echelon contingent had spotted it.

"What did you say?"

"I told him it was none of his business. He asked if his agency had come up in our discussions. I honestly told him no. He told me that if it ever did, I was to contact him by putting a potted plant on the balcony of my apartment."

"Seriously? He's using tradecraft from *All the President's Men*?" I laughed. Keith would get a kick out of this when I told him.

"I don't find this very amusing. What have you gotten me into?"

"Nothing yet. Not until I give you more information about that hypothetical we discussed."

"Am I in danger?"

"I hope not, but don't know for sure. Want me to arrange some Echelon protection for you?

She smiled pertly. "No thanks. I'm arranging for FBI protection. Logan said that if I know what's best I'll cooperate with him. I took that as a threat—and the FBI protects its US Attorneys."

"Alright, let me know if he makes contact again."

"I will. And please get me the information I need to get these people."

"Eventually."

PART THREE

THE TRIAL

CHAPTER 27

The legal field is riddled with Latin terms. Many, if not most, are unnecessary; they could just as easily be expressed in English. I remember the first term I came across in law school. I was reading a court opinion for our first day of classes (yes, law students get assignments before classes begin!). The judge used the term *inter alia* in his opinion. I was so excited that I was going to learn my first Latin legal term. I ran to my copy of Black's Law Dictionary (no internet back then) and looked it up. "Among other things." My first thought was, "Couldn't the judge have just said that?"

Anyway, one such term of art is *voir dire*. *Voir dire*, when applied to choosing a jury, is simply the questioning of a juror by the attorneys on opposing sides of a case to determine if either attorney would like to have a particular juror struck from the panel. It is also used during trial to refer to the preliminary examination of a witness, usually an expert. If the side who has not asked the expert to testify would like, they can question the expert to determine his or her credentials before the court rules on whether the witness may in fact give an expert opinion.

At the beginning of *voir dire*, when we are questioning the jury panel as a whole, I like to play a little game. I tell the members of the panel to imagine they are chosen for the jury. And then, instead of listening to all the evidence, the prosecution and the defense only give opening statements and then both sides rest. I tell them I am going to give them three choices on voting—guilty, not guilty, or not enough information to vote.

As you might expect, unless someone wants to avoid jury duty, nobody raises their hand for guilty. Also, very few raise their hands for not guilty. The vast majority choose "not enough information."

I then tell that majority that under the law they must apply as jurors, they are wrong. I explain that under the scenario I gave them, they have a duty to vote "not guilty." That's because the Commonwealth has the burden of proving my client (I use the client's first name at all times) guilty beyond a reasonable doubt, while the defense has no obligation to prove anything. None. Even if the prosecution had presented a case and the defense had not, if the jurors don't think it's enough to meet the "beyond a reasonable doubt" standard, they must vote not guilty. I remind them that a vote of "not guilty" does not mean innocent. It just means the prosecution has not proven its case beyond a reasonable doubt.

Most jurors at this point are nodding slightly, agreeing with what I am saying, because they are familiar with the concept of proof beyond a reasonable doubt. But usually in a jury pool, there are some who either look skeptical or have no expression on. In most judges' courtrooms I can get away with looking at the prosecutor and the judge and then saying, "Neither the prosecutor nor the judge have objected to or stopped me from telling you this."

I then ask whether there are any prospective jurors in the panel who feel that if the defense does not present any defense, they cannot vote "not guilty."

By the way, during the entire *voir dire* everyone from my office who is with me in the courtroom is taking notes so that I don't have to pause to write down the important information regarding which juror said what or raised their hand in answer to which question. Or which looked skeptical about voting "not guilty" in the absence of evidence.

Because the prosecution wisely charged Allen's case as a non-capital murder, which meant the DA's office wasn't going to ask for the death penalty, each side was allowed seven peremptory challenges to jurors. That meant if we didn't want a particular juror—call him Juror #X—we didn't have to provide a reason. Juror #X was automatically removed from the jury panel. But before we used any peremptory challenges, we first had to challenge any jurors for cause. That meant we had to provide a reason why we believed the juror would not be able to impartially decide the case by following the judge's instructions at the end of the trial. As you can imagine, that was not easy. But one challenge for cause that was easy for me to make was to challenge those who raised their hand to say they could not vote "not guilty" if the defense did not present any evidence. And Tom successfully challenged for cause one juror who believed that wives were property of their husbands and there was no crime if a husband killed his wife (!).

In the Crosby case, a jury was empaneled after one day of *voir dire.* I found that to be an about average amount of time for murder cases I had handled where the prosecution wasn't seeking the death penalty. Each side used their seven peremptories. As trial attorneys, our job was not to pick a jury that was demographically representative of the population. Our job was to pick a jury that would be most receptive to the arguments we planned to make. To do that, we used actual knowledge of jurors in the jury pool based on answers to the questionnaires they filled out in advance as well as what they had said during *voir dire.* But that didn't give us enough information. As a result, we often had to rely on stereotypes.

Usually when I represent a criminal defendant, I want a jury of poor people and African-Americans of any wealth level. Both of those groups tend to be more skeptical of law enforcement and have the "prove it to me" attitude that all criminal juries should have. However, they are also more skeptical of wealthy people. Allen is filthy rich, as am I. So, in this case, I did not want any poor people or African-Americans on the jury. Two things helped me accomplish that. First, Montgomery County does not have a high percentage of prospective jurors who are either poor or African-American. Second, Tom decided to not take a chance on having poor or African-American jurors. Sometimes using peremptory strikes is a little like a chess game. If it's your turn to tell the judge that you are or are not striking a juror, you don't want to use a peremptory if you think your opposing counsel will use theirs for that same juror. When the first African-American prospective juror presented, I had to announce first. I did not use one of my peremptory challenges. Tom looked at me for a few seconds before he used one of his. So I knew I did not have to use any of mine on African-Americans unless Tom ran out of his. I did the same when it came to the first person who looked to me to be lower-middle class, and I got the same result.

Also, usually when representing criminal defendants I want as many women on my jury as possible. As a general rule, they are more lenient than men. However, since the charges here involved a husband killing a wife, I wanted more men than women. Tom, however, wanted more women than men. Tom bettered me on this: our final jury was seven women and five men, all white.

After the jury was sworn in, they were allowed to leave for the day, with instructions to pack enough clothes for a week and bring the clothes with them on Monday. Due to the unfettered publicity this case would likely generate throughout the trial, the judge had wisely decided to sequester the jury for the length of the trial. Sequestering a jury involves taking them from their normal lives, putting them up in a hotel, and making sure that they see no news or hear anyone talking about the case. This dramatically impacts the jurors' lives and their families' lives. Generally, the jurors get no access to newspapers or the internet, and no telephones. Fortunately for this jury, we estimated the trial would take only one week. For comparison, OJ Simpson's jury was sequestered for 265 days.

After the jury left, we handled preliminary matters. One of these preliminary matters was Tom's motion *in limine*—another unnecessary Latin term that is used to signify a motion heard at the start, or just before the start, of a trial. His motion asked the judge to rule in advance that any evidence concerning journalist Roberts's death was irrelevant and inadmissible. I asked to move this argument into the judge's chambers—*and* I asked for a gag rule; that is, a judge's order that prevents either party from revealing what was said. The judge seemed skeptical, but agreed to both of my requests.

After we had retreated to the judge's chambers, I explained that we believed Roberts's death was not accidental; that both Roberts and Deidre were either killed by, or on the orders of, the same person.

Tom and Judge Warren both seemed taken aback. Judge Warren sat back in her chair. "You have evidence of this?"

"I don't yet have enough evidence to meet 'beyond a reasonable doubt,' but I certainly have enough to raise a reasonable doubt that Allen killed his wife."

Tom was compelled to state his predictable objection. "Your Honor, this is merely an attempt to confuse the jury with irrelevant information."

"An opinion I am sure you will share with the jury," Judge Warren replied. "I will withhold a decision on its admissibility until it is presented." Judge Warren then looked at me very directly. "Counselor, I don't appreciate attorneys trying to confuse issues in my courtroom. You will be on a tight leash with this."

"Thank you, Your Honor," I responded.

Another preliminary matter was my own motion *in limine.* I didn't expect to win it, but I knew Tom would be expecting me to make it, and didn't want him to start getting suspicious. I argued that the murder weapon should not be admitted because there was no chain of evidence establishing how the DA's office had come to possess it.

Tom argued that it came into their possession in a plastic bag, that an Upper Dublin police officer had come into possession of it, and from that time on there was a chain of possession.

I argued that we had no way of knowing whether the real killer wasn't trying to frame Allen.

Judge Warren commented: "An argument I am sure you will make to the jury. The gun will be admitted, and you can question and argue its authenticity."

It was Tom's turn to thank the judge.

CHAPTER 28

Whenever I start preparing for a trial, I start with my closing argument. That helps me concentrate on what facts I need presented in evidence, what attacks I need to make on the prosecution's case, and, in summary, what I need to create reasonable doubt in the minds of the jurors.

The period between choosing a jury and the state making its opening statement is the time for me to review what I have. I often draw a chart, with the major points I plan to make on the left and the evidence I have, or expect will come out, listed beside those points. I look over the chart to see what, if any, gaps I have. I look first for whatever facts I can still bring out by changing a line of questioning or by the last-minute acquisition of a witness. If there is a gap I can't fill with direct evidence, I look to see if logical arguments to that point can be made by inference from evidence that will be introduced. If not, I modify the closing argument accordingly.

After I do all of that—after I know what evidence to expect (based on discovery of the prosecution's case and what I expect my evidence to show)—I lay out what I expect the order of the evidence to be. Only then am I ready to prepare my opening statement and to make a tentative decision as to whether I will give my opening immediately following the prosecution's or if I will wait until the prosecution rests to present my opening. That is a choice defense attorneys have, at least in Pennsylvania. I'm not sure whether that is true in all states.

In this case, with the prosecution bringing forth the murder weapon, the apparent lie by Allen about his walk to the ATM, and the purchase of the murder weapon by Allen, I decided I wanted to blunt that evidence somewhat in the jurors' minds by giving my opening statement immediately after Tom's. Interestingly enough, I did not see on the prosecution's list of proposed witnesses a name I expected to see—the only one I knew who could provide a motive. I did, however, know she was told to be available for the trial.

Allen and I also had to decide if he would testify. Given the strength of the prosecution's case, Allen's defense, and the strength of his reputation in the community, I had no doubt that if I couldn't get the case dismissed before the defense was due to begin, I would be calling Allen as a witness. This is what Allen and almost all truly innocent defendants want. Most defendants, even those innocent of the charges presently against them, have some criminal background or would not come off as an innocent person, especially under cross-examination. With Allen, I did not have those concerns.

I had Reese and Abby conduct research on the chosen jurors to see if there was any evidence that any of them, especially those we'd prefer not to be on the jury, had lied during *voir dire.* This is perfectly legal as attorneys always have an obligation to notify the court if someone lied in the courtroom.

As usual I was not able to get very much sleep the weekend before the trial. I made sure that my opening day trial suit, a trusting blue, was cleaned and ready for me to wear. Allen and I met in my office on Sunday, both to calm Allen's nerves and to let him know what to expect during the trial.

"I believe that the prosecution has a witness who will testify about a motive," I stated after laying out how I thought the prosecution's case would go. "And she wasn't on the prosecution's witness list."

"Can they do that?"

"Usually only if they are going to use her in rebuttal to our case, or as additional confirmation for a witness we destroy on cross-examination."

"Do you know who it is and what they will say?"

"Yes."

"Who and what?"

"I can't tell you that now for several reasons. The reason I am willing to tell you is that I want you to demonstrate an honest reaction when she testifies."

"When do you think they will use her?"

"My guess is after our case. After you testify."

"But I don't have to testify. We don't even have to present a case. Isn't that risky for them?"

"Not really. Remember, they don't have to prove motive to convict you. And Tom's analysis of the case is probably the same as mine—you have to testify."

"Can you counter her testimony?"

"I believe I can destroy her on cross."

"That's great. How did you find out about her if she wasn't on their witness list?"

"Are you ready for what's happening at trial?" I asked, ignoring his question.

By now, Allen knew that when I did not answer one of his questions, I had a reason. He did not press the issue.

* * *

"All rise."

As Judge Warren entered the court, everyone in the courtroom stood. No matter how prepared I am for a trial, I always feel butterflies in my stomach at the start. Once the trial gets underway, certainly by the time I speak for the first time, the butterflies are gone.

As Judge Warren took her seat, I looked around the courtroom to get a good sense of my surroundings. The seats were filled with interested bystanders, attorneys who had no other appointments on their calendars, curious residents who were either unemployed or retired—and I even spotted the district attorney herself. No doubt she had come to observe one of her best trial lawyers in action. I also noticed reporters and sketch artists in the courtroom. Sketch artists were there to draw what went on because cameras are not allowed in Pennsylvania courtrooms. I saw four apparent bystanders who I knew to be our guards from Echelon.

"Mr. Fanucci, would you care to begin?"

Tom rose. "Thank you, Your Honor."

Tom began his opening statement. Opening statements are a different beast than closing arguments, as the name implies. I like closing arguments better because we get to argue the inferences we want the jury to draw from the evidence that was presented. But if we talk about evidence in opening statements, all we are allowed to state is what we expect the evidence to show. And good trial lawyers use the word "expect" frequently so that there can be no objection that the lawyer is arguing instead of stating what they expect.

"Your Honor, members of the jury, Mr. Frankel. What I say to you and what Mr. Frankel will say to you is not evidence. Evidence is what you hear from the witness stand and the documents or objects that the judge allows to be admitted into the trial. As Mr. Frankel told you during jury selection, the Commonwealth has a heavy burden. We must prove beyond a reasonable doubt that the defendant intended to, and did, kill his wife. We expect to easily meet that burden. I expect you will hear evidence that on the morning of the murder, the defendant purchased what turned out to be the murder weapon, and that only the defendant's fingerprints were found on that weapon. I expect you to hear that only the defendant had an opportunity to commit the murder. I expect you to hear that at the scene the defendant lied about where he was during the murder. And I expect you to hear that Deidre Crosby was so well liked that nobody else had a motive to kill her. Which brings me to another point. Keep in mind that the Commonwealth has no burden to prove that the defendant had a motive. We only have to prove, beyond a reasonable doubt, that the defendant intentionally killed Deidre Crosby. That, I fully expect we will do.

"Now I expect that Mr. Frankel may try to confuse the issue with facts that are not relevant and with fantastical stories about a killer or killers who, for some unknown reason, killed Deidre—and possibly other victims. Don't let Mr. Frankel confuse you. When the case is complete there will be no reasonable doubt about the defendant's guilt.

"Thank you."

Tom sat.

Judge Warren turned to me. "Mr. Frankel, would you like to give your opening statement now or defer it?"

"Thank you, your Honor," I said, standing. "I would like to address the jury now."

"Your Honor, members of the jury, Mr. Fanucci. What Mr. Fanucci said about his case is true. He will be presenting the evidence he said he will present. It will be up to you ladies and gentlemen to determine, after you hear *all* of the evidence, whether the Commonwealth has proven beyond any reasonable doubt that Allen Crosby, this upstanding law-abiding citizen, intentionally killed his wife, his best friend. Deidre Crosby. As Mr. Fanucci said, nobody had a motive to kill Allen's wife. That includes Allen.

"Keep in mind that the defense does not have to prove anything. Remember the question I asked you before you were chosen for the jury? About whether you could find Allen not guilty if the prosecution did not prove their case beyond a reasonable doubt but the defense presented no case? You all agreed you would."

I paused here, nodding. Nodding, nodding, until I had all the jurors nodding as well....

"Although I expect to present a case that will raise all kinds of reasonable doubt, I want you to remember that. If there is reasonable doubt, the fact that the defense did not prove a certain element of the case you wanted to see proven is no reason to find Allen guilty. Sometimes neither side has any evidence about a part of the case you would want to see. If there is *any* reasonable doubt by the end of the trial, you must find Allen not guilty."

I didn't want to give away too much of our case, so I concluded with this:

"The prosecution gets to present their case first. I'm sure you've all heard someone tell their side of the story, and then you conclude what the facts are. Later you hear another side of the story and you aren't too sure… yes?"

A few nods.

"Well, I'm going to ask you to try to hold off judgment until you hear both sides. Although I expect the Commonwealth to present the evidence Mr. Fanucci said they would present, I also expect that by the end of the trial you will have more than a reasonable doubt about Allen's guilt and will quickly find him not guilty.

Thank you."

Tom and I subscribed to the same theory of opening statements—the shorter the better. We have the jury's attention when we start speaking but we lose it shortly thereafter. They are always more anxious to hear the evidence.

CHAPTER 29

"Your Honor, the Commonwealth calls Officer Robert Norman."

Tom decided to go with the police officer who had first responded to Deidre's murder as his opening witness. My next move was to throw Tom a little off his stride, although I didn't expect to win my motion.

"Your Honor, may we approach the bench?"

I requested this so that the conversation would be outside the hearing of the jury.

Judge Warren nodded. "Approach."

Tom and I approached the bench.

In a low voice, bordering on a whisper so the jury couldn't hear, I said, "Your Honor, I suspect that the Commonwealth might use this witness to introduce a statement my client allegedly made to the officer before being advised of his rights."

"Is that so, Mr. Fanucci?" Judge Warren asked, turning to Tom.

"Yes, Your Honor. However, it was also before the defendant was in custody or became a suspect."

Judge Warren looked back at me. We all knew that rights do not have to be read to someone before they are a suspect in custody. Until then, any statement they have made is admissible.

"Your Honor, I would like an *in camera* hearing with Officer Norman to determine whether my client was a suspect in custody at the time he gave his statement." *In camera* is one of those unnecessary Latin terms. It means "in private." In the context of a trial, it means in the judge's chambers, or in a courtroom where the public and jury are not allowed. Given that the courtroom had the jury and was filled with members of the media and interested bystanders, the easiest logistical step in this case would be to go to chambers.

"You have reason to believe he was a suspect in custody at that time?" Judge Warren seemed interested in, but a little skeptical of, my argument.

"Based on normal policing, yes, Your Honor, I do."

"That's ridiculous, Your Honor," Tom asserted. "The investigation had not yet begun." He looked frustrated, as he wanted to get his case started.

"Your Honor," I countered, "the investigation began once Officer Norman showed up at the scene of a reported homicide."

"I have to agree with Mr. Frankel. Let's retire to chambers."

Tom and I returned to our places so Judge Warren could instruct the jury.

"Ladies and gentlemen of the jury," she began. "We must take a short break at this time. You will remain in the courtroom, as I do not expect this discussion to take long. You are not to discuss the case with each other or with anyone here. You can discuss other topics with other members of the jury but may not communicate with anyone else in the courtroom."

A quick glance from the judge to the bailiff and the sheriff's deputies who were present because of the large crowd. The bailiff and deputies then moved to stand between the jury box and the others present in the courtroom. I admired the tight ship Judge Warren ran.

The judge rose and the bailiff intoned, "All rise." We rose, and as everyone else sat, Tom, Officer Norman, the court reporter, and I headed back to chambers. Once we had all gathered inside, Judge Warren administered the oath to Officer Norman, as the bailiff had not come with us.

"Counselor"—the judge nodded my way—"you may question the witness."

Even though Officer Norman was a witness for the prosecution, it was up to me to begin the questioning, because I had made the motion to exclude part of his testimony.

"Thank you, Your Honor," I told the judge. "Officer Norman, were you the first officer to arrive at the Crosby's house?"

"Yes, I was."

"And why did you go there?"

"There was a 911 call that a woman was bleeding and non-responsive at the Crosby home."

"Officer," I continued, "where did you receive your training?"

"Well, in addition to the police academy, the department sent me to Quantico for additional training."

"And by 'Quantico,' you mean the FBI?"

Officer Norman nodded. "Correct."

"How long have you been on the job?"

"Fifteen years," Officer Norman said.

"And when you arrived at the Crosby home did you ask the defendant to tell you what happened?"

"I did."

"Did you read him his Miranda rights first?"

"No, I did not. At that point I was just trying to gather information." He seemed to understand where I was going with my line of questioning. "Your client was not yet a suspect in custody."

I ignored his observation. "Officer Norman, as a result of your training and as a result of your experience, do you have an opinion regarding who the initial suspect is when one member of a couple is murdered?"

"We have to gather the evidence first before we form such an opinion."

"Thank you for the boilerplate answer, Officer." I stared at him deliberately. "I will ask you again. Do you have an opinion as to who the initial suspect is when one member of a couple is murdered?"

Hesitation.

I turned to Judge Warren. "Your Honor?"

"Officer Norman," the judge said, "please answer Mr. Frankel's question."

Officer Norman cleared his throat. "The other member of the couple is always considered a possible suspect. But other evidence might point to someone else."

"But until that evidence is gathered," I said, "law enforcement tends to focus on the other member of the couple. Isn't that right Officer?"

"I guess," Officer Norman said, none too happy with my questioning.

I paused. "Your Honor, would Mr. Fanucci agree that his witness is an expert in policing or should I *voir dire* him as to his expertise."

Judge Warren looked at Tom. After a moment, Tom said, "The Commonwealth will so stipulate."

I turned back to Officer Norman. "Officer, I am going to ask you a hypothetical about what you would do as a police officer with your experience. When you arrived at the scene and were informed that Deidre Crosby had been murdered, if Allen had said he was leaving the house without answering any of your questions, would you have allowed him to do so?"

Officer Norman looked nervous. "I'm not sure."

"Really, officer? A woman is murdered in her locked home and the only other person there, her spouse, wants to leave without answering any questions, and you aren't sure if you'd let him go."

Shrugging his shoulders, Officer Norman said, "If you put it that way, I guess not."

I paused again.

"And isn't it true, officer, that you asked if my client had any guns in his house?"

"Yes."

"And when my client led you to his gun, you collected it as possible evidence, using rubber gloves and an evidence bag?"

"That is also true."

"What role did you think Allen's gun might have played in his wife's murder?"

Another hesitation.

Without my prompting this time, Judge Warren said, "Officer, please answer."

"Possibly the murder weapon."

I turned to Judge Warren. "It seems evident that Allen was a suspect from the time Officer Norman arrived at the residence."

"Your Honor, may I question the witness." I knew Tom would have some questions.

The judge nodded. "Proceed."

"Officer Norman," Tom began, "when you arrived, did you know anything of the circumstances surrounding the shooting of Mrs. Crosby?"

"No, I did not."

"Did the defendant say he was going to leave or did he voluntarily answer your questions?"

Officer Norman was clearly less nervous with this line of questioning. "He voluntarily answered my questions."

"What did you ask the defendant?"

"I asked him what had happened."

"So you were trying to get information, not a confession?"

"Correct." Tom paused, allowing the judge to note the officer's answer. Then he continued: "And after the defendant told you what he told you, what conclusions did you draw based on your training and experience?"

"That it was possible the defendant was the killer. That his story of being away from the house for twenty minutes, then coming back to find his wife shot to death, seemed convenient. And that any estimate of time of death would not be able to definitely narrow it down to a specific twenty-minute span."

"So it wasn't until after the defendant spoke to you that you began to view him as a suspect?"

"Actually, at that time I thought of him as possibly being the perpetrator. But we also had no evidence indicating that he was. So no, he wasn't an actual suspect."

Tom had everything he needed. "Your Honor," he said, turning to the judge, "it is clear that at the time the defendant made his statement to Officer Norman, he was not actually in custody and was only answering the responding officer's natural inquiry as to what happened. Thus, if at any time he became a suspect, it was only *after* he spoke to the officer."

"I agree, Mr. Fanucci," Judge Warren stated. Turning slightly in the direction of the court reporter, but addressing both of us, she announced: "The defendant's statement to Officer Norman will be admissible. Of course, that does not stop Mr. Frankel from cross-examining the officer on the same topic if he so chooses."

Tom and I were in unison, "Thank you, Your Honor."

* * *

So Tom presented Officer Norman's testimony to the jury. In addition to detailing his conversation with Allen and the events that occurred at the scene of the murder, he testified that a previously unknown person who desired anonymity had turned over the murder weapon to him in a plastic bag, which he then turned over to county detectives. Tom also had Officer Norman repeat several times that Allen was certain he had left his house to go for his walk after five o'clock.

My cross-examination proceeded with merciless logic.

"Officer Norman, is it true that when you discovered Mrs. Crosby had been murdered you viewed Allen as a suspect?"

Pause.

I think he remembered that he just testified that way in the judge's chambers, which was one of my reasons for getting him on record in the judge's chambers.

"According to standard police training, the other half of a couple is always a suspect when someone is killed and there is no obvious evidence pointing to anyone else," he said, "but we had no evidence linking him to Mrs. Crosby's murder, so I would not say I viewed him as a suspect."

Officer Norman was trying to separate his law enforcement training from his thinking.

"If Allen wanted to leave the scene instead of answering your questions, would you have allowed him to?"

"That did not happen, but I would not have allowed him to leave."

"So he was not free to leave when you began questioning him?"

"He didn't try to leave so I was not preventing him from leaving."

"But you would have had he wanted to leave?"

"True."

"Did you read him his rights before questioning him?"

"No, but as I said, I did not consider him a suspect and he was not in custody."

"Did you take his gun as evidence to use in a trial?"

"Yes."

"Why?"

Another pause.

Officer Norman *had* to remember what he'd just told us in chambers.

"Because I thought it was possible that it was the murder weapon."

"And if it were the murder weapon, as you thought, who do you think would have pulled the trigger?"

Officer Norman looked uncomfortable as there was only one answer he could give. "The defendant."

"But he wasn't a suspect and he wasn't free to leave?" I asked incredulously looking at the jury.

"Objection," Tom rose from his seat. "Asked and answered. Officer Norman did not consider him a suspect and he wasn't in custody."

"You've made your point, counselor," Judge Warren looked at me. "Move on."

"Yes, your Honor." I looked back to Officer Norman. "You had the gun tested?"

"Yes."

"Was it the murder weapon?"

"No."

"In fact, you returned the gun to him, isn't that true?"

"I did."

"Did you investigate anyone else as a suspect?"

"No, we had no evidence come our way that indicated anyone else might have killed Mrs. Crosby."

"Why not?"

"We investigated the victim's background and found that everyone liked her; nobody had a motive to kill her."

I paused.

"*Nobody?*" I asked, looking at the jury.

"Our investigation didn't turn up anyone."

I paused, letting that sink in. Then I turned back to Officer Norman.

"Turning now to what has been identified as the murder weapon, you said some mysterious stranger turned it over to you, already in a plastic bag?"

"I wouldn't say she was mysterious."

I raised an eyebrow. "She?"

Officer Norman realized he had made a mistake. He had just given away the sex of the unknown informant.

"Yes."

"Did you know her?"

"Not before she came in with the weapon."

"Who is she?"

Tom was on his feet before Officer Norman had a chance to answer. "Objection. The Commonwealth is allowed to maintain the confidentiality of informants who request it."

"Your Honor," I replied, "how can we tell who doctored the gun if we don't know who had possession of it before the state?"

"Okay, counselors," Judge Warren returned, "you've both summarized your arguments for the jury. Since the witness who delivered the gun to Officer Norman is not testifying, we do not need to know her identity. Move on, Counselor."

"Officer Norman, please tell me if I've got your testimony right. Once you found out Mrs. Crosby was murdered, your training told you to consider Allen as a suspect. You asked him questions without giving him his rights. You took his gun—which turned out to not be the murder weapon. You did not investigate anyone else. Your investigation concluded that *nobody* had a motive to murder Deidre Crosby. Then a woman you did not previously know showed up and gave you a gun in a plastic bag that turned out to be the murder weapon. Do I have that right?"

"Yes."

I nodded. "No further questions, Your Honor."

* * *

Tom's next witness was Robert Fitzgerald, an IT expert from KeyBank. On direct examination, Tom introduced the computer printout of Allen's bank history showing no ATM withdrawal the evening of Deidre's murder. I had a surprise for Tom with this witness. First, the normal cross-examination on the direct issue Tom presented him for.

"If I were to get access to your security system, could I access Tom's bank history?"

"Yes," Fitgerald replied, "that is how I did it."

"And, if you wanted to, could you have changed that history?"

The witness glared at me. "I wouldn't change a depositor's history!"

"Let's assume some anonymous person—or *agency*"—I paused for dramatic effect—"obtained access into your security system…could they have changed the customer's history?"

Robert Fitzgerald eyed me curiously. "In what way?"

"Could they, for instance, delete an ATM withdrawal that had been made?" I was looking at the jury as I asked that question.

"I suppose so."

I looked back to the witness. "No supposing. Could they or couldn't they?"

"Yes, they could."

Pause.

I looked through my notes and glanced at the jury. Looking through my notes was a way to let the answer sink in before I moved on to another topic.

"Did you bring with you today the digital video of the ATM at your bank that I requested?" I had done more than request it. I subpoenaed it.

"Yes."

"Your Honor, can we approach the bench?" Tom was already out of his chair as he said this. I had expected this.

"Approach."

After we both, along with the court reporter, got to the side of the judge's bench away from the jury, Tom stated his objection.

"Your Honor, we did not question this witness about any video. I object because this is going beyond the scope of direct examination."

"Counselor?" Judge Warren looked at me.

"Your Honor, the Commonwealth called this witness to present records that indicate my client might have been lying. The evidence on the video, I believe, will call into question the accuracy of the digital records presented."

Tom argued, "Defense counsel is free to do so in his case in chief but not in mine." The "case in chief" is the main case each side presents with its own witnesses, not in cross-examination of the other side's witnesses.

I rejoined, "I believe questioning the accuracy of the records is within the scope of the direct examination. The witness is in charge of all digital records at the bank, which included not only the report Mr. Fanucci introduced into evidence, but also the digital videos of their ATMs. In addition, judicial efficiency would argue for letting this witness testify now rather than calling him back during my case."

"I agree," Judge Warren said. "The questioning is allowed."

"Thank you, Your Honor," I said loud enough for the jury to hear. Having the jury think you are more on top of the facts of the case than your opponent is paramount; the same is true of the laws that are in play.

When we were back in place I asked Fitzgerald, "Did you load the digital video of the ATM in question onto the court's equipment?"

"I did."

I had Fitzgerald verify the time span covered by the video: from twenty minutes before Allen called 911 until the call itself. The screen was set up and I requested that the video be played, asking the witness to watch it.

About halfway through the recording a little static disrupted the video; then there was nothing but a black screen for a few minutes…and then we were suddenly back to the recording.

The video ended. I turned again to Fitzgerald. "Is that the video your ATM machine at the corner of Twining Road and Limekiln Pike recorded at the time in question, and on the night in question?"

"Yes, it is," Fitzgerald replied.

"Can you explain why there is an interruption in the recording?"

"Not definitively."

"Do you have a theory?"

"Objection," Tom was on his feet again. "Mr. Fitzgerald has not been admitted as an expert witness." Only expert witnesses may give opinions.

"I am willing to *voir dire* the witness as to his expertise." I was ready for Tom's objection.

"Counselor," Judge Warren stared at Tom. "He is your witness. Do you really question his credentials?" That was the best response I could have hoped for from the judge in front of the jury.

Tom paused. "I will agree to the witness's qualifications."

I smiled. Turning to Fitgerald, I said, "I will repeat my question: Do you have a theory about why part of this video turned black?"

"Yes. It looks like part of the recording was deleted."

"You mean erased?" I raised my voice and my eyebrows, looking at the jury.

"Yes."

I paused.

"Could someone—or some *agency*"—another pause—"who had access to your security system have gotten in and erased part of the video?"

The witness shrugged. "I suppose."

I shot the witness a glance.

"Yes, they could have," Fitzgerald acknowledged.

"No further questions, Your Honor."

Judge Warren dismissed us for a lunch break. Overall, I felt confident about the morning's proceedings. We were laying the foundation for our case and, I hoped, raising some doubt in the jurors' minds about the state's case. I told Allen and the team from my office to head over to the Bar Association, where I had arranged a private room for lunch. I would meet them there after I made a quick pit stop.

As I was standing at the urinal, one of the bystanders from the courtroom came over and stood at the urinal next to mine. He was a white man, tall, with a full head of dark hair. He appeared to be in his forties.

"Watch it, Counselor."

"Excuse me?"

"There is no such agency that could have done what you are saying."

I didn't miss the acronym. *No Such Agency.* I decided to play dumb.

"There might be."

"There isn't. If you make any credible case that there is, I hope your affairs are in order."

CHAPTER 30

I arrived at the Bar Association's private dining room later than expected. The Echelon team had eaten earlier, so their men stood around the premises, some outside the room, some just inside the doorway. My crew were all smiles as I entered, telling me what a good job I was doing in laying a foundation for our case through cross-examination.

"Why do you look so concerned?" Jerry asked.

Before I could answer, ten additional Echelon agents entered our private room.

"I've asked Echelon for more protection for all of us. They will accompany each of us 24/7 in our homes and our apartments, and in the office as well, of course. If we use a public bathroom, they will accompany us to the bathroom. We'll set up a new reception desk in the office, and they will staff that desk as well."

Susan looked worried. "What happened?"

"Let's just say I was warned that if I continue with the defense we are planning, I should have my affairs in order."

Now it was Allen's turn to be concerned. "I don't want you risking your lives for me."

Reese spoke up. "Is there anything better to risk one's life for than to see justice is served?"

"I'm going to ask you all again," I told the group, "if you want off this case, that's fine with me, it won't affect your employment with my firm. This very well may be a dangerous assignment, and I don't know that even the very fine people Echelon has supplied us with can protect us from the bad guys." I looked around the room. "Does anyone want out?"

I was proud of my hiring abilities. Nobody wanted out.

Susan seemed worried. "Why don't you tell the judge about this threat?"

"I trust the judge, but I don't know who she would have to tell, and I don't trust people I don't know. I've gotten us extra guards from Echelon."

I turned to Jerry. "Jerry, you are scheduled to cross the lab guy. If you don't want to be that high profile, I can handle it."

Jerry met my gaze with determination in his eyes. "Boss, I'm not backing down just because of some threats."

"Okay." I figured I could count on Jerry but had thought it best to ask him. "For all of you, if anyone manages to threaten you, let me know immediately. And if any of you change your mind and want off this case at any time, let me know."

Just then a team of waiters brought in our food while the Echelon men eyed them carefully and we remained silent while they were in the room. We ate our lunch, mostly in silence.

* * *

When everyone was back in court, I surveyed the courtroom. I didn't see the man who had threatened me. I wondered if someone had replaced him.

"All rise."

Judge Warren entered and took the bench. She gestured her hand toward Tom. "Mr. Fanucci, you may call your next witness."

"The Commonwealth calls Donna Carroll."

Donna was the lab scientist who had tested both guns. Tom was smart: he walked Donna through her examinations of both guns, the gun Allen had already been in possession of before the murder, and the second gun—the gun that turned out to be the murder weapon. Jerry would have brought up Allen's gun—the gun that *wasn't* the murder weapon—during his cross.

After Tom finished with the direct, which definitely emphasized that the second gun *was* the murder weapon, and that the only fingerprints on that particular gun were Allen's, Jerry stood up to begin the cross.

"Dr. Carroll, you said that the first gun you examined was not the murder weapon?"

"That's correct."

"Whose fingerprints did you find on that weapon?"

"The defendant's."

"Did you find anyone else's?"

Dr. Carroll frowned. "There were many smudged prints that could have been other people's fingerprints, and there were a couple that did not match the defendant's."

"And you reported your findings to the police?"

"My original report went to the District Attorney's office with a copy to the Upper Dublin police."

"Did either of those agencies send you any other fingerprints to see if you could match the unidentified prints you found on the first gun?"

"No, but I didn't expect them to."

"I see. Why not?"

"Well, for one it wasn't the murder weapon. For another, we typically find more than one person's fingerprints on a gun."

"Really?" Jerry really wasn't surprised by this answer and would have elicited it had she not volunteered it.

"Gun owners take their friends target shooting with them, and of course, the people who work at the store the gun was purchased from probably also handled the gun."

Jerry paused to let that sink in.

"Now, turning to the gun you identified as the murder weapon. Whose fingerprints did you find on it?"

"The defendant's."

"And?"

"Nobody else's."

"Didn't you just say that it is typical to find other fingerprints on guns?"

"This was one of those rare occasions when only the defendant's fingerprints were present."

"I see. Could you tell if anyone else had handled the gun, such as with gloves, or wiped down the gun after using it?"

Dr. Carroll shook her head. "No, I couldn't. But I was informed that the gun had been purchased only the morning of the murder."

"Your Honor, I would like that last comment stricken from the record as being both hearsay and nonresponsive to my question."

Tom was on his feet too. "If Dr. Carroll had been told the gun was purchased the morning of the crime, that could explain why she wasn't concerned about finding only one person's fingerprints on it."

"Your Honor," Jerry replied, "now counsel has added to the hearsay problem. And I never asked the witness why she wasn't concerned."

Judge Warren was not forgiving in her response: "The court reporter is instructed to strike the last sentence the witness said. The jury is instructed to ignore the witness's comment regarding what she was informed. Dr. Carroll," the judge continued, turning to the witness stand, "please try to answer only what is asked of you." Then she turned back to Tom. "Mr. Fanucci, please do not state any facts not in evidence in my court again."

"Thank you, Your Honor."

I relaxed. Jerry had handled the situation perfectly.

"Proceed."

Jerry resumed his cross. "Dr. Carroll, please correct me if I have any of this wrong. When you examined the first gun, Allen's, you found that it wasn't the murder weapon, and that it had both Allen's and other people's fingerprints on it. That it's expected to find other people's fingerprints on any gun—at a minimum, the fingerprints of employees of the store where the weapon was purchased. Am I stating your testimony correctly so far?"

"Yes."

"Thank you. And, Dr. Carroll, when you examined the second gun, the murder weapon, it had only Allen's fingerprints on it, and you were not able to tell if someone had wiped down the gun previously. Is that correct?"

"Yes."

Jerry nodded. "No further questions, Your Honor."

When he sat down I patted him proudly on the back.

Tom's next witness was the IT director for Clayton's. As such, he was in charge of all computerized records. Tom's direct exam went quickly, introducing a printout of the record that showed Allen purchased the murder weapon on the morning of the murder. Tom brought out that it was the murder weapon Allen purchased because the serial number of the gun purchased matched the serial number on the murder weapon. Jerry's cross was similar to mine of the bank's IT expert: if someone or some agency gained access into the gun store's computer system, they could have changed the records to say whatever they wanted it to say. Unfortunately, there was no surveillance video at Clayton's.

Tom's next witness was Dr. Christopher Lane, the county coroner. Tom had Dr. Lane testify that Deidre was shot three times at a fairly close range. The first two bullets penetrated her chest and abdomen; one of the two bullets went entirely through the body and one was stopped by bone. The third shot struck Deidre between her eyes and was fired after she was on the floor. That bullet went through the front of Deidre's skull but did not exit, stopped by the rear part of the skull after traveling through the brain. Tom also had Dr. Lane testify that his estimate of the time of death was between four thirty and five o'clock.

I began my cross-examination.

"Dr. Lane, for how long have you performed autopsies?"

"About twenty-three years."

"And is it true that most of the murder victims you have autopsied were not the victims of pre-planned killings—what's known in the business as 'hits'?"

"I think that's fair," the doctor agreed.

"Have you autopsied victims of professional hits?"

"I have."

"Is there a difference in the wounds between, say, a personal murder and a dispassionately executed professional hit?"

"Sometimes."

"Can you describe those differences?"

Dr. Lane shifted his position in the witness chair. "Sometimes in a killing that is motivated by personal reasons, the shots are haphazard, similar to what you would get as the result of a gunfight. Maybe a shot to an arm or a leg and then shots not close to each other, one or more of which manage to do enough damage to kill the victim. Also, if the killing was a crime of passion, often there are many, many wounds. Sometimes several of these wounds are inflicted even after the victim has died."

"And if a professional killer kills someone?"

"Usually there are fewer shots and they are closer together."

"What about the parts of the body that are shot?"

"Usually there are two or three close shots near center mass and a final one to the head."

"Like we have in this case?"

I asked the question of the coroner but made eye contact with the jury.

"Yes."

I paused, both to let the answer sink in and to signal a change in topic.

"Now, going back to your testimony about the time of death—I believe you said your estimate was that death occurred sometime between four thirty and five o'clock?"

"That's correct."

"And that's important because Allen told Officer Norman that he didn't go out for his walk until after five o'clock, correct?"

Tom said "Objection" at the same time that Dr. Lane correctly said, "I have no knowledge of that."

Tom, satisfied with the answer, withdrew his objection.

I continued: "Hypothetically, doctor, if Allen was at home with Deidre until after five o'clock, then your estimate of the time of death would mean he was there when she was shot and died, correct?"

I glanced at Tom, but he seemed quite happy with this line of questioning.

"Yes, that's true," Dr. Lane replied.

"Tell me, doctor, how did you form your opinion about time of death?"

"Well, generally we—"

"No, doctor," I said, "I want to know *specifically* in this case."

"Okay." Again he shifted in the witness chair. "Well, according to the reports from the scene, Mrs. Crosby was not lying in the sun and her body temperature at 6:02 p.m. was 96.65 degrees Fahrenheit. Bodies left undisturbed in an area with a temperature that is cooler than the body lose temperature at about 1.5 degrees per hour."

I interrupted Dr. Lane's testimony, more to keep the jury listening to this biology lecture than to actually get the answer to my question. "And was the room Mrs. Crosby was in cooler than her body temperature?"

"Oh yes, of course. The tech in the room measured the temperature at 68 degrees Fahrenheit."

"Okay. So you were explaining that you calculate the time of death based on bodies losing 1.5 degrees per hour?"

"Yes. So in Mrs. Crosby's case, if you subtract her temperature of 96.65 at 6:02 from 98.6, you get a 1.95 degree difference. And if you divide that by 1.5 degrees per hour—the rate that bodies lose temperature—you get one hour and twenty minutes before the time the temperature was taken as the approximate time of death."

"So that would have been what time?"

"Four forty-two p.m."

"If you can be so exact here on the witness stand, how come your estimate had a thirty-minute range?"

"Well, the precise time of 4:42 assumes that the victim's body lost temperature at the exact average rate that bodies do. But rates vary slightly. Hence the range."

"I see. And what about the victim's starting temperature?"

"I don't understand your question."

"Well, doctor, what if Deidre Crosby's internal temperature wasn't 98.6 degrees when she died?"

Out of my peripheral vision I saw Tom reach for a file. I was fairly certain it was the file I had provided him. Until I asked that question, Tom had no idea what relevance the file had to the case.

"The estimate would still be good if the temperature of the victim's body started anywhere between 98.2 and 99 degrees. That's another reason I give a range."

"What if Mrs. Crosby's temperature at the time of death was over 99?"

"That would mean she died even earlier."

"And what if her temperature was under 98.2?"

"That would be highly unusual. But that would mean she died later."

"Could she have had a beginning temperature under 98.2?"

"It's possible...but she would have had symptoms of something wrong."

The wording of my next few questions were suggested by Keith based on a movie we both love, *A Few Good Men.*

"What kind of symptoms?"

"There are many possible."

"Fatigue?"

"Definitely."

"Headaches?"

"Possibly."

"Intolerance to cold and heat?"

"Could be."

"I see." I reached for the file on my desk. "Doctor, I am showing you what has been marked as Defense Exhibit 3, and I ask you to open the file."

I handed the file to Dr. Lane then walked back toward the defense table.

I faced the witness. "Doctor, inside that file are a series of three documents that have been certified as records from the last three doctor's visits Mrs. Crosby had before her death. Please look at the first record and find the section labeled 'Reason for Visit.' "

"I see it."

"Please read it to the jury."

Tom knew better than to object based on hearsay because I would just bring in someone from Deidre's doctor's office to testify to the accuracy of the records.

"'Patient complains of fatigue, headaches, and intolerance to both cold and heat.' "

I paused.

"Now please look at the examination section."

"I see it."

"Please tell the jury what Mrs. Crosby's temperature was at that doctor visit."

"Ninety-seven-point-eight."

"Now please turn to the second of the doctor's visits and tell the jury what Mrs. Crosby's temperature was then."

"Ninety-seven-point-eight."

"Now please turn to the final doctor's visit Mrs. Crosby had before she was murdered. What was Mrs. Crosby's temperature at that visit?"

"Ninety-seven-point-nine."

"So the average of Mrs. Crosby's temperatures is..." I intentionally didn't finish the question because I wanted Dr. Lane to do so.

"About ninety-seven-point-eight-three."

I nodded. "You didn't have this information when you estimated the time of death, did you?"

"No, sir."

"Does this information change your estimate?"

"Yes."

"In what way?"

I could see the doctor do a mental calculation.

"It would change it by about half an hour."

"To be clear, what is now your estimate of the time of death?"

"Five o'clock to five thirty p.m."

I paused.

"As an expert, let me ask you this hypothetical. Assume, as Allen told the first officer to arrive, that the following facts are true: first, Deidre Crosby was alive when Allen left for a walk a few minutes after five o'clock; second, when he returned approximately twenty minutes later, she was lying dead on the floor. Would those facts be consistent with your revised time of death?"

"They would."

I paused and nodded as I looked at the jury.

"No further questions, Your Honor."

This ended the first day's testimony.

The defense team remained in the courtroom as it was emptied so we could discuss the day's events. As we were in the empty courtroom instead of in our secure office, we were careful to not discuss our planned defense. Generally, we felt that the day had gone as well as could be for the defense. We had established that the time of death was consistent with Allen's story. However, the Commonwealth had presented evidence that Allen lied about where he was when Deidre was killed and that he had purchased the murder weapon the morning of her murder. They had also presented evidence that only Allen's fingerprints were on the murder weapon.

Although our cross didn't present any new evidence other than time of death, it did raise questions... *if* we could get the jurors to believe that one or more NSA agents were out to get Allen.

As we walked out of the courthouse, we discussed our next steps and how we were going to begin our case, but not in such detail that anyone listening in would know exactly what we were doing. It seemed to me that the Commonwealth was probably ready to, or almost ready to, rest their case. Although some murder cases take more time than Allen's case, this prosecution was being presented with documentary and scientific evidence that wasn't complicated. There were no eyewitnesses for the prosecution to call as witnesses. We had to be ready with our motion to dismiss, and with the beginning of our case after that motion was denied. We expected it would be denied because Tom met the prosecutorial standard of presenting evidence that, if believed by a reasonable juror, proved each element of the crime.

We had walked out of the courthouse on the side facing Main Street; now we headed down the many marble steps. We had parked in the garage across the street.

About halfway down the steps, a shot rang out. We all hit the ground

CHAPTER 31

We scrambled back up the steps then ran zigzag back to the courthouse. The Echelon security team ran backwards behind us, their guns drawn. Blood was coming out of Allen's shoulder. We got safely inside the courthouse lobby without hearing any additional shots.

An ambulance and the Norristown police came quickly. EMTs dressed Allen's wound, which fortunately was a simple in/out wound. Abby and Susan were shaking but calmed down after the EMTs covered them in blankets to counteract shock. I was fairly shaky myself.

Allen was taken to the hospital; several members of the Echelon crew and police security were guarding him. The rest of us were taken to a secure room in the District Attorney's office.

Tom walked into the secure room.

"Jeez, Josh, if you wanted a delay, you could have filed a motion."

Tom was smiling. I wasn't.

The next moment Tom became serious. "Are you alright, Josh? Any pains? Tightness of chest?" Apparently I was pale enough to cause Tom concern.

I looked at Tom. "How can I be alright? Look at the danger I'm putting my people in!"

"It seems whoever it was, was aiming for your client, not your people."

"Too close for comfort. Whoever it was doesn't care about collateral damage. How's my defense sounding now?"

"It could just as easily be someone who doesn't like wife-killers."

I glared at him. "Have you ever had anyone else accused of killing their wife shot at on the courthouse steps?"

"Not that I know of. Do you want to provide me with more information so we can research what you've been saying?"

"I trust you, Tom. However, I don't know who in your office, including your investigators, could be compromised by the group I'm talking about."

"You have referred to them as an 'agency'—yes," he said purposefully, "I caught your dramatic pauses every time you mentioned 'agency.' Are we talking about a government agency here?"

I paused. "Can we talk hypothetically, without you talking to anyone else, including people in your office, not excepting your investigators?"

"If that's what you want, but I don't do much investigation so I don't know how much I can help."

"Right now, I'm a bit panicked. I could use advice from a good friend even if he happens to be trying the case against me."

"Okay." Tom nodded to reassure me he was on my team with this. "So which agency are we speaking about?"

"I've been advised, in the men's room of the courthouse, no less, that there is no such agency that can do what I'm alleging."

"Well then…" Tom started, stopped—and then I saw recognition click in his eyes. He let out a low whistle. "Shit, Josh, what have you gotten yourself into?"

I shrugged. "Just pursuing justice."

* * *

Judge Warren cancelled court the next day, telling jurors to relax, enjoy themselves; but she reminded them that they were not permitted to talk with anyone about the case. The jurors found their newspapers and news magazines with more holes in them than they had expected; no television or wifi was available either. Their cellphones were confiscated. They were not allowed to be any place where they might overhear the general public. In fact, they were not allowed to be any place where the general public might be encountered. Some felt like they were in prison. A very nice prison with room service.

Meanwhile, security was tightened in and around the courthouse.

Police were quick with their investigative work. They did me the courtesy of keeping my team up to date about their findings. After passing through Allen's shoulder, the bullet embedded itself into one of the courthouse steps. Given the angle of the shot, police believed it came from the third floor of the parking garage across the street. It turned out there was only one shot. The sniper left the weapon on the garage floor. The serial number was filed off. No fingerprints were found on the weapon or on the bullets left in the gun—many criminals don't think of protecting their bullets from their fingerprints. I wondered why the sniper took that shot instead of waiting for us to enter the garage and getting a Ruby/Oswald shot as they walked by us. Ruby was the Dallas bar owner who killed Lee Harvey Oswald, President Kennedy's assassin, at close range in a garage. Perhaps the shot was meant as an additional warning but not meant to kill? Or could it have been set up by Allen with a sharpshooter, meant to convince us that Allen was innocent?

Tom and I had another good conversation after court was postponed, as only two adversaries who trusted and respected each other could have. Tom was still not convinced that the NSA was out to get Allen, pointing out the same thing I had wondered about—the sniper shot versus the more accurate close-range shot that would have been available if the would-be assassin had waited for us to walk into the garage. He did let me know that when court resumed on Wednesday, he was going to rest the State's case. He believed he had presented proof that Allen had intentionally killed Deidre.

"But what motive did Allen have to kill her?"

"We don't have to prove motive."

"I know that. I'm not asking for legal sufficiency of your case. I'm asking for the internal logic of your case. He had all the wealth, not her. They were best friends, never cheated on each other, never argued in public."

"Although what you say may or may not be true, I am not planning to present any motive in our case in chief."

"I see."

Tom had just confirmed what I suspected. He was saving what he thought was a surprise witness for rebuttal after our case rested. "Well, I think I raised questions about your proof. Maybe I'll just rest and argue the logical inconsistency to the jury."

"Please do that."

We both smiled, knowing that although I had raised questions, there was no evidence to support the conspiracy theory I presented unless we provided some evidence on defense. Any questions I had raised about the State's case were not evidence, as Tom would no doubt remind the jury in closing argument if I did not, in fact, present evidence.

The defense team met in my conference room Tuesday afternoon. Again, I offered to let anyone who wanted off the case to leave it. Not only did I not have anyone take me up on it, but almost everyone in my firm offered to help if we needed more manpower. Again, I was proud of the firm I had built.

"Okay then," I said, "is everyone ready to present our case? Anything you think we might have missed?"

Abby spoke up. "Someone has to say this, so I guess I will. What if he's guilty?"

I looked at her in surprise. "You verified with the clerk that Allen bought his gun the day after the murder. Reese verified the child labor at the factory. And Allen was shot. Explain all that."

Abby started hesitantly. "Well, he's very rich. He could have paid the clerk at Clayton's to say what he wants him to say. And maybe he invested in the company with child labor because it was a good investment but he's willing to throw them to the wolves for an interesting alibi. He's also wealthy enough to hire a sharpshooter to shoot him where it won't do much damage. If it were the NSA agents trying to silence him, why didn't they wait until we were in the garage where they could have killed him?"

Everyone silently pondered Abby's hypothetical.

"I'm not saying I necessarily believe he's guilty, but I'm also not convinced he's not," Abby clarified.

Jerry was doubtful. "Would he really have had himself shot?"

It wouldn't be the first time I had been fooled by a client into representing them, thinking they were innocent when they were guilty. In my mind I reviewed what I knew about the case, what I knew about Allen, and how Allen appeared to me.

"Okay. Abby's argument is possible, but my judgment is that he's not guilty. As you all know, I have been fooled by clients in the past, but not frequently, and not recently. It is possible I've been fooled. But I don't think so." I looked around the room. "Does anyone want off the case for any reason, including Abby's possibilities?"

Everyone was silent.

"Abby, are you okay continuing on the case?"

"Yes. I just wanted to bring up those possibilities I've been thinking about."

"Okay, thank you for expressing what you are thinking." My words weren't trivial; I appreciated the frankness my staff members felt they could address me with. "Now, back to our trial strategy. We'll start with Allen and move on to our factual and character witnesses. Reese, are you ready to testify in case we can't get your photos and documents in with Allen's testimony?"

"Yes, boss," Reese answered.

"Abby, is Bob ready?" I was concerned that Bob might not want to contradict what Clayton's electronic records said. After all, the gun shop was his employer.

"He says he is. Although I owe him a lunch after he testifies."

Everyone chuckled.

"How about the neighbors, Abby?"

"They're ready as well. I went through the basic order of the questions you will be asking."

"Reese, how about the PECO employee?"

"He's ready."

"Susan, do we have enough copies of Reese's European evidence for Tom, Judge Warren, and the extra one I asked you to have ready?"

"All ready, boss."

"And enlargements for the jury?"

"Yes, sir."

I let out a relieved breath then smiled to all of my team. "Seems like we're ready. Let's go in tomorrow and win this."

CHAPTER 32

After Allen was shot Monday afternoon, Judge Warren had issued an order allowing our Echelon security to keep their guns with them in the courthouse and in the courtroom. Previously, they had been ordered to leave their weapons with courthouse security then pick them up on their way out. In addition to Echelon security being seated near our team, some of their personnel were scattered in the courtroom in various disguises. I still didn't see the man who had threatened me in the courtroom, but I imagined the NSA was pretty good with disguises as well.

"All rise."

Judge Warren took her seat on the bench and then turned to the jury.

"Ladies and gentlemen of the jury. I apologize for not holding court yesterday but something came up that we all agreed required a delay in continuing the trial. I hope you were all able to relax."

Most members of the jury noticed, and were staring at, Allen's arm in a sling.

Judge Warren then turned toward Tom.

"Mr. Fanucci, you may call your next witness."

"Your Honor, the Commonwealth rests."

The judge immediately turned her gaze to me. "Mr. Frankel, are you prepared to begin your case?"

"Your Honor, first we have a motion we would like to discuss in chambers."

"I thought you might." Judge Warren turned to the jury. "We have a matter that must be discussed in private. You are still directed to not have any discussions about this case and to not have any conversations about anything other than with fellow jurors or the bailiff."

She nodded to all officers in the court, who quietly took their place between the jury box and the gallery.

Tom and I followed the court reporter and the judge to her chambers as everyone stood.

"Your Honor," I began once the door to the judge's chamber was closed, "the defense moves to dismiss the case against Allen Crosby."

"On what grounds, Counselor?"

Judge Warren's question was polite even though we all knew what grounds I would argue and that Judge Warren would deny it. We were making a record in case an appeal was needed.

"Your Honor, the Commonwealth has failed to present a *prima facie* case." Again with the Latin. In this setting a *prima facie* case means sufficient evidence had been presented to convince reasonable jurors beyond a reasonable doubt that Allen was guilty.

"Present your argument, Mr. Frankel."

I began: "Through the Commonwealth's own expert witnesses, we learned that the defendant's alibi, given immediately at the scene, is consistent with the time of death. We learned that the murder weapon, which was mysteriously turned over to the police, had only Allen's fingerprints on it, when normally, and especially with a gun so recently purchased, there would also be fingerprints of the clerks in the gun store who had handled it. We learned that nobody, including Allen, had a motive for killing Deidre. We learned that mysteriously, the video that could have backed up Allen's alibi was deleted for the time Allen was at the ATM. We learned that anyone who gained access to Clayton's computer system could have entered the murder weapons as being purchased by Allen on the day of the murder. All of this adds up to the conclusion that any reasonable juror would have a reasonable doubt as to Allen's guilt."

Judge Warren looked to Tom for a response. "Mr. Fanucci?"

"Your Honor," Tom said, "the Commonwealth has presented evidence that the defendant lied about his alibi. The fact that if someone hacked into the bank's system, they could have changed the records, is not evidence that someone did. Similarly, the fact that if someone hacked into Clayton's computer system *they* could have changed *their* records is not evidence that someone did. The fact that the defendant's alibi stated immediately to Officer Norman is consistent with Deidre's time of death is not a surprise if he's the killer, since he would have known when he killed her. And, although our witness stated it was 'unusual' for there to only be the defendant's fingerprints on the gun, it is not beyond the realm of possibility."

Judge Warren rendered her verdict without fanfare: "I agree with the Commonwealth. Although the arguments you presented are all good arguments I assume you will argue to the jury, Mr. Frankel, the Commonwealth has presented a *prima facie* case. Let's return to the courtroom."

We proceeded back to the courtroom and Judge Warren repeated her question to me.

"Mr. Frankel, are you prepared to begin your case?"

"We are, Your Honor."

"Call your first witness," Judge Warren instructed.

"Your Honor, the defense calls Allen Crosby."

Allen walked to the witness stand and took the oath. The jury watched intently as the bailiff helped Allen rest his slinged left arm on the Bible. Once he was sworn in, Allen sat down in the witness chair.

I began with some basic questions. "Allen, how long have you lived in Montgomery County?"

"Except for my years at Wharton, my whole life."

"Before this case, have you ever been arrested?"

"No, sir."

"Not even as a juvenile?"

"No, sir. I've never been in trouble with the law."

"Okay. Before we get to the facts of this case, I want to review a contact you had with the law in the late 1970s and early 1980s."

"Objection, Your Honor. What is the relevance of something that happened thirty or forty years ago?"

Tom just wanted me to say it for the record.

"Your Honor, as counsel well knows, the defense is allowed to put the character of the defendant into play. In this case, we wish to demonstrate Allen's sterling character."

"Yes, I'm sure Mr. Fanucci knows, and I know—and now the jury knows. Objection overruled."

"Thank you, Your Honor."

I turned back to Allen.

"Please tell us about the contact you had with the law back then."

Allen led us all through the Abscam story. The jurors sat riveted, especially those who were too young to remember the scandal. When Allen got to the point where he was offered the bribe and went straight to the FBI, several jurors smiled, and a couple of the older jurors nodded as though recalling the event.

Now I led Allen step-by-step through his getting very wealthy. This had to be done carefully, emphasizing his hard work and his intelligence combined with what he learned at Wharton. My questioning about Allen's real estate developments concentrated on the jobs they provided, or the much-needed affordable housing they provided for the middle class in Center City. After that, we moved on to his trips overseas.

"Was real estate development the only way you accumulated your wealth?"

"No," Allen replied. "At Wharton I learned about evaluating businesses. I took some of the profits I earned in real estate and invested them in companies that looked like they had a good future ahead of them."

"Were these businesses all in the United States?"

"At first, yes. Then I gradually started investing in foreign businesses as well. I learned that, in addition to doing my due diligence with the paperwork, it helped if I met with the management team of each company and saw the business in actual operation, especially if I were going to invest a great deal of money."

"Were businesses receptive to you coming and seeing them in operation?"

"Oh yes. When word got around how much I was investing in companies I believed in, I would even be invited by companies I had not yet researched. By the late 1980s I was traveling a good part of the world, wherever there seemed to be an opportunity."

"Did there come a time when the areas of the world you traveled to expanded?"

"Yes. After the Soviet Union broke up in the early 1990s, I started going to see companies starting up in Eastern Europe; they were just experimenting with capitalism."

"Did you invest in those?"

"Some of them. The ones that treated their workers fairly and seemed able to succeed in the business and national environment in which they were doing business."

"I am about to ask you a yes-or-no question, and I want you to just answer it either 'yes' or 'no.' At about that time, did you have further contact with our federal government?"

"Yes."

"Your Honor, may we approach the bench?"

I was about to make an unusual request, especially for such a high-profile case.

"Approach."

When Tom and I were at sidebar along with the court reporter, I stated my request.

"Your Honor, this next contact with the federal government involves a secrecy agreement Allen signed. If he speaks about his activities publicly, he could be criminally charged. However, his testimony in this matter is vital to his defense. I suggest that we close the courtroom to all but court staff, the jury, and the Commonwealth and defense teams, as well as members of the bar. I request that you issue a gag order to all those remaining, instructing them not to speak about what was said. With one exception."

"What exception?" Judge Warren raised her eyebrows at this.

"Janice McGuire is in the courtroom."

"Yes, I noticed that," the judge commented as Tom looked at the pews. He spotted our US Attorney.

"Some of what might be presented, including some hard evidence I plan to introduce, could form the basis of a federal prosecution. Therefore I ask that she be exempted from the gag order so she can direct her staff as to what needs to be done to pursue such a case. In addition, there are two FBI agents with her, here as protection. I ask that they be allowed to remain."

Judge Warren looked concerned. "Has she been threatened regarding this case?"

"Without going into details, yes, she has been."

Judge Warren paused for a moment, taking in the seriousness of what I had just told her. Then she gazed at Tom. "Mr. Fanucci, what do you have to say to Mr. Frankel's unusual—and somewhat complicated—suggestion?"

"I object for two reasons, Your Honor," Tom answered. "The public has a right to know what goes on in a case with such a high degree of public interest. And I don't see the relevancy of what Mr. Frankel has told us to the defendant's trial for murdering his wife."

"Let's deal with the relevancy issue first," Judge Warren replied. "If it's not relevant we do not need to decide whether to close the courtroom."

"Your Honor, if I might," I said. "I could make an offer of proof as to what I expect to be testified to and how it is relevant to our defense."

"Go ahead, Counselor."

"Your Honor, I expect the defendant to testify that he did some covert work for the National Security Agency. That while doing this work, he encountered misdeeds by at least two members of the NSA. And that he tried to bring these misdeeds to light. It will be reasonable, based on events that transpired after that, to argue that a cover-up went into effect leading directly to Deidre Crosby's murder and an attempt to frame Allen for it."

"Wow." Judge Warren was taken aback. "Is this related to the shooting of your client outside the courthouse?"

"We believe it is, Your Honor."

"I see." She pursed her lips, taking a moment before announcing her decision. "Okay, I will rule it relevant. Now for the more difficult decision about a secret court proceeding. Counselors, I see, understand, and agree with both of your arguments. Can we come to some kind of agreement that would satisfy all interests?"

"Your Honor, I have a suggestion." I had been ready for Tom's objection. "After the testimony, before we reopen the court to the public, perhaps the three of us can agree on a summary of the testimony to release to the public?"

"Mr. Fanucci, would Mr. Frankel's suggestion satisfy your concerns?"

Tom looked at me. It was times like these that my reputation among, and my relationships with, others who pursue justice comes in handy. Tom, very reluctantly, said, "I suppose so."

"Okay, then we are in agreement. Step back counselors."

After we were back at our respective tables, Judge Warren continued.

"We are about to take a fifteen-minute recess. During this recess, I am directing the court officers to remove anyone who does not have a direct professional relationship to this case, or any member of the bar."

There was instant grumbling throughout the courtroom. Immediately, Judge Warren leaned over, whispering to her bailiff. Following their gazes, I could tell the judge was directing the bailiff to allow the FBI agents accompanying Janice to remain in the courtroom.

* * *

After fifteen minutes, Judge Warren returned to the bench.

"For those of you who chose to remain, you are under strict orders not to discuss what you are about to hear with the general public, the media, your friends, your neighbors, your loved ones—anyone. Jurors, you have no choice about whether to remain. You are about to hear testimony that, if made public, could endanger our national security, lives, and, possibly, federal prosecutions." Judge Warren glanced at Janice before continuing: "At some point after the testimony, you will all be given a summary agreed to by all parties regarding what you may say outside this courtroom about the testimony. If you are not in agreement with that, please leave the courtroom now."

Judge Warren paused, giving everyone a chance to leave the courtroom. Nobody rose to leave.

She nodded to me.

"Okay, Counselor, proceed."

"Thank you, Your Honor."

I could feel the attention of everyone in the courtroom shift to me, more so than at any time since opening statements.

I approached the witness stand again. "Allen, please tell us about this further contact you had with the federal government."

"A gentleman who said he had an investment opportunity for me made an appointment to see me. After he was seated in my office, he pulled out an identification card. It identified him as Terry Logan; the card indicated he worked for the NSA."

I glanced back at Janice and saw her eyes widen a bit.

"What does 'NSA' stand for?"

"The National Security Agency."

"I see. What did Mr. Logan want?"

"He proposed that while I was exploring investment opportunities around the world, I keep an eye out for illegal or dangerous activities. Especially in Eastern Europe. He suggested I express an interest in these companies and invest heavily in them so that I could obtain as much information as possible. Then, whenever I arrived back in the states, I would report to him what I had found. He also told me he would send me on trips to investigate companies the agency already had damaging information about."

"During the course of your career, did you invest in organizations engaged in illegal or dangerous activities as a regular course of your business?"

Allen shook his head. "No, not at all. In addition to being immoral, they're too risky an investment."

"Then if you followed Mr. Logan's request, wouldn't you lose money?"

"He assured me that the US government would reimburse me for any losses I suffered."

"Without going into details that might endanger national security, did you agree to do this?"

"Yes, I felt it was my patriotic duty."

"Okay. Again without details, was there ever a time when you reported to Mr. Logan that a business you investigated was engaged in illegal or dangerous activities?"

"Yes."

"Did that happen more than once?"

"Yes."

"Approximately how many times did it happen?"

"More than a dozen times."

"Did Mr. Logan say what the NSA would do about these businesses?"

"No. He would just thank me for the information."

"Do you know whether the NSA did anything about them?"

"I suspect they did."

"Objection, Your Honor. The witness is testifying as to what he thinks someone did."

Judge Warren said, simply, "Sustained."

I resumed my questioning undeterred. "Okay, Allen. Did Mr. Logan ever tell you that he investigated any of the businesses himself after you reported on them?"

"No. He never said that."

"Do you know what happened after you reported your information to Mr. Logan?"

"Always, those businesses would be hurt in some way."

"Hurt?"

"Their offices might burn to the ground at night when nobody was there. There might be a raid by the local authorities that shut their warehouses down. More recently, their network might suddenly become infected by a computer virus that disabled all of their operations."

"And something like that happened to every business you reported was engaging in illegal or dangerous activities?"

"Yes," Allen said. "Until very recently."

"Okay, before we go into those details, I have a few more questions." I paused, clearing my throat and allowing the jurors a moment to take in all that they were hearing. "After something untoward happened to those companies, didn't you lose your investment?"

"I did."

"Did you ever get reimbursed for your losses?"

"That's not what it said on the check."

"What check?"

"About two weeks after an incident shut down a business I reported on, I received a check in the mail from the US Treasury."

"Was the check for an amount equal to your loss?"

"No. It was equal to my loss plus ten percent."

"And did it say on the check what it was for?"

" 'Consulting Services.' "

"Okay. Now did you ever meet anyone higher up in the NSA than Mr. Logan?"

"Only his direct supervisor."

"Do you know his name?"

"Lyle Curry. At least that's what he said his name was."

"Do you doubt that his name was Lyle Curry?"

"Only because he's in the NSA… I don't know if they go by their real names."

"I see. So Terry Logan and his supervisor, Lyle Curry, are the only two people you met who work for the NSA?"

"As far as I know. I'm not sure NSA employees always identify themselves as such."

"Okay." I nodded. "Now, getting back to your recent encounter—you said that recently nothing had happened to a certain company you reported on?"

"Yes. This wasn't a company they sent me to investigate. However, I had heard of a business in Slovakia which had low overhead and a good profit. I don't want to go into details but it was a business I believed would be in high demand in Eastern Europe, so I went to investigate."

"Did the owners agree to meet with you?"

"Yes. By now my reputation as a wealthy American investor had gotten around."

"How did that meeting go?"

"The owners were very anxious to impress me. I asked them how it was possible for their overhead to be so low. They said they would show me, and then they asked me to follow them out to their factory floor. Once we were there I was horrified. There were children…young kids who looked to be five or six years old, chained to the machines they worked on. The owners smiled. One of them volunteered that they didn't have to pay the children anything: they were slave labor. In addition, when they got older and more rebellious, in their early teens, say, the owners sold the children to sex traffickers. That added to the company's profits."

"What did you do?"

"It was difficult, but I hid my horror and made a six-figure investment in their company. When I flew back to the states I immediately reported to Terry Logan."

"What did Mr. Logan say?"

" 'Thank you for the information.' Just as he always did. I assumed the matter would be taken care of. But weeks and months went by and I hadn't heard anything."

"What did you do?" I asked again.

"I had already planned another investigative trip in Slovakia. When I finished that trip, I decided to drive out to see if the company I had reported on was still in business, still using slave labor. As I drove up in my car, the door to the administration building opened. I saw Terry Logan and Lyle Curry step out, leading a group of about five teenagers. The teens had their hands behind their back."

"Were their hands bound?"

"I wasn't close enough to see, and I didn't want to be seen by Logan and Curry. I was glad that I always use vehicles with tinted windows, especially in Eastern Europe. Terry stopped and glanced my way, so I maneuvered my car to park in one of the executive's parking spaces. Terry and Lyle put the teens in the back of a van and then climbed in the front and drove away."

For a third time I asked, "What did you do?"

"I decided to walk into the company as if I were checking on my investment. Answering my inquiries, the owners bragged that they had just sold five teens. I asked who they sold them to. They didn't want to tell me, but they informed me that the head of the organization they sold them to was a friend of US presidents."

" 'Presidents.' Plural?"

"Yes, they said the current president and at least one prior president."

"Continue," I said, nodding.

"I asked if the organization that buys the children comes to pick them up. They said no, the same people who sold the young kids to the company acts as a go-between and take the teens to the organization that uses them as sex slaves. I asked if that's who I saw leaving as I drove up, and they said probably because the go-betweens had left only a few minutes before I came in. They bragged that they had a great relationship with those two men: they supply whatever workforce they need."

I paused to let all this sink in. The jury looked fascinated. I turned toward Abby and nodded to her. She rose and took a sealed envelope to Janice. At the same time, I took a file folder and gave it to Tom.

"Your Honor, may I approach the witness?"

"You may."

I took a photograph and handed it to Allen. "I am showing you what has been marked as Defense Exhibit 4. Do you recognize it?"

"Yes." Allen nodded. "This is the administrative building of the company that is using the child slave labor."

I handed Allen a second photograph. "I am now showing you what has been marked as Defense Exhibit 5. Do you recognize it?"

Again Allen nodded. "Yes. This is a picture of the children on the factory floor, chained to their machines."

A third photograph. "I am showing you what has been marked as Defense Exhibit 6. Do you recognize anyone in it?"

"On the left is Terry Logan and on the right is Lyle Curry."

"Your NSA contact and his supervisor?"

"Yes."

"Do you recognize where they are?"

"Yes, they are in front of the administrative building."

"Your Honor," I said, turning to Judge Warren, "we move the admission of Defense Exhibits 4 through 6 and ask that they be shown to the jury."

Judge Warren looked to Tom. "Any objection?"

Tom replied: "Other than renewing my objection on relevancy, no."

"Objection overruled. The exhibits are admitted and may be shown to the jury. Bailiff, please hand the photographs to the jury." She now turned to the jury. "Jurors, you may pass the photographs among yourselves. When finished, please hand them back to the bailiff."

The bailiff handed the photographs to the jurors. After each juror in turn had an opportunity to view the photographs, I continued.

"What did you do after learning of all the new information from the owners?"

"Well, I knew reporting it to Logan or Curry wouldn't do any good. I had never met their superiors, but I wasn't sure that would matter, because I didn't know how high up the illicit operations went. I figured the best thing to do would be to shed light on it by trying to publicize it."

Again I turned to Judge Warren. "Your Honor, we've now completed the part of the examination of this witness that needed to be conducted in secret. I suggest we have Mr. Fanucci cross-examine on the testimony thus far and then retire to draw up a summary."

"Mr. Fanucci?" Judge Warren asked, again turning to Tom.

Tom shook his head. "No questions, Your Honor."

I had thought Tom might not want to cross-examine on this portion of Allen's testimony. Especially if he planned to argue to the jury that it wasn't relevant to the charges.

"This courtroom stands in recess. I remind all of you to not discuss what you've heard here with anyone not in this courtroom. Bailiffs," she added, "do not let anyone enter the courtroom yet."

We retired to Judge Warren's chambers.

* * *

After discussion, some argument, and lots of editing, Tom, Judge Warren, and I agreed on the following summary:

> *The defendant, Allen Crosby, testified to interactions he states he had with people employed by the government of the United States. As part of those interactions, Mr. Crosby states he encountered illegal activities that were being conducted by the people with whom he had contact.*

This summary was printed out, copied, and distributed to everyone in the courtroom, along with printed instructions that stated anyone who was present and who revealed more than this summary—"except in the event and in conjunction with any prosecution resulting from this information"—would be held in contempt of court. That freed Janice to do her job. The instructions also stated that anyone who tried to get someone who was present to reveal more information would likewise be charged with contempt of court.

Copies of the instructions were also made to be distributed to the press and anyone else who entered the courtroom.

Tom, the court reporter, and I reentered the courtroom. The doors were opened for the press and anyone else who could fit in the remaining seats. Janice seemed to be getting up to leave; I sent Abby back with a handwritten message:

You'll want to hear the rest.

Janice sat back down.

After the courtroom had filled to its capacity and the cameras were turned back on, Judge Warren entered. We stood until she had taken her position at the bench. She then read out loud the summary and emphasized the secrecy of all additional details. Then she turned to me and said, "Mr. Frankel, you may continue with your examination."

"Thank you, Your Honor."

I turned to Allen.

"Mr. Crosby, you testified that you wanted to shed light on the information you had about illegal behavior by employees of the federal government. How did you plan to do that?"

"I knew a young, aggressive reporter for the *Inquirer* who I believed to be honest and would love to do a story like this."

"Did you tell the reporter what you had discovered?"

"I did."

"And—?"

"He was fascinated. But since I had no proof other than my say-so, he said he had to do his own investigation."

I nodded. "What was the reporter's name?"

"Paul Roberts."

A murmur rose through the courtroom. Judge Warren banged her gavel twice to restore silence.

Once the courtroom had fallen quiet again, I said to Allen: "Paul Roberts…the reporter who died mysteriously?"

Tom immediately jumped to his feet. "Objection, Your Honor. There is nothing mysterious about dying from carbon monoxide poisoning from a space heater."

"Your Honor," I replied, "as we will show, that cause of death is questionable."

"Until you show that," Judge Warren returned, "I will sustain the objection."

Although she sustained the objection, I could tell Judge Warren was fascinated.

I had asked my question about Paul Roberts in case any of the jurors did not recognize the reporter's name. Now I rephrased my question. "Allen, is Paul Roberts the *Inquirer* reporter who died a week before Deidre was murdered?"

"Yes."

"And how long before that did you go see him?"

"About a week before that."

I paused.

"Okay, let's move to the week of the murder. The murder occurred on a Tuesday, correct?"

"Yes."

"You heard the testimony presented by the Commonwealth that said you purchased the murder weapon on the morning of the murder?"

Allen shifted defiantly on the witness stand. "I heard it but it's not true."

"Did you purchase any weapon at any time on that day?"

"I did not."

"You are familiar with Clayton's?"

"Yes. It's the shop where I buy weapons, and where I go to shoot. They have an indoor shooting range."

"Did you go to Clayton's for any reason on the day Deidre was killed?"

"No I did not."

"At any time that week did you buy the gun that has been identified as the murder weapon?"

"I'm not sure."

A soft murmur in the courtroom.

"How can you not be sure?"

"I did buy a gun of that make and model. But I did not take note of the serial number."

"I see. And when did you buy that gun?"

"The morning after the murder."

"So that would be Wednesday?"

"Yes."

"But Clayton's records show that you bought the murder weapon Tuesday morning...and that you didn't buy any weapon on Wednesday. Can you explain that?"

"The records are wrong. Maybe someone changed them."

"How can you be so sure you bought the gun on Wednesday and not on Tuesday?"

"Well, as Officer Norman said, he took my gun Tuesday evening to have it examined to determine whether it was the murder weapon. It wasn't, but they had to examine it to make sure. Later, after the officers left my house, it occurred to me that Deidre's death could have been an attempt on my life carried out by the people I had contact with in the federal government."

"Wait," I said, turning to the jury, "are you saying that you thought employees of the federal government might be trying to kill you?"

"The thought occurred to me. After all, I knew about their illegal activities. And I suspected that Paul Roberts was killed because he was investigating what I had told him."

"But Paul Roberts died because he had an unventilated space heater, didn't he?"

"That's what the reports said—but I didn't necessarily believe that was true."

"Okay, so you said it occurred to you that you might be a target. What did you do then?"

"The next morning I drove to Clayton's to buy another gun. After the police confiscated my gun as possible evidence, I didn't have any protection."

"I see. What make and model did you buy?"

"A Glock 17."

"The same make and model as the murder weapon?"

"Yes, and the same as the gun I was used to, the gun taken by Officer Norman."

"Did you go to the police with your theory about being the target?"

"No."

"Why not?"

"First, I realized how crazy it would sound to someone who didn't know the background to my story. Second, I still didn't know whether it was true. And third, I didn't want to risk the police investigating and letting my government contacts know I was accusing them of serious crimes, and I didn't want them revealing the other information I knew."

"Okay. What, if anything, did you do Wednesday night?"

"I went to the Jarrettown to have a few drinks."

"Tell us about that."

"While I was at the bar, another patron recognized me from the news about Deidre's death; he offered to buy me a drink. I let him. I had a couple of drinks and talked to the man."

"Had you ever seen him before?"

"Not that I remember."

"Did you get drunk at the Jarrettown, Allen?"

"No. And in the past I've had much more to drink than what I had at the Jarrettown, and I did not get drunk."

"Okay. What did you do when you left the Jarrettown?"

"I drove home."

"How long of a drive is it from the Jarrettown to your home?"

"About five to ten minutes."

"Were you feeling any effects from your drinks?"

"Not on the drive home. But shortly after entering my house I started feeling woozy. I remember heading to my bedroom. The next thing I remember was waking up the next morning, lying across my bed fully clothed."

"Was there anything else unusual about how you woke up?"

"Yes. I had a Glock 17 in my hand."

The murmur through the courtroom was louder this time. I let it continue for a few moments before resuming my questioning. Judge Warren seemed fascinated and didn't pound her gavel for silence.

"What did you do then?"

"I checked where I kept my gun at night. A Glock 17 was right where it should be; I assumed it was the one I had bought Wednesday morning. But now I'm not sure which of the two guns is the one I bought."

"Okay." I nodded my encouragement. "Tell us what happened Tuesday evening, from the time before the murder until the time the police arrived."

Allen laid out the events just as he had described them to me. I exhibited for the jury's benefit an enlargement of a map of Allen's neighborhood showing the woods in his backyard, the bank with the parking lot, and the path through the woods Allen took to the bank. I asked Allen to point to specific areas on the map as he testified. After he had reached the point where he was recounting his call to 911, I interrupted.

"Your cell phone was on the coffee table?"

"Yes."

"You had left it there when you walked to the bank?"

"Yes. I don't usually carry it when I go for a walk. I don't want to be interrupted from the peace and quiet."

"So if someone were tracking you by the location of your cell phone…."

"They would have thought I was home."

I paused to let that resonate with the jury.

"Is that why you thought you might have been the target?"

"That was part of it. After the police left and I laid down to rest I was thinking about death, particularly unexpected deaths. I thought of Paul

Roberts's death the week before. And then suddenly it hit me. What if Paul Roberts's death was not actually an accident? What if his investigation tipped off Logan and Curry that I was trying to get the story out? What if they were trying to keep it from coming out? Then I thought of my cell phone and the fact that if someone was trying to kill me to keep me from going to another reporter, they would have thought I was home. Especially if they were in front of the house, since I left my house through the back to go to the ATM."

"Objection, Your Honor." I was surprised Tom had let Allen's testimony get as far as it did. "This is speculation by the defendant."

"Your Honor," I replied, "this testimony is not speculation. It is what Allen was thinking and demonstrates the timing regarding the second gun as necessarily occurring after the murder, not before. It provides his reason for buying another gun."

"I'll overrule the objection." I sensed a reservation in Judge Warren's voice. "But let's move on, Counselor. I think the witness has described his thinking on this subject well enough."

I wasn't going to object to the judge's reasoning, expressed in front of the jury. "Thank you, Your Honor."

"Allen, did you kill your wife?"

"No, I did not."

"Did you ask anyone else to kill your wife?"

"No, I did not."

"Did you have anything to do with the murder of your wife?"

A pause. Tears welled up in Allen's eyes. And then, an unexpected answer.

"I think I did." I looked at him in surprise as he continued: "If I hadn't pushed to get the information released, or if I had held a press conference to let the public know what I knew instead of trying to play Deep Throat by giving the information to a reporter, Deidre might still be alive."

I decided Allen's words were a stronger ending than just another denial.

"No further questions, Your Honor." I didn't need Allen to furnish any more information to bolster our case; I wasn't quite finished with his testimony, however. "May we approach the bench before the cross-examination?"

"Approach."

After Tom and the court reporter took their positions next to the bench, I said, "Your Honor, I believe that Mr. Fanucci might ask Allen what he did with the gun that he found in his hand on Thursday morning."

"Ya think?"

Judge Warren could be sarcastic at times. Especially when the jury couldn't hear.

I went on, carefully.

"The answer would involve attorney-client privilege; and so I would like to preempt the question."

Silence fell around the bench for a few seconds. Both Tom and Judge Warren realized that for the answer to the question to even remotely be connected to attorney-client privilege, Allen had either given the gun to me or asked me what he should do with it.

Tom spoke up. "Your Honor, if the witness asked counsel what to do with the gun and followed his advice, he could answer what he did with the gun without revealing any conversation he had with counsel."

"That is true." Judge Warren looked at me.

"I obviously cannot reveal if Mr. Fanucci's hypothetical is true. All I can say is that an honest answer to that question would require Allen to waive attorney-client privilege."

"Well, Counselor, why don't we wait to see if Mr. Fanucci asks the question and what your client's answer is before we have this conversation?"

"I was hoping to get the sidebar out of the way before Mr. Fanucci's cross," I replied, "and maybe avoid the awkward moment when Mr. Fanucci asks the question and Allen refuses to answer."

"Sidebars are not for avoiding awkward moments for murder defendants being cross-examined by the DA," Judge Warren stated simply. "Now get back to your places."

After we were back in place, Judge Warren said, "Mr. Fanucci, your witness."

"Thank you, Your Honor.

"Mr. Crosby, you've told us a great deal about your imaginary theory of what happened. Do you have any evidence for any of what you have told the court?"

"Objection, Your Honor." Surely Tom knew he wasn't going to get away with this. "There is no evidence that what happened to Allen is imaginary— and it is up to me, not the witness, to introduce evidence."

Tom quickly responded: "As to the imaginary part, I was referring to the defendant's theory that the United States government is out to get him, and that government agents killed his wife and a reporter for the *Inquirer.*"

Judge Warren clearly did not condone Tom's explanation. "I sustain the objection. Mr. Fanucci, you know better than to try those rhetorical tricks in my courtroom."

I made sure to offer my gratitude to the judge. "Thank you, Your Honor."

Tom returned to the matter at hand. "Mr. Crosby, you've testified that you did not kill your wife and that you had no reason to kill her, isn't that so?"

"Yes, Mr. Fanucci, it is."

"To the best of your knowledge, was your wife ever unfaithful to you?"

Allen did not flinch in his answer: "No, she was not."

"Were you ever unfaithful to her?"

"No. We were best friends and loyal to each other."

"I see. Do you know anyone named Loretta Woods?"

"No I do not."

"You never had an affair with her?"

"I've never had an affair with anyone."

"And you didn't give her the murder weapon to hide?"

"No!"

"Then what exactly did you do with that gun you conveniently found in your hand Thursday morning when you woke up?"

Allen remembered his line perfectly. "Upon advice of counsel, I claim attorney-client privilege."

"You refuse to answer?"

"Upon advice of counsel, I am claiming attorney-client privilege."

"How did the police get the gun?"

"Honestly, I have no idea."

"If counsel gave you advice and you followed it, you must tell the court what actions you took with respect to the gun, and you don't have to refer to the conversation you held with counsel."

Allen reacted perfectly by saying nothing.

I stood.

"Your Honor, is the district attorney really trying to give legal advice to the person he is prosecuting?" I saw a couple of grins on the jurors' faces. "Shouldn't he be asking questions on cross?"

"Please ask a question, Mr. Fanucci" Judge Warren encouraged.

Tom persisted with his questioning of Allen: "If counsel gave you advice and you followed it, you must tell the court what actions you took, and you don't have to refer to the conversation you held with counsel, isn't that so?"

"Your Honor, now he's asking for legal advice from my client, who is not a legal expert."

Again, more grins from the jurors.

"Mr. Fanucci, move on."

This time Tom obeyed Judge Warren's instructions. "Didn't you tell Officer Norman that you walked to your bank to take money out of your ATM at the time your wife was killed?"

"Yes," Allen said, "because it's true."

"Can you explain why the bank's records show no withdrawal from your account on that day?"

"No."

"And you told us today that you bought a gun from Clayton's the day after the murder?"

"Yes."

"Can you explain why Clayton's records have you buying the murder weapon on the morning of the murder?"

"No, I cannot."

"Can you explain why Clayton's records have you buying no weapon on the day after the murder?"

"No, I cannot."

"This whole story you've told, about your escapades for the federal government and telling Paul Roberts about the supposed illegal activities you found...that's all pretty convenient for you, isn't it?"

"Convenient?" Again I was impressed with Allen's stoic response.

"Well, the computerized records show no ATM withdrawal, the computerized records show you purchased the murder weapon the day of the murder, and so you concoct this whole story blaming an agency that has the capacity to change computerized records. Isn't that convenient?"

"It's the truth."

"Any evidence to back that up?"

"Excuse me if I'm wrong, Mr. Fanucci, but isn't eyewitness testimony evidence?"

"What eyewitness do you have?"

"Me."

"The one person accused of murder!"

"The one *falsely* accused of murder."

"Do you have any evidence that Paul Roberts was murdered?"

"No, just my suspicions based on what I told you."

"What you told us today?"

"Correct."

"Did you go to the police with your suspicions?"

"No."

"So today, more than six months after his murder, is the first time you are stating this theory publicly?"

"Yes."

"Nice story."

It was a good line. But I couldn't let it stand unchallenged. "Objection, Your Honor. Counsel is badgering the witness." Allen was holding up well, but I wanted to give him a short break and point out to the jury exactly what Tom was doing.

"Sustained," Judge Warren ruled. "Mr. Fanucci, stick to questions."

"Mr. Crosby," Tom said, "I will summarize the way I understand your testimony today—and I ask you to correct me if I have anything wrong. You, a renowned public figure, conducted covert investigations for the federal government. You discovered a couple of federal agents were engaging in illegal activities. You didn't go to their supervisors. You didn't go to the FBI like you did decades ago when you saw violations of federal law. You didn't even go to your local police. You told your story to a young reporter for the *Inquirer*—who ends up dead one week later. Yet you didn't suspect anything until your wife was murdered. Conveniently, you weren't home during the twenty minutes she was attacked. You say you withdrew money from an ATM, but your bank has no record of any such withdrawal. You say you purchased a gun the day after the murder, yet Clayton's only has a record of you purchasing the murder weapon on the day of the murder. You went out drinking the night after the murder, when some stranger bought you a drink. You woke up the next morning with a gun in your hand, but the gun you bought the day before was where it should have been. And the gun Officer Norman took from you, the gun you purchased, and the gun you woke up with are all the same make and model. Yet you won't tell us what you did with the gun you woke up with because of attorney-client privilege. Do I have your testimony correct?"

"Well, you took my testimony and combined it with your evidence," Allen replied accurately. "It's pretty much correct."

"Pretty much? What do I have wrong?"

"I went to the Jarrettown the night after the murder to have a couple of drinks. That's where the stranger bought me a drink because he recognized me and knew my wife had been killed. I didn't 'go out drinking when a stranger bought me a drink' the way you said it."

"Okay, with that correction do I have your testimony correct?"

"Yes, that's what happened."

"Pretty convenient. No further questions Your Honor."

"*Pretty* convenient?" Allen said. "I got—"

"Your Honor, I am finished my cross," Tom stated flatly. "I did not ask the witness a question."

"Mr. Crosby, please try to only answer questions." Judge Warren instructed. "Mr. Frankel, any redirect?"

"Yes, Your Honor. Thank you." Again I approached the witness stand. "Allen, what were you about to say about Mr. Fanucci's comment 'pretty convenient'?" Although no trial lawyer should ask questions in court that he doesn't already know the answer to, Allen was smart and hadn't said anything that would damage his case so I took a chance to ask him this.

Allen had tears in his eyes. "What I did got my wife and a young reporter killed. There are no records of my work for the government. The bank records were altered to make it look like I am lying. Clayton's records were altered to make it look like I am lying and that I bought the murder weapon. I get arrested and am standing trial for killing my best friend, my wife. And I can't provide any evidence other than what I tell you. I don't consider that 'convenient.' "

I paused, allowing Allen to compose himself.

"Allen…do you remember seeing the video from the ATM machine earlier during the trial?"

"Yes."

"And did you pay attention to the approximate time period when you would have been there, withdrawing money?"

"Yes."

"Did you see yourself withdrawing the money?"

"No."

"Why not?"

"Because the video went black from just before to just after I would have been there. Now that's what I call *convenient.*" Allen's voice cracked. I could see he was holding back tears again. But a couple jurors smiled at Allen turning the word "convenient" back on Tom. I decided that was a great comment to end on.

"No further questions, Your Honor."

"Any re-cross, Mr. Fanucci?"

Tom was finished too. "No, Your Honor."

"Mr. Frankel," Judge Warren said, "do you have a witness with shorter testimony you can call now, or should we adjourn for the day?"

"Your Honor, I do have one witness here whose testimony I don't expect to take long."

"Alright," Judge Warren said. "Call your next witness."

"Defense calls Bob Coleman."

Tom conferred with the other members of his team. Then he looked up toward the judge. "Your Honor, I object. There is no Bob Coleman on the defense's witness list."

I nodded to Jerry. He stood.

"Your Honor, this witness is in rebuttal to a prosecution witness."

"I'll allow it."

Bob was sworn in and Jerry conducted the examination. We were setting Tom up and hoping he'd ask the right question on cross.

Bob was obviously nervous. He rubbed his hands along the knees of his pants as though working out his anxiety.

"Bob, where do you work?"

"At Clayton's gun shop."

"In your work at Clayton's, did you meet Allen Crosby?"

"I did."

"The prosecution has said that Mr. Crosby came into your store on the morning of his wife's murder and purchased a Glock 17. Mr. Crosby says that it was the morning after his wife's murder when he did that. Do you know which, if either, is correct?"

"Yes, he came in the morning after his wife's murder."

"And he didn't come in the morning before?"

"No."

That was all Jerry needed. "No further questions, Your Honor."

Judge Warren turned to the prosecution's table. "Mr. Fanucci?"

Tom looked over at me and at Jerry, trying to read our faces.

"Thank you, Your Honor," he finally said.

As he rose and walked toward the witness stand, Tom continued to look at me and Jerry. I guess we had great poker faces because Tom went exactly where we wanted him to go....

"Mr. Coleman, you say that you remember which day the defendant purchased a gun in your store?"

"Yes."

Tom glanced at us again.

"You do realize this was more than six months ago?"

"Yes."

"Were you the only one on duty at the counter on the morning before the murder?"

"Yes."

Another glance. Tom took the plunge.

"So how do you remember, more than six months later, whether it was a Tuesday or a Wednesday when the defendant purchased a gun from you?"

"I don't remember the day of the week."

"You don't?" Tom smiled.

"No. I just know he didn't purchase a gun the day of the murder and that he did purchase a gun the next day."

Tom hesitated.

"No more questions."

Good call. The first rule of cross-examination is to not ask a question you do not already know the answer to. He violated it a bit by asking Bob how he remembered whether it was a Tuesday or a Wednesday when Allen had bought his gun. But he wasn't going to press his luck by asking the next obvious question.

That fell to Jerry—and he was ready for it.

"Redirect, Your Honor?"

"Proceed," Judge Warren said.

Jerry set in: "Mr. Fanucci has made a big deal about you not knowing what day of the week it was when Allen bought his gun and questioning your memory, didn't he?"

Bob sighed. "I guess so."

"Can you tell the jury how you can remember that Allen bought the gun after the murder instead of before the murder?"

"Because when Mr. Crosby came in to buy the gun, he told me about his wife's murder and that his gun was taken by the police to make sure it wasn't the murder weapon. He felt unsafe without a weapon, so he wanted another Glock 17."

Jerry paused to let that sink in. Assuming the jury understood the implication, Bob's testimony should have given them reasonable doubt about whether Allen had purchased the murder weapon.

"Are you aware that Clayton's official records show that Allen purchased the murder weapon the morning of the murder, and that he did not purchase any weapon the day after?"

"Yes."

"What do you have to say about those records?"

"They're wrong."

Jerry nodded. "No further questions."

"Mr. Fanucci?" Judge Warren inquired.

"Nothing further, Your Honor."

Another good call.

"Okay," Judge Warren said, wrapping up the session. "We will now recess until tomorrow morning. Jurors, I remind you to not speak with anyone, including each other, about this case. And I also remind everyone in this courtroom that the testimony during the closed session of court shall remain secret except for the approved summary you all have. Any violation of this order will result in contempt-of-court charges at the very least. Court is in recess."

CHAPTER 33

When we met after court on Wednesday, we discussed among ourselves that we thought the day has gone as well as could be expected. Tom landed some points in cross about Allen's story being unbelievable and "convenient,, but we thought Allen's response to the word "convenient" was as effective as it could have been. We all congratulated Jerry on his handling the redirect of Bob to bring out the reason he was so sure that Allen had purchased the gun the day after the murder. We had hoped Tom would fall for asking the question himself on cross-examination, but he was too seasoned for that. However, Tom's best move would have been to say "No questions." Then in his closing he could have argued about how much time had passed since the murder had taken place, and how Bob was being asked to distinguish between two days that were only one day apart. There would have been nothing we could have done to introduce Bob's information about why he was able to recall which day Allen had purchased the gun in question, because redirect can only take place after cross-examination. A risky move that paid off...and more proof that hindsight is twenty-twenty.

We adjourned until the next court session on Thursday.

* * *

Our first witness was Marge Tablou, next-door neighbor of the Crosbys. Jerry and Abby had prepped her. And in fact I let Jerry handle the direct of all the neighbors.

Jerry started: “How long have you lived next door to the Crosby’s?”

“Eleven years, about,” Mrs. Tablou answered.

“Do you know Allen Crosby?”

“Oh yes, he is always quite friendly.”

“And did you know Deidre Crosby?”

“Yes, she was a doll!” Mrs. Tablou did not believe in mincing words. “It’s a shame what happened to her.”

“Do you know other people in the community who also know Allen and Deidre?”

“Yes, because all the neighbors on our street got together at one or another’s house each month.”

“And have you discussed with your neighbors the character of Allen Crosby?”

“We did, sometimes.”

“And do you know what Allen Crosby’s reputation for truth and honesty is?”

“Yes,” Mrs. Tablou said, beaming, “it is absolutely perfect!”

“Absolutely?”

“Yes…I would stake my life on whatever he says.”

“So you would have no doubt about the truth of anything he told you?”

“Absolutely no doubt whatsoever.”

“And did you also discuss with your community Allen’s reputation as a husband?”

As ever, Mrs. Tablou did not disappoint: “Allen was absolutely devoted to Deidre. You could tell as much whenever you saw the two of them together. They’ve been a couple since they were in high school.”

Jerry smiled with approval. “If someone told you that Allen Crosby was having an extra-marital affair, would that be in concordance with the community’s opinion of him as a husband?”

“Absolutely not!” Mrs. Tablou had straightened her back as though she had personally been offended. “Whoever said that would be lying.”

"Okay." Jerry was satisfied with what he had heard from his witness so far. "I would like to direct your attention to the evening of the murder."

"Such a shame...." Mrs. Tablou lamented again.

"Yes. Did you notice anyone in your neighborhood who is not usually there?"

"Well, a PECO truck was parked across the street."

"To your knowledge, was anyone in your neighborhood experiencing any trouble with their electric power?"

"Not that I know of."

"Did you see any utility workers climbing any of the utility poles in the neighborhood?"

"No."

"Did you see *anyone* in the truck?"

"It looked like there were two people inside."

"Did you see them get out of the truck at all?"

"I didn't see them get out."

"Was the truck still there when the police showed up?"

"No, they left shortly before that."

"About how long before that?"

"About half an hour or so. I heard the truck moving. I glanced out the window and saw it heading to Twining Road."

"Thank you." Jerry nodded to Mrs. Tablou. "No further questions."

"Mr. Fanucci?"Again Judge Warren invited Tom to start his cross.

"Thank you, Your Honor....Mrs. Tablou, let's start with the day of the murder. Did you watch the PECO truck the entire time it was parked there?"

"Heavens no!" I smiled. Mrs. Tablou was determined to be as effusive on cross as she had been during Jerry's direct. "I did glance out the window once in a while."

"So, as far as you know, the people in the truck could have gotten out and performed some electrical work while you weren't looking, isn't that true?"

"I suppose so."

"Now let's turn to the defendant's reputation in the community. The people you spoke with about him—these were also neighbors?"

"Yes, it's our neighborhood group that gets together."

"So your opinion was based on seeing the defendant in social gatherings with his wife and neighbors?"

"I guess that's true."

"Let me give you a hypothetical question. If the defendant were having an affair, do you think he would share that information with his wife and neighbors at a social gathering?"

"He would never do such a thing!" Mrs. Tablou insisted again.

"Objection, Your Honor." Jerry should have been on his feet before the answer came out. "Mrs. Tablou has not been qualified as an expert behaviorist with knowledge of Allen Crosby's information-sharing habits."

"Sustained. The jury will disregard that question," Judge Warren instructed.

Of course the jury wasn't going to forget the question, which was why Tom asked it.

"Okay, Mrs. Tablou, let me take you back to the evening of the murder again. Is your house closer to KeyBank than the Crosby house, or is it farther away?"

"A little closer."

"So if the defendant were to go to KeyBank through the woods, he would have to walk behind your property?"

"Yes."

"Okay, good." Tom then dramatically picked up his legal pad and a pen and got ready to write. "What time did you see him walking through the woods in the direction of the bank that day?"

"I didn't."

Tom looked shocked. Of course, he already knew what her answer was going to be.

"You didn't see him walking to the bank?"

"No."

Tom paused, pretending to be confused.

"Okay, what time did you see him walking back from the bank?"

"I didn't."

"So you, his next door neighbor, closer to the bank than the defendant's home, didn't see him walking to or from the bank that evening?"

"No."

Tom shrugged. "Then I have no further questions for this witness."

We called a total of six neighbors, all of whom testified approximately the same way on direct and cross. Tom did his shocked-response routine for the three neighbors who lived closer to the bank than Allen.

When the neighbors' testimony had finished, the court adjourned for lunch. Over our meal the defense team discussed that morning's developments in the case. Again, we thought it was going pretty well. Some concern was raised over who Loretta Woods was and what evidence Tom had of an affair. I told them to let me handle that.

After lunch we called Gene Clark, a PECO employee. I asked him to explain his duties at PECO, which included functioning as the IT officer.

"Mr. Clark, at my request, did you bring any records with you today?"

"Yes, I did."

"What records are they?"

"Records of where all our vehicles were on a particular day."

"And is this particular day the same day as the murder in this case?"

"Yes."

"Do your records show any PECO vehicle, truck, van, or car on Timber Road in Dresher, Upper Dublin Township, on the day in question?"

"No they don't."

"Do your records list *every* vehicle owned by PECO?"

"Yes, they do."

"And all vehicles are accounted for?"

"Yes."

"Well, let me ask you this. Were any of the vehicles on that day working near that neighborhood? Could workers have stopped there to eat lunch?"

"None of the vehicles were near the Township of Upper Dublin on that day. It would have been out of the way for any of our workers to drive there to eat lunch."

"Thank you," I said. "No further questions."

Tom was on his feet quickly. "Mr. Clark, do your workers have to report in to tell you where they are taking a break?"

"No, just that they are."

"Thank you, no further questions."

My turn again. "Your Honor, I would like to recall Dr. Christopher Lane to the stand."

Dr. Lane was reminded that he was still under oath as he took the stand.

"Dr. Lane, did you autopsy a reporter, Paul Roberts?"

Dr. Lane nodded. "I did."

"And did you bring those records with you to court as I asked?"

"Yes."

"What was your conclusion as to Paul Roberts's cause of death?"

"Carbon monoxide poisoning."

"What information was your conclusion based on?"

"His cheeks were a bright red, he was in otherwise good health, and he had an unventilated space heater in his apartment."

"I see. I am going to ask you a hypothetical. If Mr. Roberts had a ventilated space heater, would you have come to the same conclusion?"

"I'm not sure. We would have had to do more tests."

"From the evidence you found, could you rule out all other causes of death?"

"Well not all. Obviously we could rule out stabbing or shooting."

"Could you rule out cyanide poisoning?"

Dr. Lane paused while he thought. "No, I guess not."

"Are you familiar with cyanide poisoning?"

"Somewhat."

"How can cyanide be delivered to someone?"

"Any of three ways—gas, liquid, or solid."

"From your education, can you give us some examples of how cyanide was used as a poison?"

"Well, probably the most famous case is the use of cyanide gas in the Nazi death chambers. But intelligence agencies also tend to give their agents cyanide pills so that they can commit suicide in the event of capture. And there are reports that certain agencies have devices that deliver cyanide gas quickly to a particular subject, say if you engage them in conversation and puff on something that looks like a cigarette or a cigar. And actually regular cigarettes and cigars also emit a certain amount of cyanide gas."

"Intelligence agencies, huh?" I said, looking directly at the jury.

"Yes. In fact, Alan Turing, the British spy worker who broke the famous Enigma Code during World War II, killed himself by injecting cyanide into an apple and eating it."

"An apple?"

"Yes."

"Is there any way to tell if someone died that way?"

"You mean by eating a cyanide apple?"

"Yes."

"Well, cyanide leaves very few traces. The victim's skin might turn bright red, but that is similar to how many poisonings act, including carbon monoxide poisoning. If the coroner performing the autopsy has an extremely sensitive nose, they might detect an almond-like smell while dissecting the brain. The best way to determine whether cyanide poisoning is the cause of death would be to examine the apple itself for residual cyanide."

"So then if someone were to murder someone with a cyanide-laced apple, for instance, the smart murderer would then get rid of the rest of the apple?"

"I guess that's true."

"No further questions."

"Dr. Lane, again…what was the cause of death of Paul Roberts?" Tom was quick to get to the point.

"Carbon monoxide poisoning."

"It wasn't cyanide poisoning?"

Dr. Lane paused—and I swore I could see a bead of perspiration on Tom's forehead as he waited for the answer.

"Well, I actually can't rule that out."

I knew Tom was upset with that answer; but Tom, ever the professional, acted as if it was the answer he expected. "But that wasn't your professional, official conclusion, was it?"

"No."

"No further questions."

Tom had done the best he could after Dr. Lane's equivocation.

Next we called Sandy Shelton, Paul Roberts's landlord. Under Jerry's skillful questioning, Mr. Shelton testified that after Roberts's death, he sold everything in the journalist's apartment to a man for cash. That he provided the man with a copy of the itemized list the police had given to him as to what was found in the apartment, including the trash in the can right next to the desk Roberts was found dead at. And that included on that list was an apple core. Jerry also had him verify that the apartment loft was equipped for a ventilated space heater.

We provided one more witness for a very brief testimony; then Tom crossed him even more briefly. We called an administrative assistant from the records department at Paul Roberts's credit card company to testify that two months prior to his death, Paul Roberts purchased an Ashley Hearth Products 17,000-BTU Wall-Mount Liquid Propane Vented Convection Heater. Tom's cross-examination consisted of pointing out that one didn't know whether that heater was ever installed in Roberts's apartment or if he bought it as a gift.

It was late in the day, so Judge Warren adjourned court until Friday morning. To our team, the case still seemed to be going as well as possible.

CHAPTER 34

On Friday morning we called six more character witnesses for Allen. These six were business acquaintances. Three were people Allen had done deals with. The other three were competitors. All testified that Allen's character was beyond reproach, and if it would be okay with their corporate attorneys, they would agree to a deal with Allen based on a handshake.

Tom's cross on those character witnesses was along the lines of what he tried to bring out with the neighbors—that if Allen were having an affair, he would not have shared that information with any of them.

At the end of that testimony, approaching lunch hour, I said, "The defense moves in evidence all documents we used in questioning each witness."

Tom had no objection. The documents were admitted.

"The defense rests," I said.

Judge Warren called us to a quick sidebar. "Are you ready to close after lunch?"

Tom said, "Your Honor, we have a rebuttal witness."

I pretended to look surprised.

Judge Warren granted what I thought was a reluctant, "Okay." She then asked us if we had the jury instructions we each requested her to use. Tom and I both handed our instructions to her.

Judge Warren then adjourned court for a lunch break.

Over lunch, I explained to the team that Tom had a rebuttal witness. Jerry asked, "Who do you think it is?"

"My guess is this mysterious Loretta Woods."

Abby asked, "Shouldn't she have been on the witness list?"

"Not if they were going to use her only for rebuttal of Allen's testimony. And the character witnesses'. Just as our rebuttal witnesses didn't have to be on our witness list."

Abby persisted, "But wasn't he taking a chance? What if Allen hadn't testified?"

"Tom knew very well that Allen had to testify. If he hadn't gotten on the stand and denied killing Diedre, with the evidence the Commonwealth had, it would have been a sure conviction."

We returned from lunch and I was prepared. I wanted my IT guy's expertise available so I had Keith meet us in the courtroom. And, anyway, this was all his idea.

Judge Warren instructed, "Mr. Fanucci, call your witness."

"Your Honor, the Commonwealth calls Loretta Woods."

Loretta Woods entered the courtroom. She was a striking woman dressed in clothing that displayed her curves but that nonetheless leant her a professional demeanor. The bailiff administered the oath and Ms. Woods sat in the witness box.

After the preliminaries, Tom got to it.

"Ms. Woods, do you know the defendant?"

"Yes, I do.

Allen looked at me and shook his head vigorously.

"How do you know the defendant?"

"We met at the Upper Dublin Community Day last year."

Allen smiled and wrote on the pad we had between us *I wasn't there.*

I wrote, *I know that.*

"What happened at Community Day?"

"We started talking. Instantly we really liked each other. We found we had similar tastes in literature and music. Politically we were in agreement. After Community Day we periodically met for lunches to continue talking."

"Did your relationship get past this 'friendship' stage?"

"Yes. We first started kissing on greeting and parting. Then it got more serious."

"In what way did it get more serious?"

"We started meeting for sex. We expressed our love. Allen said that he wanted to marry me but that getting a divorce would be bad for his business and personal reputation."

"How did you react to that?"

"I wasn't happy. I wanted more, and Allen knew it."

"As it got close to the date of the murder, did Allen say anything that indicated his thinking had changed?"

"Yes. He told me he had an idea about how he could get out of his marriage and eventually marry me."

"Did he say what that idea was?"

"No, he just told me to park near the KeyBank ATM and wait for him that evening."

"Did you do that?"

"I did."

"Did he come to you that evening?"

"He did."

"What happened then?"

"He handed me a paper bag and told me to hide it somewhere. Then he turned and hurried back towards his house."

"Did he tell you what was in the paper bag?"

"No."

"What did you think was in it?"

"Well, since he had just used the ATM, as he was walking to me I thought it might be money. But when he handed it to me, I knew it wasn't."

"How did you know that?"

"It was too heavy for money."

"Did you look in the bag?"

"I did."

"What was in the paper bag?"

"A see-through bag with a gun inside it."

An audible gasp went up in the courtroom. Although my staff was trained to not react to testimony detrimental to our client in the courtroom, I could see the fear in their eyes. If believed, this witness would provide motive and an explanation of how the murder weapon went from Allen's possession. The woman who turned it over, we could see coming, would no longer be the "mysterious stranger" I had termed her.

Tom walked over to the evidence table. "I am showing you what has been marked as Commonwealth Exhibit 4 and has previously been identified as the murder weapon in a plastic bag. Is this what the defendant handed you and asked you to hide?"

"It looks like it."

"Did you hide it?"

"At first."

"What do you mean by 'at first'?"

"Well, I was scared about why Allen wanted me to hide it. Then I saw on the news that his wife had been murdered that same evening. I wrestled with my conscience for a few weeks and then decided to take it to the police."

"During the time you had it, did you take the gun out of the plastic bag?"

"No. I didn't even take the plastic bag out of the paper bag."

Tom seemed satisfied. "No further questions, Your Honor."

Judge Warren trained her gaze on me. "Mr. Frankel?"

"Your Honor, as you know this witness was not on the Commonwealth's witness list and was therefore a surprise. I do have a few questions based on this witness's story, but I also would like some time to be able to investigate this witness."

"How much time do you need?"

"One week should be sufficient. We will also need any information the Commonwealth has about this witness, including any statements she gave the police."

"I object Your Honor." Tom was once again on his feet. "Counsel just wants the jury to forget what the witness said."

"Your Honor, I doubt the jury will ever forget the story this witness came up with."

"Mr. Frankel, do as much of your cross as you can now. Mr. Fanucci, get Mr. Frankel everything you have about the witness. Then we will adjourn until Monday morning. You will have the weekend to do your investigation."

"Thank you, Your Honor." Tom and I spoke in unison.

"Good afternoon, Ms. Woods," I said, approaching the witness.

"Good afternoon."

"Did you say you first met Allen at Community Day last year?"

"Yes, I did."

"Please describe that encounter."

"I don't remember all the details."

"Please tell us all you remember."

Loretta Woods immediately broke eye contact with me and moved her eyes to look at the ceiling, making eye contact with…nobody. I was hoping observant jurors noticed that. To emphasize it, I turned my head toward the ceiling as though to see what she might be looking at.

"Did something on the ceiling attract your attention?"

"What?"

"Well you were looking at me before I asked you for details of your meeting and suddenly you looked at the ceiling."

"Objection, Your Honor." Tom, of course, recognized my tactic for what it was. "Counsel is badgering the witness. It doesn't matter where she is looking."

"Objection sustained." Judge Warren sighed with impatience. "Mr. Frankel, let's assume the jury is paying attention and there is no need to question the witness as to whether she is making eye contact."

"Yes, Your Honor."

That was the best comment I could have hoped for from Judge Warren while sustaining Tom's objection. Apparently she noticed the shift of Loretta Woods's focus as well.

"Okay. Ms. Woods, you've had some time to come up with what you want to say. Tell us about your encounter at Community Day last year."

"Well, we were both standing at one of the tables, and Allen said something funny."

"What did he say?"

"I don't remember."

"Okay, go on."

"I laughed at his comment and we started talking. We talked for the rest of the day."

"And what did you talk about?"

"You know, just chitchat."

"No, we don't know. That's why I'm asking."

"About our interests in books and music and politics."

"And what are Allen's interests in books and music and politics?"

"Very similar to mine."

"Okay. That may be true, but it is not a very helpful answer. Tell us *specifically* what those interests are."

"Objection, Your Honor." Tom was doing his best to ward off my inquisition. "The defendant's interests in books and music and politics are not relevant to the murder of the defendant's wife."

Before I had a chance to respond, Judge Warren said, "Overruled."

I said, "Thank you, Your Honor." I chanced a comment too: "Mr. Fanucci has again given you some time to come up with an answer. What did Allen tell you his interests in those three topics were?"

"The conversation was last year. I don't remember exactly."

"But they were the same as your interests?"

"Yes."

I looked at the jury. They looked as confused and amused as I had hoped.

"Okay, let's move on. You said over time you met for meals and coffee and got even closer—and then you started meeting for sex as well, is that correct?"

"Yes."

"Where and when did these meals, coffee, and sexual assignations take place?"

"During weekdays so his wife wouldn't notice him missing."

"I mean on what dates and in what locations specifically did you meet?"

"I didn't keep a record of the meetings. I don't remember."

"Okay, when you went to the bank to meet Allen and you parked close to the bank, where did you park?"

"I'm not sure how to describe it other than 'close to the ATM.' "

"Well, you know that the bank parking lot allows a lane for cars to go by between the ATM and parking, correct?"

"Yes."

"And then there are three rows of parking heading out away from the ATM?"

"Yes."

"And the middle of those rows is directly in line with the ATM, correct?"

"Yes."

"Did you park in that middle row?"

"Yes."

"And how many spaces away from the ATM were you parked?"

"I was in the first space."

"The one right next to the lane for cars to go by the ATM?"

"Yes."

"What kind of vehicle were you driving?"

"An SUV."

"Do you know the make or model?"

"It's a Cadillac Escalade."

"What color is it?"

"Black."

"Your Honor, I request that the video screen be set up so that we can view the recording at the ATM again."

"Your Honor, we've all seen the video already." Tom knew exactly why I wanted it shown. "This is a waste of time."

"Your Honor," I countered, "apparently Ms. Woods has not seen the video, and I would like to use it as part of my cross-examination."

Judge Warren's decision came fast. "Objection overruled."

Our team sat quietly while the video screen was set up and the video cued to about five minutes before it went black.

"Ms. Woods, this is the video taken from the ATM camera just before and just after Allen used the ATM." I hit the PLAY button followed shortly thereafter by the FREEZE button. Although the video was in black-and-white, one could clearly see a small white sedan parked in the space described by Loretta Woods.

I pointed to that car. "Is this your black Cadillac Escalade?"

Most of the jurors smiled.

Woods looked away in disgust.

"Your Honor, could you please direct the witness to answer the question?"

"Ms. Woods," Judge Warren said sternly, "please answer Mr. Frankel's question."

"No, that is not my car."

"The video isn't showing any other car near the ATM…so where's your Cadillac?"

"This must be either before or after I was there."

"Okay."

I pressed the PLAY button. We all watched as the small white sedan stayed parked up until the blacked-out part of the video began. I fast-forwarded the video to the end of the blacked-out section and hit PLAY again. The white sedan was still there. Parked. No Cadillac Escalade in sight.

"This is just after Allen used the ATM. Where's your Escalade?"

"I must have left already."

"So, you are saying that during the time the video is blacked out, the small light-colored sedan left, you pulled into the same space, Allen used the ATM and handed you the bag, you checked what was in the bag, left, and the small sedan returned and parked in the same place?"

"Yes."

"I'm sorry, I didn't hear you. Did you say 'yes'?"

"Yes!" Ms. Woods said again, with more spirit than I thought she might have at this point.

I paused to change topics.

"You said you and Allen were in love?"

"Yes."

"Would you describe him as the love of your life?"

"Yes."

I walked behind Allen's chair at our defense table. "Is this the Allen Crosby you are talking about?"

"Yes."

"I only ask because he has no memory of ever meeting you or knowing who you are." I knew what was coming next but I wanted the jury to hear that.

"Objection Your Honor. Mr. Frankel is testifying instead of asking questions."

I smiled mildly. "I'll withdraw the comment.... Your Honor, I have no further questions for this witness until Monday morning."

Judge Warren adjourned court until Monday morning with her typical warnings to the jury.

After Judge Warren and the jury cleared out of the courtroom, Tom approached the defense table and handed me a file containing copies of all the information the Commonwealth had about Loretta Woods. He had come prepared.

At the meeting after court, I told Abby and Reese to find out all they could about Loretta Woods, and I told Keith to find out anything he could about her online presence. They responded, "Yes, boss."

Jerry said, "Her voice and mannerisms seem familiar…."

"Interesting," I said. "If you figure out why, let me know."

Susan made eye contact with me but said nothing. We adjourned for our weekend of work.

CHAPTER 35

Late Saturday morning, as directed, Reese went to the address listed for Loretta Woods. It was the bottom apartment in a two-story white suburban home converted into first- and second-floor apartments.

Reese knocked on the door. No answer.

He tried the cell number for Ms. Woods that Tom had given us. It went immediately to voicemail.

Reese peered in the window, between the blinds, and observed a bare apartment, no furniture, nothing of a renter's possessions. He snapped some quick pics of the empty apartment with his cell phone. He also took a pic of a security camera outside the building. I immediately had Reese deliver a subpoena to the landlord to appear Monday with the video recording covering the time span from Friday after court until the time Reese appeared on Saturday, along with all rental records for Ms. Woods's tenancy.

Keith brought me all the Facebook records for Loretta Woods. I made sure to remind him he needed to be a witness Monday to introduce these into evidence, since Woods wouldn't be there.

Jerry came to my office. "I know who Loretta Woods reminds me of," he said.

"Good. I was hoping it wouldn't take you very long. For your sake, let's not talk about it."

After Jerry left, Susan came in. "Did he figure it out?"

I looked at her. "Yes. Did you?"

She looked offended. "Of course!"

I smiled. Susan was always bright and observant.

She asked, "How did you pick her?"

"She acted all through high school and college. She was a drama major and planned to go into acting professionally. Then she got married and her husband put the kibosh on her plans."

"She didn't look like herself."

"It's amazing what hair dye, a new hairstyle, colored contacts, and a new style of dress—plus a little swagger—can do."

"Where is she now?"

"Someplace safe, I suppose."

Susan smiled then left my office.

CHAPTER 36

When we resumed court on Monday morning, Loretta Woods did not show up. Of course, this was not a surprise to anyone on the defense team. In chambers, Tom asked for, and received, a recess for the police to go to her apartment to see if she was there. I argued that my investigators had been there on Saturday and found an empty apartment so there was no need for the delay. Judge Warren granted a one-hour recess.

To nobody's shock, the police came back and reported that they found the same thing Reese had found—an empty apartment. I said that Woods's testimony was potentially damaging enough that, even though (maybe even especially *because*) she was not here for further cross-examination, the judge should allow us to reopen the defense case to present evidence to impeach her testimony. Tom knew there was no way to prevent that. He sadly acquiesced.

Tom's delay helped us. Instead of me calling my investigator as a witness to say that Loretta Woods's apartment was cleaned out, I called the officer Tom had sent out to check on her. He reported what he found, and Tom had no cross-examination.

Next I called Woods's landlord. He testified that shortly after the murder, Woods showed up and gave him cash in advance for a one-year rental of the apartment. He had no forwarding address for her and, in fact, did not know she had moved out until contacted by my investigator. I also asked him if he had brought the digital video from his security camera.

"Yes, sir."

"And does it cover the period from Friday afternoon until Saturday afternoon?"

"Yes it does."

"Did you watch it before coming to court?"

"I did."

We had spoken before court began, so I knew exactly where to tee up the video.

"I am going to show a portion of that video now and ask you to identify if it is the same video you obtained from your security camera."

I played the video for about a minute, showing a black Escalade pulling to the front of the building followed by a small, unmarked moving van. I stopped it there.

"Does this appear to be the video you brought to court today?"

"Yes, it does."

"I will play it from this point on and ask you to narrate what you can identify in the video. Before I hit PLAY, can you tell what kind of vehicles are in this picture?"

"It looks like a black Escalade and a van."

"Are there any markings on the van?"

"I can't see any."

"Okay, please tell us what you see." I pressed PLAY.

The landlord narrated that the woman who got out of the Escalade was Loretta Woods; also, two gentlemen climbed down out of the truck. When asked, the landlord said he didn't know if he knew the men, because at no time did they allow their faces to be seen by the camera. All three proceeded to empty furniture and boxes from the building and then drove away.

Tom had no cross.

I then called Keith Cross to testify about Loretta Woods's social media presence. He testified that he could only find evidence of her social media from shortly after the murder until the day she disappeared. Tom's cross brought out that the social media confirmed her relationship with Allen. My redirect asked Keith, as an IT expert, whether everything on social media is true. Jurors smiled even before Keith let out a laugh and told us all that a high number of people lie on social media.

I then called the chair of the medical records department for Abington Memorial Hospital.

After the preliminaries, I asked, "Did you bring to court the records for Allen Crosby?"

"I did."

"It has previously been introduced that October eighteenth last year was Upper Dublin Community Day. Is that date in Mr. Crosby's medical records?"

"It is."

"Please tell the court what it says about that date."

"The records show that Mr. Crosby was admitted to the hospital on Friday, October seventeenth and discharged on Sunday, October nineteenth."

"So he was an in-patient in your hospital on Saturday, the eighteenth of October?"

"Yes."

Tom had no cross-examination.

I then, again, rested the defense.

We adjourned for lunch with the judicial command to be ready for closing arguments when we return.

Over lunch, I entertained suggestions and discussions regarding the closing. I scribbled a few notes, but most of the good ideas I had already included. I ate mostly in silence and left about half the lunch on the table.

Then we set out for the courthouse.

CHAPTER 37

In Pennsylvania, the defense presents their closing argument and then the Commonwealth presents theirs. The Commonwealth gets the last word, so it is important for the defense to anticipate what will be said and to counteract it. I always try to do that. Usually I'm successful. Sometimes the Commonwealth throws me a curve.

But before closings for Allen's case began, I had to have one more conversation with the judge, Tom, and the court reporter without anyone else present. It didn't exactly go as planned.

"Your Honor, in my closing argument, I will be discussing my client's relationship with the NSA. For the same reasons that his testimony could not be public, I would like to close my argument to interested spectators."

"Mr. Fanucci?"

Tom said, "Are we going to have to come up with a public summary of Mr. Frankel's argument to distribute?"

"Mr. Frankel?"

"I don't think so, Your Honor. Given that argument isn't evidence, there is no need for the public to know."

"But the right of the public to know what is being said during any trial is not limited to specific parts of the trial," Tom noted. "I won't agree to having to summarize Mr. Frankel's closing even if he were to agree to that."

Judge Warren tried to find a compromise. "Mr. Frankel, can't you simply refer to an unnamed government agency?"

I thought through my planned closing. “I think I can, Your Honor.”

Judge Warren was happy. “Problem solved.”

After we were all back in the courtroom, Judge Warren called on me to begin my closing.

I approached the jury and paused a moment before starting. “Your Honor, ladies and gentlemen of the jury. Thank you for your close attention to the evidence presented in this case. I will make a final argument about what I think the evidence shows or doesn’t show. Then Mr. Fanucci will do the same from the Commonwealth’s perspective.

“What we say to you is not evidence. And if what we say is not what you remember, go with your memory. We are here to argue what we think the evidence shows. I will show you why I think it is clear that you should come back with a verdict that Allen Crosby is not guilty of killing his wife.

“I want to address the Commonwealth’s last witness first. Ms. Loretta Woods appeared out of nowhere after the murder. She paid one year in advance in cash for her apartment shortly after the murder took place. She had no social media presence before the murder and then started posting how she was Allen’s girlfriend. She told us where she parked the night of the murder. Yet the video showed a different car in that place. She told us Allen was the love of her life largely because of the interests in music and literature they shared, but she couldn’t remember what those interests were. She said they met at Community Day, but Allen was an in-patient at Abington on Community Day. After I started questioning her story on Friday, she disappeared with the help of two men who were savvy enough to not let their faces be seen on the security camera. As Judge Warren will instruct you, if you think a witness lied about any part of their testimony, you are permitted to ignore their entire testimony. If I were you, I would completely discount her testimony and concentrate on the rest of the evidence. And if you discount her testimony, there goes any motive Allen would have for killing his best friend and loving wife. And she’s the one who gave the murder weapon to the police. Given the circumstances and her lies, this helps prove Allen’s theory that he is being set up.

"So what else did the Commonwealth present? Well, they presented evidence they think means Allen lied to the police. Remember, Allen said he walked through the woods to the ATM and withdrew money? They presented a computerized report that said he did not withdraw any money. However, even their witness admitted that the computerized report could be incorrect if it were hacked. That witness also brought with him the video from the ATM that night. It amazingly went black just before Allen said he got there until after he would have left. Was that a coincidence…or was it done by the same people who hacked into the system to change the bank records? As many detectives say, 'I don't believe in coincidences.' Even their surprise witness, the mysterious Loretta Woods, says that Allen went to the ATM for a transaction that night.

"The Commonwealth presented evidence that the gun Allen had in his home was not the murder weapon. However, the gun that their surprise witness, who shouldn't be believed, turns over to the police *is* the murder weapon. You heard the lab tech dismiss other partial fingerprints found on the gun in Allen's home because usually there are other fingerprints on guns. Even if the owner didn't let anyone use his gun, often the gun clerk's fingerprints, or at least partial prints, are found on the gun. What did the tech find on the murder weapon? Only Allen's fingerprints. No clerk's full or partially smudged prints. It's as if someone wiped down the gun before Allen's fingerprints showed up."

I paused to let that sink in.

"Speaking of the murder weapon, the Commonwealth presented computer evidence that Allen bought that gun on the morning of his wife's murder. He didn't. The clerk from Clayton's remembers the conversation he had with Allen when he purchased a weapon—and it was the morning after the murder, not before. Remember that conversation? Allen told the clerk that his wife had been murdered the night before and that his gun had been taken by the police for examination, so he wanted to buy another for protection. Although this couldn't be the murder weapon, the fact is that Allen bought no weapon on the day of the murder and did buy one the day after the murder. Obviously, when the computerized record of the purchase was hacked to change the date, the serial number was also changed to be the murder weapon's.

"Do you remember the testimony that the Commonwealth's coroner presented? He said that Deidre was killed with two shots to the chest and one to the head, similar to what he finds with professional killings and not at all what one would expect from a crime of passion. And after he learned of Deidre's medical history, he revised his time of death to between five p.m. and five thirty. That was the time of Allen's walk to the bank.

"Now, remember that the defense did not have to present any evidence. That if you did not find the Commonwealth's evidence proof beyond a reasonable doubt you have to vote 'not guilty' even if we had chosen to present no evidence?"

I nodded and looked at the jurors. Several nodded back.

"Well, let's look at the evidence we presented anyway. Allen told us about his work for a certain government agency and his attempt to bring wrongdoing to light. This is consistent with his behavior during the Abscam investigation. He told us that two men who worked for the agency he worked for were involved in illegal activities, and he went to Paul Roberts, an *Inquirer* reporter, about it. The next week the reporter was found dead. Although the coroner concluded the death was caused by carbon monoxide poisoning, he had incomplete information. He didn't know that Mr. Roberts had a vented space heater, which prevents carbon monoxide poisoning. He also didn't know that Mr. Roberts was investigating allegations against a government agency which will do *anything* to protect its secrets. You heard the coroner say that cyanide poisoning is a common method that government intelligence agencies use to kill. You heard the coroner say that Alan Turing died by cyanide poisoning of an apple. You also heard that there was an apple core in Mr. Roberts's trash can, and that everything in the apartment, including the trash, was purchased with cash by a mysterious stranger.

"You heard that several of Allen's neighbors noticed a PECO truck parked on the street across from Allen's house. None of the neighbors noticed either of the people in the truck working on any electric wires, and the truck left shortly before the police arrived after the murder. You heard the PECO employee tell us that no PECO trucks were anywhere near that street, or even Upper Dublin Township, on the day of the murder. Who were those mysterious men?

"Now you may be wondering why these men killed Deidre Crosby instead of Allen Crosby. I wondered that too…until I realized that Allen had left his cell phone in his home when he walked to the bank. A logical assumption could be made that the two mystery men had come to Allen's home to kill him and thought he was at home because they had traced his cell. When Deidre answered the door, they could have come in, saying they worked with Allen. When they realized he wasn't home, and in fact saw his cell on the coffee table in the living room, they changed plans. They killed Deidre and intended to frame Allen.

"By the way, you also heard neighbors, personal acquaintances of Allen and Deidre, tell us how strong their marriage was and how Allen has a reputation in the community, being of outstanding character. You heard business acquaintances of Allen, both people he worked with and people he competed with, tell you that Allen's reputation was that his word was as good as a bond. That they would not hesitate having simply a handshake agreement with Allen.

"So, after Mr. Fanucci speaks to you, you will have to decide whether all these facts give rise to a reasonable doubt of Allen's guilt. I expect that Mr. Fanucci will review the evidence he presented. But remember as he does so why his evidence is suspect and does not amount to proof beyond a reasonable doubt. In fact, I would suggest that, given Allen's character and the strength of his marriage, the evidence presented by us as to what happened is more reasonable than to assume that Allen killed Deidre. Whether you agree with that or not, you have to agree that there is a reasonable doubt about Allen's guilt, and you must return a verdict of not guilty.

"Thank you."

I returned quietly to the defense table. Judge Warren looked to Tom. "Mr. Fanucci?"

"Thank you, Your Honor." Tom cleared his throat and approached the jury box. "Well, that was some story we heard. It reminds me of how squids operate in the ocean. If they are in danger, they squirt dark ink into the water to confuse the predator that is looking for them. Don't let the defense's story confuse you.

"We showed you that the defendant lied when he told his story to the police. And that he lied to you, ladies and gentlemen, when he testified on the stand. We presented documentary evidence that the defendant did not withdraw any money from the ATM. So the time of death is not relevant since the defendant did not go to the ATM. We presented documentary evidence that the defendant bought the murder weapon on the morning of the murder. We presented scientific evidence that the defendant's fingerprints were on the murder weapon. As the defense points out, if you believe a witness lied, you are permitted to discount their whole testimony.

"This conspiracy theory of a government agency doing dastardly deeds in Eastern Europe might make a good plot for a movie. But is it reasonable? That's what you have to ask yourself. Did the defense raise a reasonable or an unreasonable conspiracy theory to try to throw doubt onto the Commonwealth's case, which is based on documentary and scientific evidence?

"And let's look at how convenient the defendant's story is. The only witness who could verify it is Paul Roberts, a reporter who is dead. How convenient. The government agents happen to come into the defendant's house during the twenty minutes Allen Crosby is out. How convenient. The agents do not have enough patience to wait for him to return from his twenty-minute walk. How convenient. A famous person died half a century ago of a cyanide-laced apple and there was an apple core in the reporter's trash can. How convenient.

"Let's look at something else convenient. According to the defendant, he went drinking in a bar where there happened to be a mysterious stranger who may or may not have drugged him. How convenient that he chose that bar. He woke up the next morning with the murder weapon in his hand but didn't report this to the police. How convenient that he remembers that for the trial. And he wouldn't or couldn't tell us how that weapon ended up in the hands of Loretta Woods, who turned it over to the police. He says he didn't know her. How convenient that a stranger who disappears turns the weapon in to the police.

"When you retire to chambers to think about this case, don't let all these confusing stories cloud your judgment. The evidence you heard from the stand is this: One: the defendant lied about withdrawing money from the ATM. Two: the defendant's fingerprints were on the murder weapon. Three: nobody else had a motive to kill Deidre Crosby. Four: there is no evidence that anyone except the defendant had an opportunity to kill Deidre Crosby.

"When you concentrate on the actual evidence instead of the unbelievable story put forth by the defense, I am sure you will do your duty and find that the defendant is guilty of murder beyond a reasonable doubt.

"Thank you."

CHAPTER 38

The most difficult part of any trial is waiting for the verdict. There is a general, but not absolute, maxim that the shorter the jury deliberates, the more likely the jury is to return a guilty verdict. The longer it takes, the more likely the trial will end with a hung jury or an acquittal. In some cases I hope for a hung jury. In this case I was hoping for an acquittal. And I hoped it would be quick.

We went back to the office to catch up on work that had fallen by the wayside during the trial. The trial took a lot out of me. I felt like an olympic swimmer must feel after a grueling meet, waiting for his lungs and stomach to catch up with the rest of his body....

Before we began work, we met in the conference room to discuss the case in general. I began with a piece of mail that had been delivered. "Do you all remember Lynn Warner, the client we represented who wanted to go into witness protection?" I had the attention of all around the table. "We received a thank you postcard from her today."

"What did it say?" Jerry was at the edge of his seat.

I picked up the card and read, " 'Thanks for everything. LW.' "

"Where did it come from?" Susan was curious.

I glanced at it. "Zip code 1-9-1-5-3."

"Isn't that the airport?" Jerry asked.

"I believe it is."

"When did she send it?"

"It's postmarked Saturday."

There were nods around the table.

"Okay, so how did we do as a team on this case? Anything we could have done better? Anything we did better than usual? Let's do the post-mortem before we get back to work."

Around the table my staff offered their opinions, mostly good, some on improvements we could have made in our presentations or our methodologies.

"I thought your cross of Loretta Woods went really well," Jerry said with a smile. "It was almost as if you knew how she would answer your questions."

The group chuckled nervously.

I ignored the laughter. "It did go well."

After all the discussion, analysis, hand-wringing, laughter, and shared memories were over, we all got back to work.

CHAPTER 39

Tuesday morning, I was in the office by seven thirty. The jury hadn't deliberated for very long on Monday before adjourning for the evening. I went back to handling routine practice matters, such as seeing prospective new clients while working on cases I had already accepted. I also checked around the firm to see if anyone needed to kick around ideas on cases they were working on.

Most of the prospective new clients turned out to either be guilty or lying about material facts. A typical example was Michael Garvey, a walk-in I had on Tuesday.

Susan had knocked on my door and stepped into my office.

"There's a gentleman out here who would like to retain your services."

"Have him fill out an IC form."

"He's working on it as we speak. He was arrested for burglary last night and just got out on bail. He says he was arrested because he was walking in the area wearing a hoodie."

"Seriously?" I said. "We'll see."

Michael Garvey shuffled into my office with dreadlocks draping down his back and his jeans halfway down his backside without a belt. He looked like the stereotypical "thug" right-wing politicians rail against. Except Michael Garvey was white.

He sat down in the chair in front of my desk even though I was standing, ready to shake his hand and introduce myself. Susan had brought me his file with the IC form.

"Hey, whassup?" Michael said.

"My name is Joshua Frankel," I returned. "What's yours?"

"It's there on that paper."

I nodded silently. "So tell me what happened."

"I was at my boys' place. Left to walk home and five-o picked me up." I bet the creators of the seventies TV show *Hawaii Five-0* never thought they would influence our vocabulary.

"Thanks for bringing the charging papers." I gestured to them. Susan had included them with the IC form. "They say you broke into a home intending to steal things but left when the alarm went off."

"I didn't bust into no home! Call my boy. He'll tell you I was at his house."

It was like pulling teeth but I got all the information from Mr. Garvey that I needed.

"Here's your agreement to have me represent you. We'll investigate, and if it looks as you say, we'll enter our firm as your defense counsel. However, if I find you lied or we think that you're guilty, we will not be representing you. Do you understand?"

"Yeah, man. I didn't do nothin'. That's why I came to you."

"Okay then."

After Mr. Garvey had left, I called Abby in to give her the file and tell her to work it up preliminarily. She understood that meant 'should we represent him?'

Susan knocked on the door. "The jury has a question."

Jerry and I arrived at the courthouse before Allen. Tom was already there. The judge called Tom, Jerry, me, and the court reporter to chambers while the courtroom was starting to fill with reporters and bystanders.

"They want Loretta Woods's testimony read back to them." Judge Warren looked a little annoyed.

"Your Honor, her testimony was completely discredited, and she skipped out on this court," I objected.

"But it is of record and therefore evidence in the case." Tom was hopeful.

"Mr. Fanucci is correct, Mr. Frankel."

"Then I ask that it not only be her direct testimony, but the cross, as well as the officer's testimony and the landlord's testimony, including the narration of the video."

"Your Honor," Tom countered, "that will leave us here all afternoon."

Judge Warren was skeptical. "It probably won't take that long, Mr. Fanucci. It seems like a fair request to me." She obviously did not believe Woods's testimony.

When we went back to the courtroom, Allen was sitting at the defense table. The jury was led in and Judge Warren explained to them that, in fairness, they would hear all of the testimony pertaining to Loretta Woods.

We sat there while the court reporter read back the testimony. I watched the jurors. Most of them seemed to glaze over at the reporter's unemotional rendition of the courtroom drama. A few seemed to pay rapt attention. They must have been the ones who wanted it read to them. The jury was then returned to deliberate, and we were dismissed.

I grabbed lunch through a drive-through window at a fast food joint then headed back to the office. Abby was waiting for me.

"Not good news, boss."

"What now?"

"On the potential new client."

"Garvey?"

"Yup."

"Since we haven't entered our representation yet, it can't be that bad."

"True. And I don't think you want to enter it."

"Tell me."

"First I called his alleged alibi witness. When I explained why I was calling, he replied"—she looked at her notes to get the exact wording—" 'Look, I don' wan' my nigga to be in trouble, but I got enough trouble with five-o without perjuring myself.' I explained that I did not want him to perjure himself and was just checking out the alibi. He replied, 'Well, I ain't his alibi.' "

"Really? He referred to his white friend as 'my nigga'? Okay. But just because his alibi doesn't check out doesn't mean he's guilty. He might have thought he needed an alibi so he made one up."

"True. But the arresting officer, Romeo Bergstrom, was available so I asked him what happened without telling him the alibi. He said that he stopped Garvey because he matched the description a neighbor gave him of someone rushing from the scene when alarms were sounding."

"The description could have been 'white guy in a hoodie.' "

"There's something else," Abby noted. "I told you that I didn't mention the alibi to him." She handed me a map. "Here's a diagram that Bergstrom drew for me about his observation of Garvey just before he stopped him."

I looked at the map. There were x's and arrows showing the direction that Bergstrom said Garvey was traveling. It showed him climbing up the steps from Old York Road to Edge Hill Road and then traveling northeast. I knew that was trouble. The attempted burglary was just off Old York Road *south* of those connected steps. However, Garvey's alleged alibi was southwest on Edge Hill. If he had been coming from the crime, he would have traveled exactly as Bergstrom described. If he had been coming from his alleged alibi, he would have been on Edge Hill the whole time.

I asked Susan to step in. "Please call Mr. Garvey and tell him we will not be able to represent him as he lied to me today."

"Will do, boss."

No other calls from the courthouse about jury developments the rest of Tuesday. I was a little concerned.

CHAPTER 40

Wednesday morning at 10:15 Susan came in without knocking. "Jury's back."

"Verdict or question?"

"Verdict."

This time the whole defense team came to the courthouse with us. We asked Allen if he wanted us to pick him up but he said he was near Norristown so he would show up on his own.

We left the office. It's a short two-tenths of a mile down Office Center Drive to the E-ZPass slip ramp onto the turnpike. We rode silently as there wasn't anything to discuss now. I had our Plan B—a motion for judgment of acquittal notwithstanding the verdict—in my briefcase, in case the jury found Allen guilty.

We got off at Norristown then drove to the courthouse and parked. We walked up the steps of the courthouse, came through the lobby, and entered the courtroom. This time Allen was already there, as was Tom. Reporters were already there.

When the bailiff saw we were all there he went back to tell Judge Warren.

The judge entered the courtroom. "All rise," the bailiff instructed.

Once Judge Warren was seated she asked that the jury be brought in. After the jury was seated, Judge Warren asked, "Members of the jury, have you reached a verdict?"

The foreman stood and said, "Yes, Your Honor." I was happy to see who the jury elected foreman. It was someone who seemed to accept Allen's testimony.

"Please hand your verdict slip to the bailiff."

The bailiff gave the slip to the judge. I always try, but I have never been able, to read Judge Warren's face when she reads the verdict. I mean that lady should be a professional poker player!

"Ladies and gentlemen, as to the only count, murder in the first degree, how say ye?"

"Not guilty."

The foreman had not taken the dramatic pause one sees on courtroom dramas.

There was a murmur in the courtroom—quickly silenced by a rap of Judge Warren's gavel.

"Say one and all?"

"Yes, Your Honor," the foreman said as the other jurors nodded in agreement.

Judge Warren gave the jury her closing remarks. "Thank you all for your service and your attention in this unusual case. You are under no obligation to speak with anyone, including the lawyers, about the case or your verdict. But now that it is over, you may. However, you may still not discuss the details of the closed courtroom session. You may only refer to the summary of that testimony. You are dismissed."

A sheriff's deputy led the jury out.

"Mr. Crosby," Judge Warren then said to our client, "you are dismissed from the court's jurisdiction. You may pick up your passport at the Clerk of Court's office, and you may leave. This case is now over."

She rapped her gavel and we all stood as she left.

We congratulated each other, and Allen and the reporters left after we told them we would give our statements to the press outside. Allen gave me a big hug.

"I will be forever grateful." He choked up with tears in his eyes. "It's been horrible not having Deidre…and then being blamed for her death."

I told Allen it was a privilege to have served him. "Justice was done," I said

Tom wandered over as Allen left to pick up his passport.

"You know, Loretta Woods's testimony is really suspect."

"Well, Tom, glad you are starting to see it my way now that the jury has agreed."

"I mean, your client claimed attorney-client privilege about where the gun got to and suddenly it's turned in by Ms. Woods with her story. After hearing all the testimony and your client being shot, I understand that your client may very well have been innocent, but don't you follow any rules?"

"Not when justice is at stake."

Tom looked at me for a few seconds, then broke into a grin. "Don't tell anyone in my office but that's the thing I like best about you. Justice is why I became a prosecutor."

That triggered an idea in my mind. But before I could say anything on our way walking out of the courtroom, Tom asked, "How did you think of doing that anyway?"

"Without necessarily answering your question, do you like to watch movies?"

"Some."

"Have you ever seen *Witness for the Prosecution* starring Marlene Dietrich, or *Chicago* starring Richard Gere?"

PART FOUR

THE AFTERMATH

CHAPTER 41

About a week after the trial I invited Tom to come to lunch in my conference room. His integrity made him insist on paying for his portion of the meal.

"Tell me more about your choosing the prosecutor's office to pursue justice," I said.

"Well, I learned in law school that criminal defense attorneys need to 'zealously' represent their clients whether innocent or guilty. But prosecutors can use their discretion about whether to drop charges, lessen charges, raise charges, or prosecute the original charges based on the evidence and what the predicates of justice dictate. So I thought that's where I wanted to go."

"How's that working out for you?"

Tom chuckled. "Sometimes it works, sometimes not. Actually, overall, not too well."

"Why not?"

"Well, there's pressure to close every crime and to keep our conviction percentage up. The idea is to overcharge so that defendants will be more willing to plead guilty to something— and every plea we get counts as a conviction."

"If that convinces a guilty person to plead guilty, isn't that pursuing justice efficiently?"

"I'm afraid we're convincing innocent people who can't afford to mount a defense as thorough as the prosecution to plead guilty to an act they didn't commit, out of fear of being convicted of something even worse. Also, once we have the conviction in hand, the police stop investigating the crime as the case is considered solved."

"I see...What are you doing about it?"

"Not sure. I've stayed in prosecution while colleagues put in their couple of years to get experience and then go out either on their own or join other firms. Always hoping I could get back to making decisions based solely on justice. But my boss wants those closed cases and high conviction rates."

I stared at him with a certain amount of sympathy. "I can see two possible paths for you, if you want unsolicited advice."

"Sure. What two possible paths?"

"Well, first, I can see you running for District Attorney."

"Against my boss?"

"Well, it would be uncomfortable for you to stay in the office while you did that," I agreed.

"Uh, huh. Okay, what's your second idea?"

"You could come work for me, either while you run for DA or on a more permanent basis."

Tom appeared shocked. He stared at me. "I didn't realize this was a job interview. Is that a job offer?"

"If you want it to be, it is."

Tom paused, thinking. "You only take cases of clients you believe are innocent, right?"

"Sort of. They are either innocent or justice requires that they be found not guilty."

"If they are guilty, how can justice require a 'not guilty' verdict?"

"I admit it is the rare case that this applies to. But sometimes people try self-help remedies when they should go to the police. And some criminal laws should not exist, since there is no wrong being committed. Or both the alleged victim and the defendant are equally guilty."

"Can you give me an example?"

"Well, how about the old criminal law adage about two people voluntarily entering into a fight. The one who loses becomes the victim and the winner becomes the defendant."

"Very true. How about an example of a criminal law in place when no wrong is being committed?"

"Victimless crimes."

"So-called 'victimless' crimes actually have victims."

"Well, let's discuss that. How about a user of illegal drugs. Who is the victim there?"

"Both the user and society."

"How so?"

"The user is hurting his health. And society is deprived of whatever contributions the user could have made to society."

"Is it really the province of the criminal justice system to label as 'criminal' an activity that hurts the person who is doing the activity, but nobody else? Most attorneys majored in political science—did you?"

"I did."

"So let's think back to the political philosophy that our country was founded on."

"Oh no, you mean Locke, Rousseau, Hobbes, and all those?"

I smiled. "Don't worry, it won't be painful. Do you remember the term 'state of nature'?"

"I do. Wasn't that when there was no government and people could do whatever they wanted?"

"Yes. It was imagining a situation in which whoever was strongest could impose their will on others. Beat them up. Kill them. Take anything they wanted. With nobody to protect the weaker person."

"Okay. And this has to do with drug abuse how?"

"Be patient. I'll get there. Do you remember the term 'natural rights'?"

"Sure. Those are the rights we all have just because we exist. Religious people call them 'God-given rights.' And no person, and no government, has the right to take them away."

"Good. Now as Jefferson stated when laying out the philosophy of our new country, among these natural rights are the rights to life, liberty, and the pursuit of happiness. Locke, writing a hundred years before Jefferson, listed some natural rights as life, liberty, and property." I paused. "Do you remember what a social contract is?"

"Isn't that the idea that in moving from a state of nature to one in which we have a government, the people agree to give up some of their right to do whatever they want and, in return, the government will protect everyone's natural rights?"

"Exactly. That's what our constitution and, by extension, our criminal justice system, are based on. It's like the old adage that your right to swing your fist stops at my nose."

"Yeah."

"So, is my natural right to liberty being protected by the government when the only possible person I might harm is myself?"

"What about society's right to benefit from the full abilities of the drug user?"

"First, *does* society actually have a right to benefit from our individual abilities? What about a person born wealthy who chooses to not pursue anything that benefits society as a whole, just leaves his money in the bank and lives off of it?"

"Well, society really cannot force someone to work if they don't want to."

"Why?"

"Because of individual rights."

"'Individual rights' is a nice phrase, but doesn't it go back to my example: the rights to swing your fist ends at my nose. That if my nose isn't there, you have the right to swing your fist?"

"I see the comparison. The wealthy person not working is not actually harming society so they have the right to do that."

"My point exactly. Now let's move on to your assumption than anyone who uses illegal drugs is a nonproductive member of society. I don't think all illegal drugs are the same. Marijuana is a Schedule 1 drug and is therefore illegal under federal law. Do you know how many people actively contributing to society use marijuana?"

"But the law is catching up to that. States are legalizing it. And what about the harder drugs like heroin or PCP?"

"So you think that someone who chooses to use those harder drugs might be a danger to themselves?"

"Yes. Can't government protect us against self-destructive behavior?"

"Putting aside your question about whether 'government' can do that, should we really label those users 'criminals'? Isn't that what involuntary mental health commitment systems are for? To protect someone who is a danger to themselves?"

"But those systems don't have the resources to handle all the drug users."

"Not my problem. They still shouldn't be labeled a 'criminal,' subject to the effects that label has on their employment, housing, their right to vote, and other areas."

"I see your point. What about other victimless crimes?"

"Okay. Let's take prostitution. If a woman chooses to have sex with as many people as want to have sex with her, is that illegal?"

"Not if she isn't charging money for it."

"Exactly. So why should it be a crime just because she realizes she had a commodity that is in demand and chooses to benefit financially rather than just giving that commodity away?"

Tom seemed genuinely impressed. "I never thought of it that way."

"Also consider the irony that if one accepts money for sex and for someone to film it and distribute it, then there's no crime due to the right of expression."

"That's true."

"In addition to the natural right of liberty, I think those alleged crimes touch on our right to bodily integrity. We should have a right to control our bodies as we see fit without the government making that a crime."

"After this discussion, I'm glad I'm in the homicide division and don't have to worry about prosecuting people for victimless crimes."

I chuckled. "But you're part of an organization that is involved in doing just that."

"True. And you think I should try to become the head of such an organization?"

"Actually, as the DA you could set prosecutorial standards for your office that would deemphasize victimless crimes while putting more of your resources into prosecuting actual criminals."

"I could."

"But that's up to you. What I would really like is to have you join our firm."

"I can tell you that your firm is the only one I would consider joining."

"What do you need to know to help you make up your mind?"

"I'm not sure." Tom paused to consider that question. "Would I get to decide whether or not I accept a case?"

"Yes. You will always have the option of saying you do not want to handle a particular case. I find people do their best work when they want to work on what they are working on. However, you won't be able to prevent the firm from handling a particular case. Anything else?"

"I didn't really come prepared for this." Tom shook his head as though still in disbelief at the quick turn of his fortunes. "I'll have to think about any other questions I have."

"One thing you should know," I added. "In our pursuit of justice there are no rules or laws that we let stand in our way. You have to be okay that you are with a firm that acts that way."

Tom looked at me. "None?"

"None. Of course, not everyone knows about everything that is done. Sometimes people suspect, but we try to give as many people as possible plausible deniability by compartmentalizing information."

"I would have to think about it," Tom said honestly.

"I wouldn't hire you if you didn't," I replied honestly.

"Anything else I need to know?"

"How about if I give you a tour of our two floors and introduce you to the people you don't yet know?"

We spent the rest of the afternoon wandering the office and talking to people in my firm. When we finally parted Tom promised to seriously consider my offer. I also told him what his salary would be. His eyes widened at the figure. It was considerably more than he was making and was probably more than he could make with any other Montgomery County firm. And more than he would make if he were elected the DA.

CHAPTER 42

Janice was heavily investigating the case against the NSA agents. She had the FBI out looking for Terry Logan and Lyle Curry. According to the NSA, the two agents had completely dropped off the NSA's radar at about the time of the trial. If they indeed had done what Allen accused them of, they were rogue agents who were not acting at the direction of the agency.

She also was investigating the "friend of presidents" who Allen claimed had been on the receiving end of a sweetheart deal. She couldn't yet tell me what information she was discovering about him.

Allen called me about a month after the trial.

"How's the innocent man doing?" I asked.

"Recovering. Thank you again for all you did and the risks you took."

"You're welcome."

"I had a visit today from someone identifying himself as an NSA agent."

"Really?" I was concerned. "Any threats?"

"No, he actually apologized for my experience. He also wanted me to know that Logan and Curry were rogue, and that they were the only ones involved. He said both the company in Slovakia and the child slavery ring were being taken down as we spoke, and that I would be getting reimbursed for my investment losses."

"Interesting. I wonder what they are covering up. Sounds like Logan and Curry are being made the patsies for this."

"He also said that Ms. McGuire will be learning of their location shortly."

"Interesting." I wondered if Janice had already learned of their location.

Allen and I got off the phone after agreeing to meet for dinner in the near future.

I called Janice.

"Any news on the case?"

"How did you know?"

"A little birdie told me."

"So you know they are dead?"

"What?" I hadn't seen it coming. "No! Tell me."

"This morning we received an anonymous tip that Curry and Logan were hiding in a motel near Reagan International. So I contacted DC, and Justice sent out local FBI agents to catch them. I received a call about ten minutes before you called. They found them in a room, each dead of a single gunshot wound through the temple. Apparent suicides."

"You buy that?"

"We'll see if there's any evidence of it being anything other than that."

"Remember this. The guy that threatened me in the courthouse men's room was neither Curry nor Logan."

"I remember."

CHAPTER 43

Inspired by both the relationship Allen and Deidre had and the unpredictable nature of life represented by Deidre's sudden death, I visited Susan unannounced one evening.

"If I knew you were coming I would have made dinner," she said as she opened the door.

I leaned down—and an overeager Taco jumped into my arms. I stood and looked directly into Taco's eyes.

"Taco, do I have your permission to ask Susan to marry me?"

Taco licked my face, which I took to be permission. I turned to an astonished Susan and held out the ring. "Will you marry me?"

"What will people say at the office?"

"I hope they'll congratulate us. Let's find out."

The next day I called an all-firm meeting. Susan and I announced the news. The general response seemed to be, "It's about time."

Later in the day, Jerry and Abby came into my office.

"What can I do for you?"

"Well, after your announcement this morning, we wanted to let you know that we are dating." Jerry seemed uncharacteristically nervous in saying that.

"Congratulations, although I'm not surprised."

"We weren't sure how you'd feel about two people in your office dating." Abby stated this matter-of-factly.

"I've never had a policy against it. As a practical matter, with the time we spend doing what we do, I'm amazed when people have time to find a relationship outside the firm. And after Susan and I made our announcement, it would be kind of hypocritical for me to object, now wouldn't it be?"

Jerry was all smiles as the two of them left my office.

CHAPTER 44

Two weeks went by without any news. Then, one morning, Susan said, "Janice is on the phone."

I picked up. "Well hello. Anything new in the investigation?"

"FBI agents have just placed Jeffrey Andrew Peisted under arrest for running a child trafficking organization."

"Wow." Jeff Peisted was well-known in financial circles—and yes, he was a friend of presidents.

"That's not all."

"There's more?"

"We think he was in the area when Curry and Logan died."

"You think he did it?"

"That's what we are trying to figure out."

Remembering pictures of Peisted from the news I said, "Peisted wasn't the one who threatened me in the courthouse."

"Still investigating."

* * *

The next day, Janice called again.

"I just got a call that Peisted is dead."

"How?" I asked.

"They *say* he killed himself."

"With your emphasis on 'say' I assume you don't buy it."

"He was on suicide watch."

I let out a low whistle. "What happens now with the investigation?"

"It gets harder. But I'm determined to get to the bottom of it."

"Be careful, Janice." I was worried for my friend.

"The FBI has my back."

"But you don't know how far this goes."

"There is no certainty in life. All we can do is the right thing, pursue justice, and let things fall where they may."

"You're my hero."

A NOTE FROM JULES

Thank you for reading my book. Since this is my first novel, I would love to hear any comments about it. You can write to me at Jules@julesmermelstein.com.

Also, I have some particular questions about the novel and your reactions to it. If you are willing to answer those, please mention that in your email to me. And as I write sequels in this *Pursuing Justice* series, I would love to be as collaborative as possible with my readers. I honestly look forward to hearing from you!

To visit my website, https://www.julesmermelstein.com, you can use this QR code:

POSSIBLE DISCUSSION QUESTIONS BASED ON JUSTICE, JUSTICE SHALL YOU PURSUE

1. Is it acceptable to violate the law to pursue justice?
   a. Why or why not?
   b. If permissible at all, when is it permissible?
   c. Are there certain laws that should never be broken under any circumstances? If so, which ones? Why?

2. Specifically, which violations of the law by Josh or members of his firm were permissible and which were not? Why?

3. Think about law and justice in terms of means and end. Law is the means our society uses in an attempt to achieve justice. At least that's the theory. In Josh's view, and the view of some of those quoted in the epitaph before the book, law is a means to keep those with power from losing their power, and those without power from getting any power or justice.
   a. How do you feel about this? Why?

b. Which of the following do you think better defines the law? Why?

    i. Law is the means our society uses in an attempt to achieve justice.

    ii. Law is a means to keep those with power from losing their power, and those without power from getting power or justice.

    iii. Sometimes one, sometimes the other depending on the particular law and the particular facts.

    1. **NOTE:** No matter which you chose above, should an individual have the right to decide for themselves what is just and whether the law is preventing justice, and then acting on that belief by violating the law? Why or why not?

4. Towards the end of the book, Josh and Tom have a discussion about victimless crimes.

    a. How do you feel about victimless crimes?

    b. Do you feel differently about different victimless crimes? For instance, Josh and Tom discuss drug use and prostitution. What other victimless crimes can you think of?

    c. Does the government have the right to label consensual actions by adults as crimes, when that can have lifelong implications for education, employment, voting rights, etc?

    d. Should victimless crimes which hurt the person committing the crime have any government restriction? Why or why not? If so, should it be the criminal justice system or the health care system that is involved?

5. Josh helped his mother, Susan, and Betsy, who were in abusive situations, in very different ways. What other ways are there to help people in this situation? Does your action depend on whether you are observing the situation (Susan), whether the perpetrator and victim are related to you (his mother), or whether it was being reported to you after the fact (Betsy)?
6. Allen had to trust Josh even though Josh wouldn't tell him everything he was doing. Have you experienced a relationship like that?

Feel free to share your thought with the author –
Jules@julesmermelstein.com

www.julesmermelstein.com